THE
NATURAL
DISORDER
OF THINGS

THE NATURAL DISORDER OF THINGS

Andrea Canobbio

Translated from the Italian by Abigail Asher

FARRAR, STRAUS AND GIROUX · NEW YORK

Farrar, Straus and Giroux
19 Union Square West, New York 10003

Copyright © 2004 by Giulio Einaudi editore s.p.a., Torino
Translation copyright © 2006 by Abigail Asher
Distributed in Canada by Douglas & McIntyre Ltd.
Printed in the United States of America
Originally published in 2004 by Giulio Einaudi editore s.p.a., Italy, as Il naturale
disordine delle cose
Published in the United States by Farrar, Straus and Giroux
First American edition, 2006

Library of Congress Cataloging-in-Publication Data
Canobbio, Andrea, 1962–
     [Naturale disordine delle cose. English]
     The natural disorder of things / Andrea Canobbio ; translated by Abigail
  Asher.— 1st American ed.
        p.   cm.
     ISBN-13: 978-0-374-21961-1 (alk. paper)
     ISBN-10: 0-374-21961-3 (alk. paper)
     I. Asher, Abigail.   II. Title

  PQ4863.A545N3713 2006
  853'.914—dc22
                                                         2005056811

Designed by Charlotte Strick

www.fsgbooks.com

10 9 8 7 6 5 4 3 2 1

To my father

THE NATURAL DISORDER of THINGS

1

THE FIRST TIME IT WAS HER VOICE, THAT FAULTY AND UNSTEADY RHYTHM—IT hypnotized me. If it hadn't been for that voice I wouldn't have paid her any attention. She used the formulaic phrases that clients always do: she had heard a lot about me, she'd seen and visited this and that, she was interested, even enthusiastic. They're always enthusiastic on the phone. Then I see that they're taken aback when they actually meet me. I guess they're thinking they have wasted their breath; maybe they ask themselves why I look nothing like my gardens, where I hide all that intelligence and elegance.

I had promised to call her back, to set a date to inspect the site, but I kept putting it off. A week later it was she who called me again, at the same time, apologizing for calling so late; it was as if the ghost of her garden, the naked and abandoned garden, appeared to her in a dream, at the same time of night each week, demanding retribution, and her sense of shame and guilt drove her to seek some remedy.

Again I didn't have the strength to say no to her; I didn't want to take on a new assignment, but I couldn't do without one, and I would have ended up refusing two or three offers at random before being compelled to accept perhaps the least interesting of the lot. I promised her we'd meet that Friday; she shouldn't worry, I wouldn't forget her. But in fact that's just what I intended to do: I was slumped on the sofa in the center of the kitchen, with no energy to clear the table, staring into space, and I lied to her so easily because I'd also finished eating the food on the plate for the guest. Usually I'm lucid as long as I'm at my own place at the table, sitting on the chair: that's why the guest's spot is on the sofa, so he can sink into it.

Elisabetta Renal apologized, complaining that she could never reach me when she called my house and didn't have my cell-phone number—I hadn't given it to her the first time; I pretended not to notice and didn't give it to her on the second call either. I stared at a pile of bread crumbs half hidden by the broom that had been propped against the wall several days earlier, and the line of busy ants at work, like a writer's ellipses heightening the suspense in a sentence . . . but the coup de théâtre never came. I wouldn't remember this call the next day, even though it was the second in a week; I wouldn't remember her and her childlike voice, her apologies for ringing so late, the clichés and commonplaces; I wouldn't remember how much I liked the way she uttered these social banalities, with a child's pauses and hesitations and sudden bursts of speed.

Her voice was so beautiful and promising: there was no way that voice could lie. There was no need for it to be rhythmic and regular; no need for it to be balanced; it seemed not to know that it could ever go off balance, that people might ever beg or attack. And for just an instant after hanging up, when I went back to staring into space, staring at the crumbs and at the ants, I imagined listening to her voice in the dark and falling asleep inside it; I imagined her leaning over my ear and pouring words—her stories—into my head.

Five days went by, and I was in the car with Witold; we'd had an argument and maybe I'd offended him, and then something distracted me like a wave of melancholy; I almost rear-ended a truck carrying yogurt, and I stopped and got out to take a closer look at an old abandoned factory. Was it abandoned? I don't know. The sun was shining in a cloudless blue sky, it wasn't yet very hot, and the block of reinforced concrete gave off an air of cheerful ruination; there was a touching detail in the courtyard of the watchman's house: a laundry line strung with faded little pajamas and shorts and T-shirts. My mood had changed now, and I turned back to the car (Witold was bolted into his seat, staring straight ahead) and saw the yellow arrow, camouflaged by an explosion of forsythia, with "Villa Renal" written on it, and then I remembered Elisabetta Renal's voice and decided I wanted to hear it again.

I shift the car into gear, back up, turn into the road that runs alongside the possibly abandoned factory, and drive in silence for three minutes and thirty seconds, up and down the sulky hills, before Witold, without looking at me, asks where we're going. I tell him about the two phone calls, and I lie and say that I'd asked around and the client seemed promising: maybe it will turn into a job for the springtime and part of the summer. Witold, with his impoverished-noble profile, his eyes locked on a pair of pollarded willows facing each other across a twenty-yard gap, each one as sad as an only child. After a bit he remarks that one doesn't go to meet a new client wearing dirty work clothes. I feel that I've made an effort to make peace with him; it's fine with me if he wants to be in a huff, so I say that his innate elegance will save face for both of us. He goes gray and smoky like an illegal building being demolished, dynamited and imploding.

I turn left and pass under a brick archway without any gate or caretaker; we're on the property, but the house isn't visible, and we run along beneath the elms, lindens, and horse chestnut trees flanking the dirt road that sinks into a shady little valley. I shout above the crackle and crunch of the tires to say that the fat cows who own this place will produce enough milk to get us through the whole winter, and guffaw because Witold doesn't like cynicism (not even false cynicism)—he's a guy with no sense of humor, he doesn't like a pat on the shoulder, an ambiguous wink, an insinuation (he doesn't understand insinuations), or vulgarity, whether explicit or implicit. He's really quite a heavy character. And I'm about to push on and provoke him further when a powerful blow strikes my side window; my Renault R4 wobbles from the impact, but I keep it on the road and try to understand what's happening.

It took me ten or twenty seconds to see it, maybe because of the dust we kicked up, maybe because it was running alongside the car. It was a dog jumping and butting its head against the car, trying to sink its teeth into the side mirror, where it saw flashes of an enemy dog's ferocious face. It wasn't barking, just baring its teeth and throwing itself against the door and the side window, certain it would manage to break through. Witold yelled at me to stop, stop, I might run it over, and I obeyed, sort of: I slowed down sharply, and the dog found himself running ahead, followed by the slow-moving car, surprised and excited as if he'd proved he could defeat us, as if he'd already won.

Then he turned his head, leaping from side to side in a dance of death, challenging me to speed up again, to run him over. I don't know what came over me, because I wasn't upset or afraid—I *was* scared, but not scared of the dog (I felt quite calm and lucid about the dog); what I was actually scared about was the garden of perfectly tended hedges and flower beds that stands in the center of my reasoning mind, a garden that allows for nothing anomalous, asymmetrical, excessive, or banal; from the center of that garden came the impulse to push down on the accelerator, and my right foot acted on the impulse: the R4 speeded up suddenly, and the dog didn't expect it, he dodged out of the way too late.

I'd never felt what it's like to run over a dog; I'd hit a rabbit and two cats, but you hardly notice such small animals. A dog makes you feel his death beneath the chassis, and especially with an R4, which is built from the same tin they use for canned tuna, you feel the bones breaking and the fur tearing and the innards bursting, or anyway you're supplied with a full range of sounds from which you can choose the sounds of a dog breaking apart. When we got out, though, he was in one piece, dead but not bleeding: dust and crushed stone had already smothered the wounds. It was a German shepherd, coated with dirt, eyes wide open.

When Witold is agitated he talks in the infinitive without conjugating his verbs, and he kept saying: "Why to speed up? Why to speed up? Bad thing to kill their dog. How to explain now? Bad sign, to kill pet. Poor dog. Poor dog to become white ghost." I looked at the dog, and I let Witold vent, jerking his head about and fingering his sideburns. Then I pointed out that the dog had no collar and no tags—he was a stray, and probably rabid. Who said he was a household pet? Witold stopped talking. We spread newspapers in the rear bed of the station wagon, put on gloves, and loaded in the dog; I didn't want it to be left there in the road. There were no fresh signs of damage on the R4, or if there were they were indistinguishable from the old ones.

But my decision to go looking for Elisabetta Renal wasn't a sudden decision at all. Six days had passed since her last call, and in that time I'd convinced myself that I knew her voice. I'd convinced myself that I had to hope I knew her voice, and with all my strength I'd decided that I must believe it and *make* it be the voice of a woman I'd encountered five months earlier, left in the emergency room of a hospital, and never seen again. She never got in touch to thank me (she didn't know my name), I never got in touch to see how she was doing (I didn't know hers). Neither of us was particularly in touch that night . . . we're never particularly in touch and alive (well, I should speak only for myself—I don't know her: I'd seen her for two hours, five months ago, but it's like she's an old friend, as if I'd always known her).

So, five months ago I'm sitting in my car, parked diagonally inside a painted parallelogram at the far end of the parking lot of a mini-mall.

It's an old place, originally built as a supermarket surrounded by boutiques but later raised in status out of provincial ignorance, so it's now a hybrid that has expanded around a rickety nucleus. I wouldn't go in there even if I were fresh out of milk or razor blades, and I'm not going in there tonight either, I'm staying outside and waiting. Also waiting, like me, is the man I'm observing from about twenty yards away, silhouetted against the lights and the reflections on the wet asphalt; he's gotten out of his car to smoke a cigarette, and he pays no mind to the mantle of wetness that falls on his shoulders. I pay no mind to the moist cold that's penetrating all the way to my bones: I don't want to turn my engine on, so I pull my down jacket tighter around me and slide down in my seat, the steering wheel caressing my inner thighs.

Suffocating fog, exhaust steaming from a car moving through the herringbone pattern of the parking lot; the faint illumination from the only two lampposts nearby, one hundred feet high, which give a dull saffron glow. And then the smoke from the cigarette of the man I'm watching: it escapes from under the brim of his hat and rises straight up from the crown as if the hat were a chimney. It's November fifth, a Tuesday like any other, and the mini-mall isn't doing very well: the parking lot is half empty. It's 7:30; the man is waiting for someone who, at this point, is probably late. I'm late too. I can't tell whether he's noticed me: he keeps his eyes down, the hat tilted to cover his face, standing immobile with his legs apart, beneath a hostile sky.

He raised his eyes when he was lit up by the high beams of the Ford Ka that appeared at the entrance of the driveway, and finally I saw the pallor of his face, the expression both tense and smug, the stout body that moved forward to the center of the roadway. I waited without anxiety for the car to pull up in front of him, to stop and let him get in, and then to move off again or stop and park. The car trotted along at about fifteen miles per hour, sending up inoffensive sprays of water on either side. Those insistent high beams, the false aggressivity, the camouflaged desire, and the tranquil, impassive man in the middle of the lane were complicit smiles that mirrored one another—maybe the smiles of a pair of lovers not necessarily in love with one another.

When it was about twenty yards away from him, the Ka stopped and its wheels turned to the right and then to the left—all the parking spots were free, there were too many to choose from; then it decided, it slid in crooked across two parallelograms, outside the lines. The lights went off, no one got out. The man didn't move. I was looking at him from behind, but I could see his surprise and uncertainty in the face of this new provocation. I thought, Now he's going to go to her. But instead he just stood there; for a moment he turned his head toward me, toward his Alfa Romeo 166, and I thought, It's not possible, he can't decide to leave.

Meanwhile, from the end of the parking lot comes the retching sound of an engine revving up fast; it's a white van, it shoots down the driveway as if it's on the highway, as if it's late with its delivery schedule—we've all gotten used to the daredevil vans, the dispatch trucks cutting you off in traffic, the pizza delivery cars running red lights. I barely see it, and the man doesn't even turn around; he just steps sideways, maybe to avoid a surprise shower of water from a puddle.

The van hits him squarely at full speed, tosses him ten yards ahead, skids sideways, wobbles across the white lines, and, instead of turning toward the exit, disappears into the other half of the parking lot, behind the supermarket.

But the image of the collision doesn't disappear, it's imprinted on the night, has created a vacuum around the crumpled body. I move only my eyes: they dart back along the trajectory of the van, and I can't get them to stop going back and forth, back and forth—there's no mouse or cursor to bring the man back up into a vertical position.

I think, What's he waiting for, with his naked head resting on the asphalt? Why doesn't he get up? I think, A living man would never be able to leap so far from a standing start, not even if he had spring-loaded shoes.

When the lights of the Ka go on, the world begins to spin normally again. The car backs angrily into the driving lane and rushes the downed body, running it over so fast that the car's tail flies up in the air as if it had raced over a speed bump. It becomes just a trail of red light exiting the parking lot, and turns onto the road outside.

Silence, and not a single eye looks out on the deserted lot from behind the luminous lids of the mini-mall. Probably there was also total silence during the accident—the first, the second, I don't remember which. I have no recollection of the sound a head makes as it's crushed beneath the wheel of a car, and anyway I was cocooned in my muffling Mercedes E270.

Here are my hands gripping the wheel, my nails sunk into the rubber, my eyes glued to the broken body on the ground. Then there's nothing here at all.

I fasten my seat belt, turn on the engine and the windshield wipers, put the car in gear, and leave the parking lot with my headlights off.

Now I have this deserted road ahead of me: the drizzle has transformed the asphalt into the viscous trail left by an enormous snail, there's scarcely any visibility, but nothing would prevent me from speeding up and zooming along the curves and the straightaways that lead toward the nearest town, leaving the supermarket lot behind me. I'm slowed down, though, by a shell that I suddenly find on my back, a guilty feeling that's like an invisible mobile home. This isn't fog, this isn't fog, if it's raining it's not fog. I keep saying the words out loud; it was my father's old litany, If it's raining then it's not fog, it's just low clouds: why "just"? Why should low clouds be any less dangerous than fog? It's important for me to figure this out, but not to show that he was wrong, if indeed he was wrong. My father is always sitting next to me—I'm accustomed to driving with him, I was accustomed to our four eyes looking at the world together, accustomed to the reaction that was a synthesis of our individual reactions (a synthesis achieved not without friction, not without pain). But at this moment I have nothing else in my head, no particular feeling, neither joy nor disappointment: just the wish, more or less, to catch up with the Ka that disappeared into the night.

So I change gears and accelerate.

I crossed paths with oncoming cars that blinded me; I passed a truck in an unnecessarily risky way, perhaps; I went through a subdivision of Mexican-Mission-style houses at sixty miles per hour; and finally, far ahead, I saw the red taillights I was after. I caught up to make sure it was she: she never went over thirty-five miles per hour, she was in no hurry, she wasn't escaping, and she went so slowly I had trouble not letting her feel I was breathing down her neck and keeping an eye on her from a distance, following her. She could have taken me to the ends of the earth; suddenly I wasn't tired anymore, I wasn't hungry; all I needed was the old protected feeling of the trees wrapped and half hidden by the spiderweb fog, while I was forced to drive with my left wheel on the center strip, but I was generally calm, curious without impatience, maybe resigned—waiting for the spider.

We go on like this for half an hour. I'm not surprised when I lose sight of her around two or three curves, but then on a downslope— where she should appear again—she's not there, not even if I push on the accelerator, and yet she should have been no more than three hundred yards ahead of me. I stop short, turn around, and with my heart in my throat start driving again in the opposite direction, and find her immediately: she has ended up in a field—she went off the road at thirty-five miles per hour, if such a thing is possible—her front wheels sunk in an irrigation ditch, the nose of the car pointed down like that of an animal drinking.

I pull over, get out, sink into the wet grass as I reach the Ka, walk around it, and glimpse the body inside lying on its side across the passenger seat, and in the windshield I find a blossom of shattered crystals. When I open the door she startles, as if I've woken her, but she doesn't get up, she groans weakly; the interior light is still working, and it illuminates her bloody face, the dirty seats, the sticky black blood everywhere. "You must always wear a seat belt," I tell her, paternally, absurdly. I drag her out unceremoniously, disregarding her protests, and when I have her in my arms, perhaps overwhelmed by the feeling of a woman against me, I lose my strength, and I let her slide through my hands and fall into the mud. Seen from above, so fragile and defenseless, she looks to me as if she couldn't hurt a fly.

I searched for a jacket or a coat in her car, but there was nothing, not even a purse; she wore only a fitted blue zip-up sweater, and it was unseasonably cold. I helped her to my car, I made her sit in it, I brushed against her breast once as I fastened her belt, and before I could think twice I pretended to make an adjustment and brushed against it again. As I drove I looked at her legs: her stockings were torn at the knees, and the unraveling runs glowed in the half-light and pointed straight up like arrows aiming under her skirt of lightweight wool. I couldn't shake an image of my head sunk between her thighs.

I took her to the emergency room, where they put her on a gurney, and in the icy fluorescent light she suddenly became a patient, the victim of an accident, with bloody scratches visible through her tattered stockings. The nurse asked me to stay, saying he would be right back to talk to me, and I nodded; I squeezed the hand of the woman, who had been whimpering and moaning all the way there, incoherent rambling that offered no clue to her identity. I told her, "You'll see—everything will be all right." The nurse agreed. As soon as they disappeared into the warren of the clinic, I walked to the exit, looking neither right nor left, and took a few indecisive steps outside. No one came running after to stop me, so I got into the E270 and took off.

Another empty parking lot. Without the cars, all that remains are the white lines on the pavement: what purpose do they serve? Where has everyone gone tonight—why don't they stay put, in the places destiny has reserved for them? When you've found a niche, dug a hideout, why go elsewhere?

Later, in a half-waking nightmare, I saw the white grid printed on my retina; the unused, useless parking lot made me dizzy, as if it were a net hanging in space; standing in the middle of the lot, I nearly got caught in it, condemned, dead, hooked like a fish, the abandoned herringbone, the deboned fish already digested and passed along from the stomach of the parking lot to the twisted intestine of the roadways, and then out the exit: the garage.

I didn't see her again.

The house jumped out at you suddenly after you drove up an avenue of plane trees that had been pruned back by a sadist but were still thick with large, soft leaves that created an oppressive tunnel. You burst out into the light at the foot of a knoll, and up there you saw yellow walls and green shutters, and for a moment your eye wanted to replace the straight lines and square frames and 1930s architecture with something older—volutes and flourishes, or columns and tympanums; you expected to find something from the 1800s when you drove across the crackling gravel and raised your eyes to gaze into the midst of all that boxwood and ivy and roses.

Every homeowner is free to treat his gravel as he pleases; I've seen people who will walk on it only in slippers, I've seen red gravel shipped in from Australian quarries, carefully polished blond gravel from Monument Valley, black pebbles from the Indian Ocean: I've seen and I respect gravel that belongs to people who are respectable and even likable. So I immediately stopped the car in front of the garage (or maybe it was a greenhouse) and told Witold that it would be better for us to walk the last few yards on foot, and even though it was a short distance and the hill wasn't steep, I was breathless when I got to the entry and I had to sit on the lip of an enormous terra-cotta planter, which held a ton of inert soil and a faded little lemon tree.

Witold frowned at my round belly and the two dark eyes of sweat that had appeared on my gray T-shirt. He said that, in his opinion, there was no one home. The shutters were closed, but it was exceptionally warm for 11:30 on a morning in late March, so maybe the owners had pulled them shut in order to protect some antique upholstery. "Maybe they're pulled shut so the fabric on the sofas won't fade," I said, and I went to the dark green door. There was no bell or buzzer, and no knocker or lion's-mouth ring to grab. For a moment I was tempted to shout for someone, but actually I wasn't unhappy to have a chance to look around the place by myself, and maybe leave without ever getting in touch. Witold had ventured around the corner to take a peek, and I gestured to him to continue on around the house; on the other side, I expected, we would find the place for the new garden that had been described to me on the phone.

From the full sun of the façade we pass into the shadow behind, walking across a rectangular terrace that extends about twenty yards out from the house, where two great umbrellas of white sunshade fabric, tightly shut, sorrowfully announce that we're here in the wrong season. We stand at the balustrade of concrete columns and study the terrain that stretches across an acre or so. The first fifty yards slope down slightly, then it's flat for thirty or forty yards, and it's closed off at the far end by another hill that rears up steeply. All around are woods of chestnut and hornbeam trees. It looks like the owners changed their minds twenty times without ever clearing away the rubble of their earlier mistakes. There are traces of an unpretentious old garden, two high walls of boxwood, a few cotoneaster and holly hedges (at such a distance, I might be guessing wrong: I'd have to go down and check what they are). Witold says, "My soul rejoices before such beauty." It's a riddle, but I don't feel like trying to solve it. I make no comment. He adds that a tractor will be needed to flatten the site. I nod.

That aside, the situation was perfect, a tabula rasa where you could invent whatever you wanted, if only they'd let you. Sometimes I'm happy to let waves of ideas wash over me, and at other times the very brilliance and promise of my ideas only arouse my suspicions. I spun around. "Let's go," I said to Witold. And as I went back to the car I planned a new phone call: I would tell her that I'd been here, that I'd seen the site; or I would pretend nothing had happened, so she'd be obligated to insist, and then I'd come again with a project already all worked out, to stun her and win her over; or I'd snuff out her hopes right away, because in the end the space was so banal that it would make an even more banal garden—it was useless to try for singularity or sophistication. That's right: maybe I'd tell her that I wasn't interested in the job.

When we got to the lemon-tree planter, Witold grabbed my arm, holding me back as if I were about to be run over by a truck. I looked at him to understand what was going on, and he gestured with his head. The sun hammered down on the distant hornbeams, and the leaves whirled obediently in the breeze—shiny and dull, shiny and dull, top and underside—so the trees shifted hues like those holographic billboards. A man had stepped out of the avenue of plane trees below us, with a hunter's vest and a shotgun slung over his shoulder. We spied on him from atop the knoll as he walked over to the R4; then, when we saw him begin to examine the car, we instinctively tried to hide behind a shrub, ridiculously, especially for anyone who might have been watching us from the house, concealed behind the shutters—the idea of it suddenly seemed very likely, now that we ourselves had become spies. The hunter walked around the car, then bent down and looked through the back window for thirty seconds, cupping his hands around his face to block out the reflections on the glass.

The dog was covered with a waterproof green tarp, and in any case it wasn't the household pet. "There isn't any dog bed or dog bowl or gnawed bones lying around—did you see any?" I whispered to Witold, whose eyes were wide open. It's odd, actually, that they don't have a dog here. We had come out into the open now, but in just those few seconds the hunter had disappeared. By the time we got down the slope and reached the R4, the man had reappeared on the path that ran around the knoll, and now he was dressed as a gardener. Dressed in a gardener's uniform, just as he was dressed in a hunter's uniform before. A big green apron, a tool belt, a straw hat, and rubber boots. O, the lost peasant traditions of yesteryear! That's an expression coined twenty years ago by my brother, and it comes in handy when you're casting a baleful eye on some faux-rustic product in the supermarket. Here were the lost peasant traditions of yesteryear: the deep, woody voice, the calcified facial muscles, and the deadened expression (instead of what people usually describe as a "lively expression"). I'd say that his neck was the most remarkable element: his ability to hold his neck as straight as a pine tree and his head immobile on his neck. Still, I couldn't understand why I so hated this man on first sight, what he could have done to me.

We introduced ourselves. He mumbled something, maybe that he'd been told we might visit. He invited us to follow him. For more than half an hour he shepherded us around the property in the broiling midday sun. He made statements like "Here we planted such-and-such, but it didn't grow." He added comments like "That spot needs a tougher plant." In the beginning he tried to speak in the local dialect, but I stopped him immediately: "Speak Italian, because," I lied, "we don't understand a word you're saying." When people arrogantly speak to strangers in dialect, it's usually just thoughtlessness, and it's best to prevent thoughtlessness.

And while we're walking across the remains of an unfinished Zen garden (the traces of white gravel stuck in mud, stacked-up cadavers of stone slabs, briars, and sumac moving in to reestablish the natural disorder), a woman dressed in red appears at the concrete balustrade and watches our uncertain rambling for a few minutes. I don't want her to realize that I've seen her—I keep the bright spot that is her dress in the corner of my field of vision and glance at her without moving my head: it looks as if she's encircled by my nose, thanks to my left eye, which stubbornly follows the movement of my right, so I close it, but the gardener catches me winking, and I reopen my eye.

The woman rests her hand on the balustrade, and it's as if she's emphasizing its concrete presence, as if she's saying, "Between me and you, fortunately, stands this barrier." It's not her, it couldn't be: she was taller (but I'm seeing this woman from a distance) and had longer hair (she could have cut it). And if it were she, she would come down to greet us, or she would motion for us to come up (would she?).

Instead she turns and goes.

Now Witold was in a good mood: he bent down to test the acidity of the soil, and he reported the results to me in a sarcastic tone, as if they were scandalous, and every time the gardener opened his mouth, Witold looked as if he was about to laugh in his face. Not only was I not enjoying myself but I was growing more irritated, and I wanted to go. Then I tripped on a root, flew through the air, and tore my T-shirt as I hit the ground. They picked me up. My dignity wounded, I made it clear to the gardener that, no offense to him, I usually dealt with the master of the house, and that I couldn't understand anything if I looked over a site in this manner, that I couldn't understand what I was being asked to invent. Consistent with his style, he didn't change expression (he had none). I pulled out a business card, the one I use for clients, and put it in his hand. It carried my cell-phone number beneath the words

CLAUDIO FRATTA

GARDENS

But it hasn't always been like this: dealing with the master of the house is a recent habit for Claudio Fratta. When I used to go around with my father, our interlocutors were the caretakers and the gardeners and the Filipina housekeepers, and we took orders from the caretakers and the gardeners and the Filipina housekeepers, and we learned the English names for the plants ("lime tree" for *tiglio* and "jasmine" for *gelsomino*) because otherwise there wasn't any way for us to communicate with the help. Since then, the Romanians have come, and the Poles and the Indians: my father would have to carry two or three dictionaries along with him now, and he didn't usually deal with the master of the house, and he didn't have business cards: when necessary, he wrote his phone number on bits of paper ripped from bags of humus; my mother furnished his car with old address books and outdated calendars, but he left them in the trunk with his tools, and, when he needed to write something down and went looking for the scrap paper, he'd reach into the recesses amid abandoned boxes and half-rotten flower bulbs and half-used bags of seed and pull out those flowered notebooks, swollen with moisture, their paper reduced to a soft, useless gray pulp.

Of all the spaces I shared with my father, the car is the one I remember best. I don't have the same intense memories of me and my father eating in the kitchen, I don't remember our bodies walking through the plant nursery or standing in the seed store where he bought his supplies, I don't remember our spines curved over one of the gardens that he looked after—that we looked after. This means that if I find myself in one of those gardens, or in the store, or in the kitchen of the old house where my mother still lives, and I close my eyes and try to feel my father's presence, I can't do it; specific memories float up, scenes and episodes that have already been labeled and filed away, and they're pale and flimsy, like pictures traced on a white wall by an eight-millimeter movie projector—ghosts. But in the car, in any car (not just the R4), my father is always with me, sitting in the passenger seat, and when I take certain shortcuts that he invented (some of which don't actually shorten the route at all, I've discovered, but go through the less corrupted zones of our landscape or are uninterrupted by intersections or stoplights, though the mileage is longer), I say out loud: "Why don't we go this way?" as if he were saying it to me, waving his knobby forefinger toward the window on his right.

I began driving with him in order to be his chauffeur. He had dislocated his ankle while pruning a pagoda tree; I was doing my second year of architecture at the university, and I had just taken two final exams (all in all, I did four finals before I dropped out) and I couldn't refuse to help him for a month; it was April, and it would have been unthinkable for him to recuperate at home: the homeowners who were least loyal and least attached to him would surely have dumped him (naturally there was an imbalance between personal courtesy and economic means: the least loyal clients were also the ones who paid the most and had the biggest gardens), and his work supported the whole family, but my older brother was a serious student and my younger one was still in high school and didn't have a driver's license, so I can fairly say that my fate was decided by pure chance, because if I had gone on studying architecture, if I had graduated, I don't know what kind of underpaid work I would have found—certainly I wouldn't have made the money I've accumulated in the past seven years. When he asked me to go around with him, I looked at my mother—who said nothing: she was engrossed in peeling potatoes or trimming artichokes, or maybe she was reading a musical score—and my father said that if I didn't help him he wouldn't know which way to turn, that he felt he was "banging his head against a brick wall," and that made an impression on me because I'd never heard him use that expression before—even though once, long ago, I had seen him actually bang his head, on purpose, in sheer desperation (and then later, of course, long after I began working with him, he did really bang his head, though not on purpose, at least I don't think so), but that was just an isolated episode, my father was the last person in the world—as everyone said—to fall apart from nerves: he seemed not to have a single nerve in his body, that's what Carlo maintained, anyway.

Carlo studied history and had decided that our father was an unconscious representative of the damned of the earth and—forgetting his history as a capitalist exploiter—tried to incite him against the employers who didn't pay him sick leave and obligated him to work when he was crippled, and who would never admit that he'd hurt himself on their property, cutting a branch from their tree. This angry brother of mine came home almost every Friday night from his university housing and would begin to mutter about the family's misfortunes, mainly using terms that no one in the house had ever heard, let alone uttered; he maintained that it was right and necessary to revolt, that the dominant class reacted to nothing except brute force, that there was no room in the revolution for the meek and the cowardly, that the proletariat would raze all the fences and throw open the gardens to the deprived and oppressed children (often he reeled off statistics and percentages about children in the South or in poor countries who were forced to work sixteen-hour days; when he started with the numbers, we felt free to stop paying attention). My father's reaction to this subversive wall of sound was uniform and constant: he had no reaction. I remember that only once, at the table one Sunday night—in other words, after two days of long-suffering silence—my father leaned over to me and asked conspiratorially, "Tell me—did he get bitten by a rabid dog?" And that was the only thing I ever heard him say, the only thing I ever heard from him or from my mother. And I wonder whether this attitude, along with the physiological ebbing of his rage and the vicissitudes of life, contributed to Carlo's current state (his giving up on the struggle, his frequent mental blackouts, his surrender in the face of the world's insistence on being the world that it is).

So in that period all three of his sons, not just Carlo but all three of us, perceived that a small injustice had been loaded onto the great injustice that our father had suffered when he lost his factory, and by then it seemed that he could not escape his fate: to suffer injustice and not protest or even react; to take a slap and turn the other cheek. The myth of his meekness and submissiveness, though, wasn't really believable for us: we had known him before, and we had seen him when he was under full sail, seated at his owner's desk in the office on the second floor of the little factory. Carlo had understood, and I had intuited, that his was a choice, a rational decision. My father walked into the storm with his head lowered and never lifted it up, not even to inveigh against whoever was hurling all that hail in his face. But his clients saw him as a good-hearted old peasant, maybe a bit luckier than the others, lucky enough to choose a more comfortable and less risky line of work, but still a country bumpkin: ignorant, obtuse, slow on the uptake, as bumpkins have been since the dawn of time. They treated him condescendingly, speaking loudly as if he were deaf (and implying that he was a bit slow); they limited their vocabularies, spoke in simple sentences, and avoided the subjunctive (maybe because some of them didn't actually know how to use it), and they always wanted to explain and explain and explain everything: they'd glance at my ever-patient, ever-calm father and decide that he needed to be treated like a child. I felt humiliated, I looked away; I made no secret of my disapproval. But my father took advantage of it. He pretended to be a dunce, and in time I learned that it's the best strategy for a gardener. Often the clients don't know exactly what they want, but they know that they want it, and they're determined to get it; the belief that their gardener is decent but just a bit stupid helps them tolerate the discomfort of not being understood.

I began by going around with him as his driver but ended up helping him on his jobs too, and I went on doing it even after his ankle healed, without it being said explicitly (not a lot of things were said explicitly in my family, and Carlo's Jacobin verbosity was all the more astounding because none of us had ever thought we could talk all day about one topic without getting bored) that I was dropping out of the university and learning my father's gardening trade. Everything about plants was a mystery to me, and my father taught me a small fraction of what I now know. He had no teaching talent, and he did many things instinctively: he couldn't have explained why dahlias need sunny exposure or why hyacinths need well-drained soil. In the beginning he told me what to do, and later he signaled it with his eyes. Little by little, I began to know more than he did. I never let him see it. But I've often wondered whether he understood it on his own, and whether his anxious determination to continue performing the most dangerous tasks was born of a secret fear (for a person like him, it could only be secret) that I might steal his trade.

Sometimes you think you've found the site you've been waiting for all your life: you've never seen it before, but you recognize it, it was waiting for you and you knew that sooner or later you'd discover it. When you come back to it the next day or even just an hour later, full of expectations, it says nothing to you, it's insipid and banal and stupid, and you're sure that those stones and that terrain will never produce anything good. So if a site ever speaks to you this way—if as soon as you lay eyes on its tufts of grass, like an unknown woman's head of hair, it tells you it's ready to become the most beautiful garden of your life—don't believe it: turn your back and forget about it. Because if destiny decides that your most beautiful garden is to rise from these very stones, this very terrain, if it is really the site you've been waiting for, destiny will seek you out and find you—maybe by calling you on the phone with a childish voice full of pauses and hesitations and sudden bursts of speed.

Witold doesn't approve of my style; I can feel his disapproval hovering in the air, and in order to criticize me without referring to the episode with the gardener, he's listing all the advantages of a job in such a place: the freedom to invent, the favorable site, the wealthy family commissioning it, and, not least, the low risk of failure (after all those errors, a simply decent garden design will look like a masterpiece). I let him talk. We're halfway down the dirt track leading to the main road when, as one might expect, my cell phone rings. It's a man's voice that I can hardly hear over the sound of the wheels on the crushed stone; I stop the car and turn off the engine.

He says he's "Rossi," as if I'm supposed to know who that is; he apologizes for the "inadequate" reception we got—his wife is out, he was working in the "studio" and he'd given orders not to be disturbed— might I have a moment to go back and have a chat with him? I reply that the reception wasn't at all "inadequate," that it's my fault for stopping by without advance notice. Rossi responds that in any case he'd be delighted to offer me a cup of coffee or even a "frugal" lunch; he says he doesn't usually lay out a whole lavish meal at midday.

"Just a moment," I say, and turn to Witold. "What time is that appointment?" I ask without covering the mouthpiece.

Witold looks at me impassively, then turns away from me; I didn't consult with him when I decided to come see the place, so why do I want his help now?

"So, we have time," I say to fill the silence. "Okay, we're coming."

Climbing the hill a second time and arriving short of breath yet again, I thought I saw the gardener waiting for us by the front door, seated on a director's chair, and I thought he was crazy. But then I immediately saw that it wasn't the gardener, and that the chair was a wheelchair. The man who was shaking my hand might have been about ten years older than I am—fifty or fifty-five—and he was handsome and grizzled: the regular lines of his eyes and nose had been shaped by nature with perfect symmetry, and his regular smile and teeth had been formed to look pleasant and to transmit a sense of confidence and calm; he had a white shirt and cardigan to signal comfort and intimacy, the absence of any problems related to practical necessities: there were no pressing deadlines, no schedules or agendas or unbreakable appointments in his life.

From the waist down, it was another story; below, his body and clothes spoke a different language: the skeletal legs drawn up and lolling to the side like inert mannequin's parts, the stained pale gray sweatpants, the bulk of the diaper at his groin, and the feet, in sneakers with immaculate soles, marooned in incongruous positions; there was an anti-bedsore cushion hidden under a towel, and the arms and prongs of the wheelchair were padded with foam rubber—the paraphernalia I knew so well, the kind of stuff buried somewhere in my basement.

Witold had immediately taken on a guilty and contrite attitude, as if he were the one who had crippled the man; I started to extol the virtues of the siting of the house, and the trees and terrain and hills and god knows what else, just so I could keep moving and not face him, and Rossi observed us in silence, shielding his eyes from the sun with his hand, his head thrown slightly back. The gardener came to our rescue, appearing in hunter's uniform again—this time his sideburns might have been trimmed shorter, as well as the gray hair on the nape of his neck—and without waiting for instructions, he grasped the handles of the wheelchair and started pushing it, moving around the side of the house, and we followed him in single file, listening to the story of the birth of the idea for a new garden where once there had been an immense meadow sloping gently to the west. On the far side, camouflaged between the two sun umbrellas, the gardener in the gardener's uniform was waiting for us—but I didn't give them the satisfaction of seeing my surprise.

"I'll lead the way," Rossi said, and the twins—the gardener and the hunter—lifted him up and ventured down the three steps, then carried him around the whole meadow, stepping over all the obstacles and moving impassively like a pair of mirror images flanking the wheelchair. They put him down at every stage along the way, so as to allow him to explain the various phases of the failure, as he called it, and it was amazing to watch these two aged laborers' control and energy and apparent lack of effort. Most amazing of all was the empty expression they shared; I thought that it couldn't possibly have been real, that it certainly hid some rich and secret interior life, that they'd trained themselves to fake an animal-like (or even vegetative) insensitivity in order to fool outsiders. Certainly that emptiness attracted me, maybe only because it convinced me of my own fullness.

Rossi spoke of his wife, if that's who she was, without ever naming her—she wanted a fabulous rock garden, she had fallen in love with the idea of a garden without plants, she had a Japanese obsession; he allowed her no more than a pronoun, and this certainly made me uneasy, because it was *she* who had called me, and maybe the husband assumed that we knew each other, indeed he seemed to take for granted that I'd been socializing with her for a while and that I would understand his ironic and possibly not-so-affectionate allusions to her volubility and her changing her mind a thousand times. We had reached the cistern, a concrete-rimmed water storage tank at the end of the meadow, and I turned toward the house, trying to imagine a garden on this site. The end point was already set: all I had to do was work backward from the water and everything would fall into place, all the way up to the villa. At that moment I saw the woman I'd seen earlier, standing behind the balustrade fifty yards from us, her arms crossed.

We go slowly back up. Swaying like a maharaja atop an elephant, Rossi tells us about a famous massacre that happened right near the cistern during the first war of independence from Austria; patriots fleeing after the defeat at Novara in 1849 took refuge here but were found and slaughtered by the Austrians. Blood in the water; crimson, vermilion, clouds of burgundy red; the burst heads flattened under the horses' hooves, gray matter drifting and twisting on the water like rags that had slipped out of a washerwoman's hands. (The hedges really are cotoneaster and holly, badly pruned.)

I don't raise my eyes until we're right on top of her, and I cannot hide my disappointment when I realize that she can't be the woman from that evening, she's not even Elisabetta Renal, and I'm hit with a suffocating fatigue. Rossi introduces her as his assistant, without saying what she assists him in, and she shakes our hands without interest and doesn't say a word. She's younger, smaller, more insignificant. She examines me from head to toe: she sees the dirty, sweat-soaked T-shirt, observes the muddy jeans and work boots, and then looks back up to stare at the rip that begins in my left armpit and runs straight across my chest like the gap in a breast-feeding shirt. She doesn't get who I am, what I'm doing there.

Again we're invited to stay for lunch, but we refuse, promising we'll come again. I say that anyway I need time to think, I'll need a week or ten days; I'm very interested in the job, but I have to think about it; I could already present a few ideas in ten, fifteen days, as well as a rough estimate; I need to think, did I already say that? I'm nearly stuttering with frustration. I look down at the ground; the gravel is of very poor quality.

"I'll let you go—but first," says Rossi when we're in front of the R4, "I must ask you a favor. Our property has recently been overrun by wild dogs, which I don't think is random chance; it seems suspicious to me.

We've already alerted the carabinieri, and any of these animals that get killed on the property are turned over to them for examination."

"It was an accident," I say.

"I'm sure it was." He draws a circle in the air with his finger. "They throw themselves under the wheels."

I open the back of the car, and the twins pull out the German shepherd's cadaver. They take it away with unreal delicacy. They're just as careful as they were when moving the wheelchair, I think as I watch them, mesmerized.

In less than half an hour we're sitting in a place called the Sternwood Steak Palace. Witold is talking about Mr. Rossi. He likes him a lot; he considers him a remarkable person. It's shocking that I forced him to go around the whole meadow in his wheelchair, those poor guys had to carry him around in the hot sun, I've got a lot of nerve not even to apologize, not even to show any remorse. But he's smiling: it's not a real scolding. Or rather, it's real but it's not serious.

"A man of lively wit, not without some singular elements in his character," he says suddenly.

I stare at him without giving anything away (naturally I can't place the quote, but if I nail it I don't want him to think that I made a wild guess).

"Manzoni," I say confidently.

"D'Azeglio," he murmurs.

Finally our three steaks arrive.

After two days (two days in which I don't have any important events or thoughts) I'm in the courtyard of my farmhouse and looking in through my window, spying deliberately on the scene taking place in my living room; deliberately even though the night is cold and windy and I'm in shirtsleeves and in order to see the room from the best angle I have to stand on tiptoes, my spine curved back like half of a Gothic pointed archway. But the spectacle before me is as irresistible as flypaper is to a fly: it's sweet and somehow definitive.

A man is sitting in an armchair in front of the fire. Two children are playing next to the armchair. Every so often one of the children, the bigger one, raises his head and says something to the man, who gives no sign that he hears him. The other boy, no more than two or three years old, uses a different strategy. Without speaking, he stops playing and goes to rest his head on the man's knees. The man doesn't react to this either, but the children don't lose heart, and a few minutes later they try again, each with his own weapons.

What did I come out here for? Finally I move away, bending down low even though there's really no need to do so. No one inside the house is going to notice me and be surprised and think that I must have slipped furtively out the back door. I reach the canopy where the cars are parked. I open the driver's door and huddle down and search the interior of the gray Renault Clio that my brother and the kids came in. I look in the glove compartment, under the floor mats, in the doorwells. I look in the trunk. What am I looking for? Signs, traces of life.

Ten minutes later I'm back in the kitchen as if I'd never left, and I'm preparing dinner for four, so all the burners are on high and the pots are sizzling and steaming and letting out various smells, and I'm in a clean checked shirt and less-than-clean jeans and gray slippers shaped like mice, which the kids gave me last Christmas, and over it all I have an oilcloth apron showing a tiger about to leap on its prey (the tiger's head covers the apron's bib, and his back feet touch the ground just at my knees), which was a gift from Carlo. The meaning of the slippers is clear—I've always called Filippo and Momo "mice," and Filippo explained to me that wearing my slippers during the week would remind me of their coming on Friday nights (every other week); but I haven't yet decided what the tiger means: I'm the tiger (because of my success at work)? Carlo is the tiger (he's slumbering, but he could awake any minute)? The tiger isn't anybody, and the meaning is in the apron itself?—i.e., I appreciate your hospitality and I want you to go on cooking for us.

But there could be yet another meaning. Filippo bounces into the kitchen, comes up to me, and says, "*First thing* tomorrow let's go visit Malik." His eyes show the pleasure he takes in pronouncing the words perfectly.

"Naturally. Durga asked after you."

He carefully considers my statement, not knowing whether to believe it, but ultimately his desire is stronger than his sense of reality. He smiles, gratified.

I bring the pasta to the table, help the kids get settled, put on Momo's bib, and go to call my brother. I find him in the same place I last saw him, sunk in the armchair in front of the fire, book open on his lap, still—I imagine—open to the same page, because he's looking at the fire and he doesn't appear to have moved a muscle.

My brother is a handsome man. He's as tall as I am, but he has straight shoulders and the body of a thirty-year-old, a nose less crooked than mine, eyes more intense (more beautiful, more intense: he doesn't have my whipped-dog eyes). Maybe his eyes, more than anything else, were the weapon he once used in his numerous, remarkable conquests (that, and his ability to stun you with language, back when he still talked). "Carlo," I say, "it's ready." And he is startled. What's ready? Nothing is ever ready, everything is in a state of perennial incompleteness. Who's ready? No one, everybody's always unprepared, taken by surprise. Things start passing you by when you're young, but you watch them go past, thinking you still have time to catch up. It's not true. You make a few attempts, and maybe manage to glimpse them again in the distance, unreachable, and so you stumble and break your stride, panting. Sometimes things take a wrong turn, and they run around the same bushes three or four times, like Winnie-the-Pooh, before they see their mistake. Unexpectedly, if fate has decided to reward you, you see the things right in front of you and you can grab them. So I became a respected and sought-after landscape designer, while my brother, at forty-five, is struggling along hopelessly at the university. His one attempt at making money (launching a website about terrorism in the seventies, www.theMoroKidnapping.com) failed for lack of funding.

"Papa: *First thing* tomorrow Uncle Claudio is going to take us to visit Durga," says Filippo. Momo mumbles something through a mouthful of pasta; he puts his pacifier in his mouth, pulls it out again, dips it into the sauce, and sucks on it.

"Fine," says Carlo. "How's Malik doing? Did his wife have the baby?"

"Not yet."

The sudden flash of curiosity about my neighbor Malik and his wife has exhausted all his energy. He doesn't open his mouth again. But Filippo's presence at the table makes the conversation easier: whenever a silence falls, he takes care of it. Carlo can participate by smiling and shaking his head like a contented and kindly paterfamilias worn out by a long day at work.

After dinner Filippo begs to stay up and play a little longer.

"Maybe it's time for bed," I say.

Carlo doesn't get involved.

Momo says: "Me me, lillonger."

"He also wants to stay up and play a little longer," Filippo translates.

Carlo heads toward the armchair.

"So can we?"

"Okay," I say, "but when it's time, you'll go to bed without a fuss."

"Tonight we'll just lay the *foundations*," says Filippo.

I dump the leftovers into the trash can and pile the dishes in the sink. For a moment I think he's using "foundations" to mean some building supports, the understructure of some toy I haven't yet seen, or some kind of Lego. Then I understand: he's talking about laying the groundwork for our game. I had promised to act out a battle with our old 1-to-72-scale toy soldiers. From the protection of a pillow-hill, Filippo prepares to massacre my troops, who are marshaled in the open field below. In this preparatory stage, Momo is the wild card. He flings himself on the soldiers that Filippo and I have already set out on the carpet and hits them with his pacifier, detonating deadly missiles on the poor fools. It doesn't ruffle Filippo; he rights the soldiers, saying, "No, Momo, this one's not dead *yet*."

Every now and then I mutter a soft reminder: "Bedtime." There are minor variations: "Filippo . . . sleep," or "It's getting late—bed." But I don't stand up, I don't make a move to pick them up and carry them to bed, I don't even raise my eyes as I'm trying to get the soldiers to stay on their feet (they're the old Airfix figures from when we were kids: they're thirty years old and have every right to be tired of fighting, but there are no armchairs for these soldiers); I pepper the game with reminders to prove that I haven't forgotten my adult duties and responsibilities. But who am I proving it to? There are only four of us in my living room, around the fireplace with the great log that takes all evening to burn: Filippo and Momo don't want to hear what I'm saying, and Carlo is lost in his own thoughts.

When the kids agree to go to bed, I'm the one who takes them upstairs. I have to put them in their pajamas, I have to make them brush their teeth, and put a diaper on Momo for the night. Filippo points out that "Momo wears a diaper at night but not in the daytime because he's *part* little." Then I have to tell them a story or a read a fairy tale, straining my eyes in the orange glow of the night-light. And even after I realize the children have fallen asleep, I stay in the bedroom for a moment, thinking about Elisabetta Renal's husband and his everyday life, what he might be doing while his wife romps around the countryside driving into ditches: peering through a magnifying glass at a stamp collection for hours, or dusting off battle souvenirs from the Risorgimento, or reading nineteenth-century aristocrats' memoirs full of enlightenment, determination, pride, and even vanity.

I go back downstairs, pour myself a glass of vodka and one for Carlo, who rarely drinks. I sit down facing him; I have to talk to him, I have to find a topic that will take his mind off things for at least half an hour—a lullaby for him. But I can't think of anything. I'm thinking about the wheelchair instead. A wheelchair is such a potent symbol of impotence that it disarms and discomfits the person who's standing. A man condemned to a wheelchair condemns his interlocutors to have some reaction: embarrassment, at least, and sometimes even guilt. A man slumped in an armchair (condemned to an armchair) presents the same kind of problem. Do I talk to him? Do I *not* talk to him? Do I lay my head in his lap?

Unexpectedly, Carlo is the one who speaks: "How can you stand being here alone all the time? How is it possible that you're my brother?"

I had often thought that Fabio wasn't really our brother (the thought was not linked to any particular event or specific historical moment, and thus scattered through my childhood; it was a thought I had on anonymous days, a thought that recurred in dull mornings at school and frustrating afternoons in the courtyard, while playing games that were never completely successful). For example, I recall my astonishment (maybe this is one of my earliest memories) when I found Fabio in a blue school smock in the nursery school courtyard during playtime. How did he get all the way there? What was he doing there? Who had brought him? I hadn't noticed anything; I was seeing him for the first time. He was in a corner, playing by himself (now I know that all three-year-olds play by themselves, even when it looks like they're playing with others); it was absurd that they'd enrolled him, absurd and hopeless. I was astonished but also worried: I feared that the teacher would get mad at me for a mistake that was my parents' responsibility alone. He wasn't fit for nursery school, and I didn't want to pay the price. I was sure that he would never grow up, that he'd never move out of the room we shared, out of our house, that he was irremediably little. They tell me that I repudiated him, that I denied to my classmates and teachers that he was my brother. Fabio didn't deserve to be treated like this: if ever there was a good kid, it was Fabio. He was hardly noticeable. Not even Carlo, who ruled me with an iron hand, was able to get Fabio involved in our games.

I'm thinking about him as I get milk for the kids, who have been up since eight, and then I get anxious because I still haven't fixed the shower faucet; it doesn't often happen, but sometimes my mess and filth and discomfort reach a critical point, and even though I usually manage not to worry about the environment I live in, I'm unable to disregard it completely. When I do worry, I'm consumed by anxiety, and this morning it's triggered by the wall plate for the shower faucet: it's come off the wall and I've already ascertained that the only way to attach it again is with ultrasuperglue, but none of the tubes of superglue that I have in the house has worked so far, so I've decided that I absolutely must go to the nearest home center with the kids while Carlo sleeps in (he'll sleep till ten, as usual).

Filippo wants to finish the battle—actually start the battle, because yesterday we merely laid the foundations, so I have to negotiate and make concessions, and the usual lures don't work; the promise of a comic book isn't enough, not even two comic books, not even two comic books and a cartoon video rental, or video purchase, not even the purchase of two videos. I have a flash of inspiration as I'm tying Momo's shoes and he's repeating the endings of our sentences ("comma-book," "bideo"): I offer Filippo the idea of building a cannon out of balsa wood and elastic bands so we can shoot glass or metal marbles at the soldiers, a precise replica of the cannon I used with Carlo and Fabio. Some-times—not always—the old toys work, proving somehow fascinating and strange to the kids; the deal is struck.

I strap the car seats into the E270 and the kids into the car seats, and I set off for the home center, which lies halfway between the nearest vil-lage and the mall, so I end up tracing the route I take every morning at 7:00 or 7:30 when I go fetch Witold, who has recently, with my help, bought a home for himself and his large family in an area of comfort-able new two-family houses. But this morning is different, because I normally drive the R4, very sleepily, all alone, and now I'm in the Mer-cedes, with the kids, and I'm agitated. The E270 changes things; obvi-ously it's faster, but that's not all: it goes faster without my realizing it, we shoot down the road as if we're flying, and Filippo points it out: he says we're going to get a *heavy* fine. I ask him how he knows that fines are heavy—has he ever hefted one? He doesn't fall into my trap: he doesn't answer. I ask him, "Do they write them up on lead paper?" And imme-diately, in a maneuver that's typical of him, he keeps me from pressing on in an area where he feels uncertain of his footing and asks whether I know how to fish for fish.

The other novelty about this morning, compared with my usual workday mornings, is the presence of Filippo, who speaks and fills the aural space with his stories, his questions, and his clarifications, and generally directs conversations according to his preferences, while Momo looks out the window with the same fascinated and rapt expres-sion that he has when watching television. There are three systems for fishing, I say, trying to concentrate and forget my anxiety: nets, poles, and underwater spearguns. Wrong—there are four: you can throw a hair dryer into the water and electrocute all the fish. I ask how he thought of that. He says that when Mamma and Papa still lived together,

Mamma had threatened to do that, to throw the hair dryer into the tub and electrocute herself. This, too, is a typical move, because if I had told him there were five systems, he would still have added another one: he has to carve out a space for himself in adult conversations, and he does so with his clarifications. Filippo is the clarification king. "You're the clarification king, Filippo," I say, and I look back without a smile to catch his eye in the rearview mirror.

"I'm the king and Momo is the prince," he says, to throw me off guard.

"Momo pimf," mumbles Momo around the pacifier in his mouth (I hadn't taken it away because I didn't want him to go wild).

But the third novelty about this morning keeps torturing me, and the trip can't distract me from it. The poplar plantations flow past, their rows as regular as battalions on parade, and they're followed by the mall, the multiplex, the disco, more poplars and cornfields, the gas station, houses, subdivisions, apartment blocks, a restaurant, garages and building supply warehouses, fences, the industrial chicken farm, the bathroom fixtures and faucets outlet, poplars and fields, scattered houses . . . But my agitation doesn't dissipate, and it's no use trying to reassure myself by thinking that I'm sure to find the ultrasuperglue I need: I can't calm down. Filippo talks about the huge ocean he crossed last summer, aboard a huge ship that cut the sea in half and killed all the fish, and I give up and admit that the shower-faucet wall plate is an alibi, a pretext—it has nothing to do with anything—that I'm agitated about other things. (The erection I get at this point could be purely physiological: I always get one at this time of the morning, especially in the car—it must be the vibrations.)

After half an hour in line, I manage to find a parking spot on the roof of the home center; then I take possession of a cart and put the kids in it and go down inside. Yes, there is such a thing as ultrasuperglue, and it glues every kind of material, including human skin, in no time flat, forever. I get balsa wood and some wide elastic bands and some small steel balls and also a garden spade, two short hoes, a fruit picker, two terra-cotta planters of dubious quality that aren't even particularly cheap—stuff I don't need, but I do have to fill up the cart and make the best of the time I'm spending here (because it's Saturday morning and the place is full of people, and I failed to think of that ahead of time). I also have to buy two straw gardener's hats that Filippo and Momo have gotten hold of. And the checkout line and the payment process (handing over my debit card, typing in my PIN, taking the receipt) magically calm me.

I remember the first time Fabio came back from the detox center: during the week, his mechanic's work at the garage gave him a rhythm and a schedule, but on Saturday morning he would begin to get agitated and move restlessly from one room to another, from kitchen to bed, up and down the hallway, rubbing his hands together, so I would suggest that we go to the supermarket. Our mother would sit at the dining table and write the shopping list on the back of a receipt that curled like old parchment, and then she'd give it to me with the money, which I would pass immediately to Fabio because I didn't want him to think I didn't trust him—they had told us it was important to treat him normally and not keep any secrets, to involve him in things. And he really did seem peaceful in the supermarket aisles (even though they weren't huge and packed with merchandise like nowadays) as he pushed the cart and checked the list against the items I took from the shelves and agreed to debate about the brands we chose, and the prices, as if we were a pair of old retired bachelor brothers.

The boys and I sat down at the café, although I couldn't recall if I'd promised them we would; it's practically an obligatory stop on our outings, and I know perfectly well it's not healthy for kids to snack all day long, but I absolutely needed a coffee because my earlier anxiety had left me with a sugar low, and the drop in tension made me a little unsteady on my feet. So I got a coffee and two fruit juices and three pastries, and while I helped Momo drink his juice, I began to hear the people around us talking about war and I raised my eyes to the TV hung in the center of the room and realized that I hadn't seen the news for three days and it was maybe a week since I'd bought the paper. I showed Filippo the pictures of the airplanes taking off loaded with bombs, but he shrugged his shoulders—he already knew about it.

"Why didn't you tell me?"

He didn't understand what I was asking him; he looked at me and laboriously chewed his pastry. Sometimes I think he's afraid people are making fun of him. How could an adult possibly not know that a war had broken out?

We went up to the roof of the home center to get the car and stood at the railing for a few minutes to gaze across the open country. There are not a lot of spots around here where one can see such a vast expanse of the region, and every time I come, when the air is still and clear, like today, I linger to contemplate the landscape as if it were the first time I'd ever seen it. There are yellow lines and blue splotches, straight black lines that halve the gray-brown fields, puffs of green, and white reflections from garages and industrial parks and warehouses. Everything is flattened out as if on an immense map without labels. Everything is more beautiful; you can't see the ugliness that is the industrial sheds, the devastation of the fields hammered by hail, the filth along the sides of the road, the dreadful taste of the Indo-Saracen style subdivisions, the garbage of the mini-mall. From here the flatland looks like a garden (seen from the right height, gardens look like worlds).

I showed the children the distant towns, roads, and hills. I get great satisfaction from recognizing places and being able to point them out to someone. But I'm not so good at it since my father died. I mix up the towns, I mix up the names, and I think simply, "the city," "where Witold is," "where my mother is," and sometimes I fear it's the fault of the wine.

Last night I dreamed I'd found a cave in the woods with three doors guarded by three dogs, like in the Hans Christian Andersen tale about the magic tinderbox. Gustavo, my old dog, was guarding the first one, Durga was guarding the second, and a strange dog was guarding the third. I know that the three doors opened onto places very distant from one another in space and time, where certain scenes from my life were played out repeatedly, but the thing that most amazed me when I awoke was the idea that a place without a name, deep in the woods, linked other places together.

When we got home, Carlo wasn't in his usual armchair; he had turned on the TV and was watching the news about last night's attack and, now that I also knew more about it because I had listened to the radio in the car, we had the beginning of a conversation, a germinal exchange of impressions. Meanwhile, long lines of refugees marched through the mud, their children and old people abandoned on the side of the road, exhausted, or covered with clear plastic sheets on top of carts towed by tractors. Without taking his eyes off the screen, Carlo told me that someone had rung the bell.

"When?"

"Half an hour ago."

"And who was it?"

"I don't know, I didn't open up in time."

"Were they in a car?"

"I didn't see."

In other words, he didn't even get up from his chair. Maybe Malik came to ask for help taking his wife to the hospital; in any case, I could still take the kids to see the animals before lunch, so I decide to call him immediately.

False alarm: it wasn't he; in fact, he can't go out and can't even have visitors. He seems very agitated, and so I press him to find out if anything has happened, if I can help in any way. He seems embarrassed, and then in the face of my insistence he blurts out a confession: Durga has diarrhea. I make light of it and ask—as if I'm talking about his future tot—whether Durga got a chill in her little tummy. But Malik is really worried: no veterinarian will agree to come treat Durga, no one knows where her owner is, far away on one of his trips, and if one of the animals dies he'll surely lose his job, now, just when his baby is about to be born . . . I reassure him. If the famous photographer fires him, I'll find him a job.

I've always been proud of finding jobs for people: I've fixed all of Witold's relatives up with work, but maybe the first life I tried to orga- nize was Fabio's. When he left school I managed to get him a job as a warehouseman at the FLD factory, and I covered for him when he be- gan to steal. Later, at the garage, I vouched for him, and I insisted on paying for the replacement parts that disappeared, even though it wasn't ever clear he was the one who took them—somebody slyly took advan- tage of the presence of a perfect fall guy. I can't believe my brother could really steal—I never could, not even when faced with the evi- dence. The only thing that ever disappeared from our house was a wal- let of gold coins. Every year for Christmas our father gave us each one coin as a gift, and he managed to keep up the tradition even after he lost the factory. The wallet disappeared. From then on, without discussing the problem, each of us began to hide the things that were most pre- cious and that could most easily be sold in secret places. And during the toughest two months, when Fabio lost control, before we succeeded in checking him into the detox center for the second time, my father and I made sure that one of us was always at home.

Technically I had not helped Malik with his job, but I'd helped him with many other practical and bureaucratic details. Finding jobs for people is my way of making friends. I don't have other friends: I've lost them all along the way—not everyone accepts help. I couldn't help Carlo even if I wanted to, unless I were willing to change fields. I think about

Filippo and Momo all the time, so I already have ideas about the jobs that would suit them, and I reflect on their characters, their inclinations, to understand what they might do or want to do, so I can begin to build a network of connections. I ought to design a garden for a famous hospital director, in case Filippo wants to become a doctor, and for an engineer, because I think Momo will have a way with numbers and computers.

For the rest of the weekend Filippo tries to imitate the sounds made by a diarrhetic Doberman, and Momo echoes him without knowing what he's mimicking. I build the balsa wood cannon, let myself be massacred in a battle with unequal weapons (the rules are established, rewritten, and broken by Filippo), I cook, I watch *The Lion King* with the kids, I put them to sleep, I dress them again in the morning, I try with very little success to get Carlo to talk. When six o'clock on Sunday rolls around, I can honestly say I'm happy the kids are going back to the city, even though when they're gone I let myself go and I eat and drink too much and get drunk and stay up late for other reasons, damaging my health. The kids are already strapped in their car seats, I've just made a joke about the cheap flimsiness of the Clio, and Carlo is saying goodbye with his window down, and I haven't once thought about who might have rung my doorbell yesterday morning. At that very moment a black Ka drives into the courtyard of my farmhouse.

Elisabetta Renal stops about ten yards away and looks at me, and I see Carlo look at her with surprise, desire, and envy.

"She must have taken a wrong turn," I say, but I can see perfectly well he doesn't believe me. Because he probably saw the same car from the window yesterday, and forgot or didn't want to tell me.

"We'll see you next week," he mutters, and he shifts into gear with a demoralized slump. And for a moment I imagine their drive home, the father's silence and the obsessive chatter of the older son. Momo will sleep.

2

THE LIGHT IS LUKEWARM AND DIFFUSE, IT'S SIX O'CLOCK ON A TRANQUIL EVENING, spring has just begun; on my feet in the middle of the courtyard, I haven't got the strength to go back indoors. The conversation with Elisabetta Renal lasted no more than fifteen minutes: she came to invite me to dinner, and she left. Then the phone began to ring, and it uprooted me from the square foot of ground where she had abandoned me. It was Witold: he always calls me on Sunday evening, and I don't yet know why, because we always make a plan for Monday on Friday or Saturday, so these calls are unnecessary—maybe he wants to check that I'm still alive, that I haven't killed myself with wine and food, or that I haven't decided over the weekend to do without him and hired an Albanian or a Kurd instead. We confirmed the appointment that we had already made for the next morning.

Going back into the house, I noticed the toys scattered around, but I didn't go near them or touch them, as if they had fallen from the sky and might explode; I pitched camp in the kitchen, set the table for two, reheated the leftover half of the roast, and ate lustily at first, sitting at my place, and then more slowly and thoughtfully, sitting at the guest's place. I stayed on the sofa until eleven o'clock (at eleven I discovered that it was already eleven), drinking a bottle and a half of wine, staring at the absent shape sitting in my place—he was completely indifferent to life's complications—and then turned on the TV to hear the latest news about the aerial attacks, flipped channels randomly a few times, and ultimately began to tremble with cold, even though I don't usually mind the cold. It can't have been caused by the wine, because I drink wine every evening, and it wasn't the war, I don't think. It can't have been the departure of the kids, which plunges me into gloom but never into panic. So the cold must come from Elisabetta Renal. I thought about her in bed without managing to get any warmer.

The next morning I went out at six and crossed the plain to the south, passing the carbonized wrecks of the weekend's accidents, the rivers and the poplar plantations stretching as far as the eye could see, a cluster of neo-Gothic villas, a hospital, tire warehouses, a restaurant-hotel, abandoned fields, a farmhouse, an organic pig farm, a pharmaceutical lab, a gated residential community, a (pretty decent) mall. When I got to the ridge of the Ossiglia house, up in the hills thirty-five miles from my home, the light was metallic, the air fresh, and I was wearing a fat winter jacket; the Poles asked me if I felt okay. From Witold's expression, I could tell that I had forgotten to bring something that I should have remembered. I pretended to look for the thing in the back of the R4 for a long time while I struggled to reconstruct last night's phone call, and finally I remembered what had taken place here several mornings ago, before we happened to go meet Mr. Rossi at Villa Renal.

That day the garden we were finishing seemed disastrous and ugly, and I paced it up and down four times without managing to explain to Witold why I was so disgusted. I had known for a week, or maybe a month, but I had ignored the problem, hoping that it would solve itself. It didn't. I shook my head mutely and swung my arms around. The garden's whole dynamic and the dialogue among its parts were ruined by one corner, one hinge that I hadn't figured out how to build right, and the garden couldn't unfold, couldn't develop; one single microscopic patch of earth—fifteen misconceived, defective square yards—was ruining everything; like a fishbone stuck in your throat, this thing kept the garden from talking and breathing. I sat down on one of the four teak chaise longues and closed my eyes. Witold pretended to be completely absorbed in his work, unloading material from the R4 without looking my way.

There was no way to correct it. Having to throw out weeks if not months of work isn't just a blow to your pride: you fear you might be making an even greater error, and it's not easy to change something if you don't have any idea of what to replace it with; but until you fix the error your mind stays tangled up in it and your feet are mired in the mud and you just can't escape. I moved close to the bed we had built, a useless web of raised rhomboid planters regurgitating moss, a stack of planters staggered across three levels and interspersed with layers of polished white stones. Enraged by my own stupidity, I said that I wanted to eliminate this monster, but Witold rebelled, in his way: he began to grumble, saying that the job was supposed to have been finished a while ago, that there was no point rethinking elements that the client had already accepted, expressed enthusiasm for, or anyway approved. I kicked at the wood, slamming the planter with my boot. I told him that he wasn't the one who made the decisions, that the garden was mine, the job was mine, that I was the boss, and if he didn't like it that was just too bad. I kicked again. I told him that Jan would have to bring the excavator the first morning he could, and in the meantime I would come up with a solution.

But now it is Monday, and in the meantime I hadn't given it another thought. Of course, during last night's phone call, Witold, who never forgets anything, had asked me whether he ought to get materials for the new bed. I didn't understand what he was talking about and hung up the phone.

Now I'm observing the scene, and keeping an eye on Witold observing the scene: he's keeping an eye on Jan flattening the earth with the small excavator that we use for big jobs, the excavator that until last year was handled only by Witold; Witold agreed to turn it over to Jan when I insisted, although he's generally reluctant to give up any responsibility, even when it means taking on greater responsibilities. Witold tends to centralize things. Sooner or later, whether I want it or not, he will become more than just my right-hand man: he's starting to reason, to choose, to suggest, and in the future we'll be able to accept four or five jobs at once instead of just one or two. He is thirty years old, and he could become a garden designer too, if only he would cultivate a healthy dose of worldly ambition, if only he would stop tolerating me as if I were his cross to bear. I'm imagining the logo of our future partnership, Fratta & Witkiewicz, which would ward off his leaving me, which would keep him tied to me for a while, when I see a bottle green Honda HRV appear at the end of the driveway that winds up from the gate to the house. Witold raises his head too. He looks at me.

"Christ, Christ, Christ," I mutter to irritate him, because I'm irritated.

Signora Ossiglia crosses the garden with one arm waving in front of her head, as if she's got an enormous feather fluttering from her hat, and shouts that she doesn't want to disturb us. She's a tall, bony, energetic fifty-year-old; I shake her hand, waiting for her to ask me what Jan's doing, waiting for her to notice the ripped-up, disemboweled planters piled in a corner, and the cone of moss ready for the dump.

"You haven't decided to eliminate the bed, have you?" she finally says.

Witold doesn't react; I look at her without speaking.

"You haven't decided to take it all apart, have you?" she repeats.

I don't know what to say; Witold can't take the tension, and he glances over at me, almost imploring me to make something up.

"It all collapsed in the night," I say. "I think some of my calculations were wrong"—I swirl my right finger and draw little circles in the air— "in the planning stage." I smile, as if it's a common accident, a forgivable oversight.

"What a pity—I liked it so."

"We'll build it again, more beautiful than before."

"Oh, I'm sure you will."

She says that she had two free hours and that she couldn't resist—she couldn't help coming up to walk among the boxwood cubes and spheres. She's referring to the bottom end of the garden. I give her a false smile of gratification (it means nothing to me) and say I'll accompany her. We set off.

I tell her about my passion for sweet gum trees, I talk about "seasonal chromatic variations," I explain the importance of alternating between fullness and emptiness, I talk about "attention to visual aspects." I don't like explaining, I don't like talking this way, but with certain clients it's the best approach: it fills up the conversation and gets it over with. Indeed, after ten minutes she tells me to go back to work, she didn't mean to disturb me (in other words, she wants to be alone). I smile, I bow slightly, and I go off. But before I turn the corner of the little wall of yellow and red bricks that marks the bottom end of the garden, before I head toward the spot where Witold and Jan are clearing away the last traces of the bed, I look back to see what Signora Ossiglia is doing all by herself. What my clients do by themselves in my gardens, when they take possession of my gardens, when I cut the umbilical cord and abandon my creatures to their adoptive parents. What my clients see in my gardens, which I'll never see, because I'm seeing other things there; concerned with my own anxieties, which are almost always useless from their point of view. What represents a whole world for me is, for them, a place that's subordinate to the house, where they can spend time on Sunday afternoons in the spring looking after plants, where they can stroll with friends, where they can stroll alone before going back into the house, a house that doesn't even exist for me (even though I pretend it's not true, and I speak of the house and the garden "reflecting each other," and "rhyming," and "creating a musical accompaniment for each other").

• • •

So this is what Signora Ossiglia did when she was alone: she bent down to caress the dwarf azaleas decorating the border of the boxwood checkerboard. I would have liked to caress Elisabetta Renal that way, yesterday evening, when she got out of her Ka: stroke her cheek and reassure her, make her understand that she had found someone to share her fears with. She didn't show the hostile, decisive character that I would expect from a person capable of running over a man with her car; she seemed instead to need help: she was in a dense panic, as if the air had clotted up around her, and she moved and spoke with difficulty. Right off the bat, she didn't say hello, she didn't pretend to ask whether I was Claudio Fratta, she didn't pretend to introduce herself; she said only "What are you doing Thursday evening?" and her voice trembled.

It was just a moment before she caught the mistake, and she thought she could still fix it: "I'm Elisabetta Renal; you're Claudio Fratta, aren't you?" But in the face of my silence she gave up and repeated, "What are you doing Thursday evening?"

She could have said, "Why don't you come to our place Thursday evening?" or "Come over on Thursday evening," or "Are you free Thursday evening?" which would have been a good middle ground. The question "What are you doing Thursday evening?" is out of place, extreme; it can seem aggressive, but when spoken in a supplicating tone, it confuses the issue even further, because it's like a feeble claw grabbing your throat: you can't tell whether you should believe the aggression or the plea for help—and indeed I couldn't formulate an answer.

I almost never do anything in the evening, so I was sure I was free that night, but I wasn't as sure that I wanted to let her know it; I didn't want to answer "Nothing—why?" and yet that seemed to be the only possibility.

Ultimately I stuttered ". . . why?" without any capital letters.

The truth was that I didn't quite understand: for a moment I thought she wanted to go out with me alone, to ask me why I had behaved that way in the emergency room. It would have been better if she hadn't come to flush me out of my nest here; the farmhouse courtyard is a sad place, and she was looking around it, seeing the planters lined up sloppily against the wall like condemned men; the tangled garden hose, all muddy and leaky; tools; watering cans; black plastic bags strewn around randomly; two piles of gravel abandoned in front of Gustavo's dog bed; and, farther off, the canopy protecting the parked cars and stacked-up snow tires and mountains of newspapers and plastic bottles. It wasn't a place that could make her fall in love with me. I'm embarrassed by my courtyard; it was as if she'd come and asked to look inside my mouth before entrusting her garden to me. The sweatshirt I was wearing was decent, but I almost never shave on Sunday mornings, and after a day of playing with the kids I must have looked as sad and rumpled as the courtyard. At least my hands were jammed into the pockets of my jeans, so I looked fairly nonchalant.

Elisabetta Renal's appearance, by contrast, wasn't sad, not in the same sense of the word, even though she was afraid. When I had seen her face last, it was ravaged and bloody, but it showed no traces of the accident now; maybe the cut on her forehead was camouflaged by her hair, or maybe they'd sewn it up so well there was no scar—I was happy to have brought her to a good hospital. I didn't understand why that face attracted and interested me so, and I'd already asked myself many times whether, if I hadn't seen it for the first time that November evening, and if I hadn't imagined its expression at the very moment when the Ka gave the coup de grâce to the man with the steaming head, that face would have the same effect on me—would I want to stroke it and kiss it and examine it closely? I don't even know whether those eyes are beautiful: they're so dark and elusive, and her gaze is ambiguous—direct and provocative sometimes, and the next instant just imploring.

"Why did you come when I wasn't there? I don't know if Alberto showed you everything—I don't know what he told you—you must come back to us on Thursday evening."

"Your husband was very gracious; I stopped by without letting him know, and even so—"

"You must come to dinner with us," she repeated, and I was more than ready to accept, I simply didn't have the time to react, not in words, and not even with a gesture or a facial expression, but I'm sure I didn't express any doubt, especially because of my relief at the idea of seeing her with her husband and postponing a tête-à-tête with her.

She must have thought that I didn't want to come, though, because she said with an offended tone, "You absolutely must."

Not even a minute had passed; I was in the middle of my courtyard, and to me it seemed clear that I would have accepted any invitation at all, but Elisabetta Renal was very agitated, and until now I hadn't found a pause in her anxiety where I could slip a word in.

"Yes, naturally, of course I'll come," I said, as if talking to a petulant client about a poorly done job.

Faced with my irritation, she did something totally paradoxical: she relaxed, smiled, slipped her hands into the pockets of her jeans, and pushed her shoulders back as if she were stretching. I smiled too. And the flowering magnolia near the entry gate smiled too, making the courtyard less sad.

"It's very strange," she said. "Do you know how I found your address?"

I shook my head.

"I found it in the phone book."

I couldn't tell whether she was making fun of me.

"You may be the only person I know who still has his name in the phone book; nobody wants to be found these days."

I smiled. I thought that if this were just an isolated thing, I could forgive her. But suddenly she seemed to have a lot to say.

"Do you know when I first heard about you?"

"You told me: from Mr. Libet, the engineer."

"Oh, that wasn't true . . . I mean, he talked to me about you, but much later . . . Once I had to go to the dentist, but there were two dentists on the same landing, I didn't read the names, and I went in the wrong door and in the waiting room were two ladies who were talking about you and this beautiful garden . . . Forty-five minutes later I realized I was in the wrong place and I crossed the landing and I went into the right dentist's office and—God, I'm telling such a stupid story!"

She covers her mouth with her hands, her fingertips on her lips, her eyes moist.

"No, absolutely not. Why is it stupid? No, go on."

She shakes her head, looks off to the side.

"And what happened at the other dentist's?" I ask slowly.

She shakes her head no. She bites the knuckles of her left fist.

"You can't leave me wondering; go on."

She doesn't move.

"Go on."

She takes a long breath and gathers her courage.

"There was a magazine, I opened it, and inside was a picture of you and an article about your gardens," she says in a single breath.

I nod. "I'm very popular with dentists."

"The thing that persuaded me," she says, regaining her confidence, "and persuaded Alberto too . . . is that . . . well, I don't know if it's true, but I read . . . the magazine said that you're there during the work, you participate . . . you don't just draw up a design . . . it said, 'He's someone who gets his hands dirty . . .'"

"I build gardens," I say. "I'm an architect and a gardener. And my hands . . . yes, they're almost always dirty . . ."

Elisabetta Renal smiles. "You'll come to dinner?"

"I'll come."

All at once she turned and got back into her car. She started the engine and only then looked at me from behind the glass. At that moment she must have realized that she hadn't even said goodbye, so she rolled down her window and asked whether their garden site really was as disastrous as she thought it was, whether there was no hope at all for it. I came two steps closer—actually so that I could get a better look at her neckline, the white edge of her bra echoed by a band of lighter skin; she wasn't looking at me anyway, and maybe she wasn't even listening, her head filled once more with the reverberations of her restlessness, or something that kept her eyes glued to the dashboard.

"It's a difficult site, but easy sites produce only banal gardens," I lied.

It was only after she was gone, when I saw the Ka disappear around the curve at the bottom of the road, that I felt all the fear she had transmitted to me. I was afraid that I would rip apart like a sheet of newsprint paper and fly away on the next breeze, and I feared the opposite too: that I might fall to the ground and spend the whole night in the courtyard, as cold as a stone; I was afraid that the ghosts of my dead would come back to punish me; that nothing would happen and that Elisabetta Renal would disappear from my life.

And to squelch that possibility (that she had sought me out by chance, that she was really interested only in my gardening work), I developed a strange conviction: that she had sought me out to make amends. To make amends for her rudeness, for example: she had never thanked me for taking her to the emergency room. But if that were the case she ought to have read from a different script: as soon as she got out of her car she should have put on a surprised expression and said, "Wait, I know you—where have I seen you before?" She didn't do that. Make amends for what, then? Make amends for a mistake? That night she had made a mistake and hadn't realized it. Had it taken her five months to figure it out? Maybe less—maybe she figured it out right away, but it took her five months to find me. Five months to invent the story about the two dentists.

Later on, trembling with cold, half awake: Why didn't she come into the house? Why didn't I offer her a drink? She could have stayed for dinner, we could have sat on the sofa in front of the fire, then I would have undressed her, held her, kissed her lips, the hollow at the base of her neck, her nipples, her belly button, her lips, the insides of her thighs, her toes. And I went back to thinking about the thousand ways I could have convinced her to stay, if I hadn't stood there as stolidly as a horse just listening to her; and I listed all the witty ways I could have countered her invitation by asking her to stay for dinner right then, with the irresistible nonchalance that some men use to get women into bed.

I go back to Witold. He's loading the debris into a wheelbarrow, pretending not to care, but actually curious to know how I plan to fill the empty space that Jan carved into the heart of the garden.

"Listen," I ask him, "do you remember whether, when we accepted this job, whether I told Signor Ossiglia something like 'Well, it's a difficult site—'"

"But easy sites produce only banal gardens," concludes Witold. "Yes, you said it; you say it to everybody—I thought you did that on purpose . . ."

"Sure, I *do* do it on purpose, but I don't want to do it too often."

"Anyway, this garden is not banal," says Witold.

Because he never compliments me spontaneously, I ask him to explain why he thinks it's not banal. And while he's explaining, I get a good idea for rebuilding the bed.

• • •

Two days at home. Witold and Jan in exile at the Ossiglias' finishing the job, I at the computer creating a design for the garden of a bank's data center; in order to do it, I would have to give up the Renal garden, but I've decided to accept that, I think, and refuse the bank, even though I don't know how to break it to Witold, and until I tell him I don't stop working on it, as if he were always here, standing behind me, peeking over my shoulder at the glowing screen.

Changeable weather, rainy afternoon, impossible to work outdoors; Witold appeared on my doorstep and dragged me out to a nursery to look at some plants. We drove back late, my head pounding with the voice of Mario del Monaco—I made the mistake of having a CD player installed with the radio in my E270, and now only Witold uses it, to listen to his operas. I stopped to eat at his house: a funereal atmosphere, everybody dismayed about the war—they've organized a rosary service for Good Friday, but fortunately Witold doesn't have the courage to invite me. So I couldn't drink; I got back in my car sober and thoughtful and kept the windshield wipers going almost all the way home before I noticed that it had stopped raining.

When I get to the farmhouse I wonder how I'll get to sleep; I turn on the computer, surf around a few sites, and later, with the screen full of eyes that stare out without seeing me, I make the mistake of clicking on the icon of the garden plan and I stay with it until 3:00 a.m., so I wake up on Wednesday in the worst possible physical state. The sky is cloudy and white, the temperature has dropped back by three months into winter, and I'm worried about the crisis in my closet.

I tumble down the slope of my day, going from the mall to my mother's house to the parking lot of a giant suburban "hypermarket."

"My mother cries all the time," I said to Cecilia.

We were in the usual spot, sitting in her Fiat Regatta. The E270, dark and alien like a stranger's car, was parked alongside. The Regatta was already full of shopping bags, but I had just arrived; the hypermarket closed at 10:00, so I had all the time in the world. Cecilia was wearing jeans and a light windbreaker with a terry-cloth lining; she was uncombed and had bags under her eyes, and she'd gained weight: it required a stretch of the imagination to find her attractive and desirable, but I couldn't help it: I was always looking for a solution that would involve me personally, a clever shortcut to becoming a father.

She gave me an inquiring look; she's always ready to interpret, to find explanations, no matter how unlikely or useless they may be.

"Why does she cry?"

"I don't know." I looked at her. "But not about the two of you."

"Not about that *anymore*, maybe, because you told me that she was already crying a year ago . . ."

"Maybe she was crying for some other reason."

She sighs. She's never satisfied by any explanation. So, to fill the gap in meaning, she has to move right on to other things: other events, other words, other feelings that need decoding. All around us cars with empty trunks drive up, and other cars depart, overflowing with provisions; that's the real purpose of this parking lot—all other uses should be prohibited, or at least discouraged.

"You found nothing?"

"No, not this time either."

"But did you look carefully? Did you check the glove compartment? Notes, condoms, porno videos . . . ?"

"I checked. Nothing." I pause. "Look, Cecilia, I really don't think there is anybody—he couldn't fake it that well."

"He couldn't? But he faked it for so long . . ."

"At my place, he spent two days in an armchair, staring into space; if he's faking it, he's never been so consistent . . ."

"It's not a question of being consistent."

"And has he written to you again?" I ask, to change the tone of the conversation and protect Carlo.

"Yes."

"What does he say?"

"The usual things."

"What?" I wanted her to tell me, as if repeating it could make her believe it a little bit more.

"That he made a mistake, that he can't take it anymore, that he needs me, that he wants to talk to me."

"Talking never hurts."

I have no idea where this phrase came from. She glares furiously at me. "Talking hurts a lot, for Christ's sake!"

"Yes, of course, but after all these months—"

"For me, nothing has changed."

Silence falls for a few minutes—but a nice silence, without any discomfort. Then she sighs and says she has to go. The cars' headlights sweep over us like a movie camera in a tracking shot: our white faces, our eyes wounded by the flash.

"Did the kids behave themselves?"

I go into detail about everything we did on the weekend; I've gotten used to producing different versions for her and for my mother—I know what each wants to hear.

"They're a couple of angels," I conclude.

"I always forget there's no point in asking you if they were good."

I open the door to get out, and again she says, "Why does Marta cry?"

Why was my mother crying today? She was sitting in the room next to the kitchen, with her sewing box open on the table, which bubbled with needles and spools tumbled together higgledy-piggledy; I'd asked her to stitch a button back onto my jacket, and she held the jacket in her lap, gazing at it pityingly as if it were dying, letting the sleeves hang down while the hem fell open to reveal the torn and threadbare lining. I pretended that the button had just popped off, but in fact I'd bought it at the notions shop in the mall, where I could also have had it sewn on, so I can't say whether my visit to my mother was an excuse to come and ask her a favor, or whether I was grasping at the button like an amulet that could give me the courage to come see her. In any case, the upshot was that my mother was crying: she starts crying during all my visits recently, and I ought to understand why, but I don't, and I can't ask her anymore—I've asked her three times, and it only makes her cry more (unless she's crying for the war refugees, like the way Witold's wife and sister do).

I spent some time telling her stories about the kids; last Sunday we couldn't come visit her because Carlo had to get them back to the city before dinner, so there had been negotiations in the days before that, and as I had tried to mediate, I'd suggested that we all meet at lunch, for once, but Carlo and my mother had discouraged me by raising a bunch of objections. I had suggested that they talk directly, but my mother would never call Carlo, and Carlo must have forgotten.

In the opposite corner of the room stands the Schiedmayer upright with a score open on the stand, and I stare at the notes (illegible at this distance) while talking to my mother, like someone on TV reading from the teleprompter: facing one way but with my eyes elsewhere. I tell her what we did on Saturday and Sunday, how much the kids ate, how much we played; I tell her that Filippo speaks so well, and that Momo is so lovable; I tell her that Filippo will always be the best student in his class (some might call him pedantic), that Momo is as sharp as a six-year-old (some might call him a nuisance). And everything I say makes her nod, with her head still bent over the gray tweed jacket, and she traces the genealogies of their personalities—the virtues this one gets from his grandfather, the defects that one gets from his great-aunt—partly because she's understood by now that there won't be any more grandchildren: Carlo has done his bit, ruinously, and I won't ever do mine, to avoid ruining anyone else.

And her eyes keep producing tears that she blots with a white handkerchief balled up in her fist, using quick, precise, repetitive swipes, trying to make it look like a casual, distracted gesture. We sit in silence for five minutes, and then I get up and step out of the room and glance down the hall toward our bedrooms and see the usual shadows, the space just wide enough for two men supporting a third man between them, repeating that gesture for all time. In the living room the French doors are open onto the balcony, the white curtain swollen with air, but the house isn't sailing, it's not a boat setting off into the future: it has arrived at its final destination and it has docked forever. I go out, lean my elbows on the railing, and look at the narrow street without sidewalks and the stage set of identical façades, white two-story houses that look like a child's drawing. A woman passes with shopping bags, raises her eyes, sees me, and doesn't greet me; even though I think I recognize her, she doesn't know who I am, or knows who I am but doesn't like my mother. And, anyway, what am I doing out here on the balcony in this cold that feels like autumn, if I'm not even smoking? A dog goes by, not hurrying, and doesn't raise his head; a minibus goes by, its windows flashing a deformed reflection of the street, the doors, the ground-floor windows, the parked cars, the dog.

I trace the events that brought me here, to figure out where I made a wrong turn, where my map was wrong. (1) This morning, the examination of my wardrobe, triggered by a vague worry about how I should dress for dinner at the Renals'; (2) the need to bring a pair of corduroy pants to the dry cleaner and have a button sewn back onto the only decent and presentable jacket I have, the gray tweed; (3) the trip to the cleaners and the notions shop in the mall.

The original button must have been sewn on badly, I think, or it must have gotten tugged unexpectedly without my realizing it, on one of the few occasions when I wore the jacket (until last year I could button it easily). In the notions shop they had offered to sew the button on, which is when I thought of asking my mother to do it: it gave me an excuse to touch base with her, better than a hasty phone call would be. Now that I'm here on the balcony with the same dog going past again, now that I have to go back in to my mother, I'm not so sure it was a good idea.

She never cried in front of us: she wasn't the type, and when she was troubled—not necessarily angry—but if she was upset by some news, by a phone call or a letter, she didn't fling herself into a chair or a bed and break down; she just kept behaving in a way that seemed normal at first, except she didn't talk (or talked less than usual) and gave us harsh, icy looks, and the implicit message was "You have no right to fall apart if I don't." Now she cries all the time—with me, not with Carlo, not with the grandchildren, whom she rarely sees and who wouldn't know what to do . . . I don't know what to do either, I don't know how to comfort people and share their pain, I'm clumsy at funerals, I shake the hands of the bereaved as if I'm congratulating them, and I'm incapable of consoling friends who've been dumped by their lovers (not that they often ask me to).

Everybody cries. Maybe even my mother cried, when she was young, but the fact that she never let this be seen (she only let us see her being confident, authoritative—not authoritarian—calm, equitable, moderate, silent in her joy, silent in her anger; her silence was completely different from my father's silence, and this still astonishes me: we were born to a pair of very different silences, and we were three very different children) meant that her children were forced to learn to ape emotions elsewhere, outside the home.

My mother never knew how to sew on a button; she didn't—doesn't—know how to cook; she cleans the house energetically but without paying attention; she irons badly. She's famous in the family for these deficiencies: she's considered an artist, and her sisters refer to her as "the artist" without rancor, simply because for many years she gave private piano lessons (even before my father's bankruptcy, but afterward her income became more important), even though she never graduated from the conservatory because when she was twenty she married my father, who was ten years older.

I think about these things mechanically (I often think mechanically about them) while I watch her, bent over my jacket; after ten minutes' work, the button she has sewn on looks like a chunky, short-stemmed mushroom, and what's more, she has used thread that's too light. I think about what she must have thought when I showed up at the door with the button in hand. She must have understood it was just an excuse. She cries.

I saw my father cry only twice. This doesn't mean I never saw him in tears: he was a master at keeping his tears balanced on the rims of his lower lids, reabsorbing them, drinking them back with his eyes, as if he were crying on the inside. But there was no doubt that he cried, that this was his way of crying, and he cried only when he lost something important. (I didn't see him, or I don't remember him, when his parents died, because my grandfather was already dead when I was born and my grandmother died when I was three years old, but I'm sure that in both cases he cried that way.)

The first time I saw him cry was when he understood that he'd lost his business. In his office above the small factory, he was standing behind the desk and talking on the phone; it was one of those old gray desk phones, and the cord from the handset kept twisting up and forcing him to lean forward slightly, almost deferentially. I heard him repeating, "Thank you, thank you, I'm grateful, very grateful, you're rescuing me, you're very kind, thank you." I remember the words very clearly for one simple reason: my mother was there too, standing between the door and the desk, between me and my father, and she was shaking her head vigorously, disapprovingly, and her disapproval was so theatrical and violent, her condemnation so strange (because my parents never argued, never: I never heard them fighting about anything serious or decisive, or for any frivolous reason) that it made my father's words interesting—the banal phrases, the thanks (even that phrase "you're rescuing me" could have been simply an expression, a rhetorical exaggeration, unusual though it was coming from my father, who never uttered a word that was fashionable or affected). My mother seemed to want to say that you should never thank anybody, ever, for any reason.

She shook her head hard; I saw her from behind, I saw my father in profile as I stood still in the doorway, breathing heavily, maybe because I had run up the stairs—even though, before getting to my father's office, I must have gone to the office of Martino the accountant, a mysterious man who was always enveloped in the smoke from his two daily packs of cigarettes, buried amid his ledgers and invoices, flanked by his adding machine and his typewriter, his magical, monumental, musical instruments. He had an address book that snapped open to the right page after you slid the pointer to the letter you wanted. He had a sharpener with a spinning handle that could devour a whole pencil in just a few seconds. He had a paper-collating machine. He always gave me some kind of gift—the stump of a green eraser, a two-inch stub of pencil—or, when he had time, he would draft me a whole battalion of soldiers using three rows of letters on his typewriter:

I don't remember whether Martino was in his office that day, whether I couldn't find him or whether I stayed with him a while, as I usually did, in his little room next to my father's room, and therefore whether my impression that I was panting when I got to my father's door is just an imaginary detail that got tacked on to the memory later. Maybe I had gotten my breath back but lost it again as a result of the tension emanating from that scene: the simple arrangement of the players; the postures of their bodies—one spine bent forward (my father, in his shirtsleeves), one spine ramrod straight (my mother, with her coat and purse on her arm); the tone of my father's words; my mother's disapproval so vigorously expressed.

My father put the receiver back in the cradle and, without looking at my mother, walked around the desk and crossed the room and stopped in front of an open gray metal cabinet. For a few seconds he pretended to file away a folder that he'd carried from the cabinet to his desk, pretended to look for something else, and then, because my mother gave no sign of giving up and leaving, and because my father sensed that her outrage was increasing, and he didn't want her to see him cry (I don't think he had noticed me), he dropped all pretense and just stood there with his back to her, immobile before the cabinet.

That was when my mother said, "And thanking him, to boot!"

Without turning around, he responded feebly, "Yes—thanking him, to boot."

Then he began banging his head against the cabinet, not very hard but making a huge noise (they're really shoddy quality, those cabinets— every time you slide the door open the whole thing shudders as if it's about to fall apart; they're all in my basement now, holding my old files), doing it not to hurt himself but to drive my mother out, to present her with something embarrassing and new and too intimate, to frighten her into thinking he was going crazy (though it was really a very controlled craziness). Or maybe he simply felt like banging his head against the cabinet because he was in despair, he was finished, he was washed up: no more work, no more factory, failure, shame.

At that point my mother turned to go, and when she saw me she wasn't at all annoyed, as I had feared (had she asked me to wait for her in the courtyard?)—she was too annoyed with my father; she took my hand, and we went down the stairs and outside. I didn't expect any explanation, and I don't think she had any intention of giving me an explanation, but when we were at the gate of the little furniture factory, when she realized what our family was losing, she bent down and said softly but angrily, "Conti. Remember that name." At first her tone made me think she was scolding me, but then I understood that she was talking about the person Papa had been speaking to on the phone.

And we went home. I don't remember if I asked for any explanation, if I wanted to know why I should remember that name. I probably said nothing, I probably thought that Mamma and Papa had simply had a fight, and that was a curious novelty (I was most curious about my father's reaction, his hitting his head against the cabinet; I thought about it a lot, and it often made me laugh), but the fight didn't worry me—it couldn't last; and I was right, it didn't last.

Two things about that scene strike me now: the fluke that put me there to witness it, and my mother's agitation, which made me into the keeper of a memory.

We rarely went to see my father at the office; even though the plant wasn't far from home, we weren't supposed to disturb him, which is why Carlo was so obsessed with Papa's work that he forced me and Fabio to play in a pretend factory where he was the boss (I threw it back at him later when he tried to indoctrinate us with his revolutionary rhetoric), and I was Martino the accountant (I had gotten myself a datebook and an address book, and I smoked fake cigarettes made of paper), and Fabio was supposed to be the workman, but really he just kept on playing his own games: making long lines of toy cars (Carlo called this "the assembly line") or Lego buildings ("the construction site"). Fabio didn't explicitly refuse to take on the job that Carlo assigned to him; he just ignored the boss's orders and went on doing whatever he wanted to do, and Carlo (I now see) was intimidated by this attitude and tried to turn it to his advantage by reinterpreting and renaming Fabio's games, annexing them to his own. I'm still envious nowadays when I think about Fabio and his extraordinary ability to isolate himself, thus making other people create justifications for him and invent a useful role for him in the common game. (One day I had the amazing thought that maybe I believe I'm doing the same thing with my gardens, but I'm not sure.)

And even when my mother stopped by the furniture factory to tell my father something urgent, it didn't mean we were allowed to go up to the offices; in good weather she left us in the courtyard to play with the two German shepherds, and in bad weather she entrusted us to one of the workmen, and we'd spend half an hour hypnotized by a piece of wood turning in the lathe. But kids take unpredictable and mysterious turns when they're playing, and the flukes that lead them in one direction rather than another are completely random (Filippo and Momo buzz around like flies), and who knows why on that day I turned up at that moment in that point in space, who knows what I'd been thinking just a moment earlier, who knows what I was doing, what I was planning to do, what had happened to me two hours before, how I spent the following day, what I was doing two months later at the same time, what I thought when I heard that the factory was bankrupt, that my father had failed and was bankrupt, that he was "a failure"? It's a mystery; I'll never know: the telephone scene, the scene of my father's despair, my mother's words going home—these memories have erased all the rest. But I was there, I was a person, I tell myself occasionally, I was thinking about other things: about comics with Mickey Mouse and superheroes, about the toys I wished I had (a Gung-Ho rifle, a Lima train set, a Graziella leopard), about Carlo bossing me around, about Fabio not being our brother, about the piano that I didn't want to learn to play because it was sad—I was there, I was a person with my own life, and I recall almost nothing about that life because everything was erased by my father's crying; but I do recall, as I've said, that later when I thought about him hitting his head I laughed hard, and I never told my brothers about what I'd seen.

I didn't even tell them about what I'd heard when my mother spoke to me. I never said that I had to remember the name Conti, I never shared my mission with them. It was a name for me, not others, to remember. I was the keeper of the memory. And I kept it well: I remembered the name, even though I never heard it spoken again by anyone, and never saw it in print until at least twenty-five years later.

Last year I read in the paper about an investment company under investigation for usury; its president was named Conti. I collected every possible article about the affair. Conti defended himself by saying he was the victim, maintaining that the magistrates were persecuting him because of his ties to a certain political faction. I was very interested in this Conti's life for a short time: I followed him around and spied on him. A few months after I began trailing him, I witnessed his death in the parking lot of a mini-mall. But I'm not exactly sure that it was the same Conti, and I have no intention of asking my mother. And I'm not sure the subject interests me anymore.

The second time I saw my father cry was the night Fabio died.

A gray and rusty blockhouse next to a subdivision of little houses protected by hatred; long cars spilling out of garages built for families with lower incomes than this; and Pharaonic sidewalks never touched by human feet—sidewalks of asphalt (because around here, in the 1970s, asphalt was seen as wall-to-wall carpeting for the outdoors). It was a little factory, or a warehouse, built with blunt martial angles and bellicosities, reinforced cement and arrow slits, and maybe with skylights on the roof that couldn't be seen from the street. There must still have been a watchman's family living inexplicably in an annex, or the owners lived there, despairing of ever selling the place or renting it out—using it to store garden tools seemed like a waste, knocking it down would cost too much, and anyway, why? But they hadn't lost faith in the future: they had procreated, and they hung out little blue jumpsuits with the other laundry in the courtyard—the kid will grow up with an idea of decayed greatness, and some corner of his mind will always have an image of the abandoned factory, the place where they never let him go play. Childhood memories: a big space that can be neither used nor demolished.

Just as I did the last time, I stop to spy on the factory; this time I do it to calm myself down, but it's my tenth attempt to get calm: each attempt starts off well but ends quickly, leaving me even more agitated than before. At home, I spent an hour in front of the mirror trying to hide the fact that I couldn't close my jacket anymore, and with all my fiddling and pressing on the button my mother had sewn, I think I made it stick out even farther: it looks like it's about to pop off again; it seems bigger than the others. Looking at myself in the mirror, I pushed my spine farther and farther back, hunched over to bring the two sides of the jacket closer together, scrunched my arms up into the sleeves, and tried to flatten my stomach, but that was the hardest thing of all—it was impossible. When my hands were in my pockets and my arms tight against my body, I managed to give the impression (especially in profile) that the jacket could be closed. I look at myself now in the rearview mirror, and the interior light shows the true shape of my eyes—sad, unpleasant, framed pitilessly by the horizontal mirror; at home I didn't feel I was so poorly built . . . my mouth and my nose might be okay, but my eyes do me in, together with the extra weight I'm carrying, which adds fat to my cheeks and under my chin.

But the very certainty that I've lost before I start impels me to turn the engine back on again and pushes me up the road; my headlights grab the blacktop and pull it in from the thick darkness of the hills, and then the road slides away under my wheels like the treadmill in a gym, and I toss the darkness over my shoulders the way a mole tosses back the earth he's dug up, and then I pass under the brick arch at the entrance to the property and down into the dusty valley, under the dark, sad green trees, and then I remember that I should piss now to avoid asking to use the bathroom before dinner. I get out, walk around the car looking for some bushes, and decide to stand in front of the headlights—I don't want to risk wetting my pants and my shoes and then show up at the house spattered with droplets. I piss right in the middle of the street, pleased by my stream sparkling in the light of the high beams.

When I came out of the tunnel of plane trees and arrived at the villa, I braked abruptly before a bundled-up figure who gestured that I should pull over to the side—I saw him only at the last minute and nearly ran him over. It was one of the groundskeepers, the gardener or the hunter (I didn't remember anymore which one's hair was shorter in the back, and which had the longer sideburns), and he was wearing—I realized as soon as I got out of the car—a dark green loden coat that was two or three sizes too big for him, buttoned up to his neck and reaching almost to his ankles. He welcomed me and said that my hosts were expecting me; his face was a stony mask, utterly normal. We did not go up the road to the knoll: instead he led me along the glass wall of the garage-greenhouse toward a little door half hidden by a climbing plant.

We entered the basement level of the house, and my guide halted uncertainly for a moment, as if he expected me to ask something and wanted to give me time to speak up. I had no intention of taking off my jacket, even though it looked dreadful. But he pointed to a small toilet where the door was ajar and the light was on and said, "If you'd like to wash your hands . . ." For a moment I thought this was what people did in truly elegant houses—that guests were always invited to wash their hands in the basement before going up to the main floor to sit at the table—but no, this was impossible. I didn't want to irritate him, though, seeing that I'd treated him badly the first time we met (if it was actually he and not his brother), so I thanked him and washed my hands.

We go up two narrow flights of stairs and reach the entrance hall. I can't square my impression of the exterior with the room that I'm in now. On the inside it's clearly an old house, from the door frames, terracotta floor, and ceiling decorations to the antique furniture and the paintings in their gilded frames. I can give it only a quick glance, because a few steps take us to the threshold of a room where I can hear a fire crackling in the fireplace: we're in the drawing room and standing in front of Rossi, who's seated before the hearth in his wheelchair. This time he smiles at me immediately, and I smile back; he shakes my hand—"What a pleasure to see you again"—and invites me to sit in the small armchair next to him. Everything is carefully arranged at just the right distance, we're at the same height, so that I don't feel he's towering over me (as I would if I were sunk into a lounge chair), or that I'm towering over him (as I would if I had chosen a stiff side chair). This skill in anticipating what the guest will do in order to put him at ease fills me with gratitude toward the master of the house, but then—I think immediately—on many occasions that same kind of consideration has gotten on my nerves and made me loathe other hosts. The fact is, I like Rossi; I like his wife, but I like him too, though in his case I don't quite understand the reason why.

"It seemed like spring was here," he says, "and instead the cold weather has come back."

The weather, the climate, the rain and the sun, the hot and the cold, unseasonal oddities and seasonal suitability—whoever invented the idea of conversations about weather gave us a huge gift; what a blessing it is to be able to talk about the weather, that bottomless well of conversation . . . what a relief.

"You don't find it chilly, with just your jacket? Would you like us to lend you a sweater?"

If I put on a sweater, I probably wouldn't even be able to slide the jacket back on. "It's strange," I say. "I never got cold even before I grew this fat; I've never felt the cold . . ."

"Oh, come now, you're not fat . . ."

I cross my legs and let myself slide down a bit in the armchair; I like the sound of his voice, I like the plaid blanket that covers his legs and makes him look like a peaceful passenger on a cruise along the Riviera. I listen to him talk about a scientific theory that links human endurance to memory: it says that any human being can tolerate the heat of the desert as well as the Tuaregs do, or the cold of a polar ice pack as well as the Eskimos do, as long as he has a mental image, a memory of himself in a certain situation; he has to persuade himself . . . just as you can persuade yourself not to feel pain while walking on hot coals . . . and indeed it's been proved that . . . I'm not following him anymore, just admiring the way he pronounces his words and the modulations of his voice.

From where I'm sitting, I can see two large paintings facing each other across the room, country scenes of torpid calm: insignificant, invisible. To the right of the fireplace, half hidden by a Chinese vase that's been outfitted with a shade and turned into a lamp occupying most of the surface of a small desk, is a late-nineteenth-century portrait of a young man with a drooping mustache and wild eyes—too much white showing in the eyeballs, a naïve artist's mistake, I think. Next to the portrait is a more interesting painting of a country house covered with climbing plants and surrounded by a dense forest of emerald green leaves; it has a dark and mysterious atmosphere, and the road that should run up to the house is closed off with a drystone wall. Is the house abandoned? Is it the house that once stood here, before it was demolished, even though they kept the furnishings, the moldings and the door frames and window frames? I squint to pick some details out of the painting's dimness, to cut the glare of the Chinese lamp reflected off the oil-paint surface. I get the sudden feeling that Rossi wants to strike me, as punishment for my distraction, and I dodge fearfully.

As he continues speaking, he raises his hand, and in the darkness at the other end of the room a doorjamb obeys him, breaking loose from the wall; it becomes solid, as if sucking in atoms from the space around it—it gathers shape and volume from the air and the light—and it becomes a human body stepping toward us. It's the hunter, or the gardener, in servant's clothing, carrying a tray and serving us glasses of port. I hadn't seen him when I walked in: he must have been standing motionless and rigid in that spot ever since I came, an iguana on a rock.

I sip at my port and slowly begin to grasp that we're not necessarily waiting for Elisabetta Renal, that this is not a friendly prelude to the dinner, that we've already begun; Rossi is already communicating to me what he thinks it's important for me to know, saying that I have to see the photos in an album, that he has to explain the story of "this" family, that he and Elisabetta have debts toward the past, and that—no matter what he and his wife might wish—the garden has to take into account the duties each of them has, it has to marry their wishes and their duties; and I shake my head, because unions have never been my specialty: I'm no good at compromises. Rossi misreads me, thinking that I don't understand.

"Yes, I know," he says. "I ought to make myself clearer." And he picks up a photo album lying on the little table next to his wheelchair, hands it over, gestures for me to open it, and begins to tell a story.

It's the life of a man from adolescence to adulthood. The man is named Alfredo Renal. The shape of his life was more or less like Rossi's: born in the fifties, coming of age in the sixties, an adult in the seventies and eighties. He lived for others, in two senses: helping them directly and planning for their future. He did volunteer work, and he pondered the sociopolitical situation. A good man, but firm. Tolerant, but practical. A dreamer, but also a realist. A man who gave of himself totally, who wore himself out in the service of his fellow man.

A dead man, I think, noticing the past tense.

A saint. One of those young upper-class saints, chaste and industrious, who died early. Some extreme perversity kept him from taking advantage of the wealth he was born with. I have some flicker of memory—I might have heard of him. A saint for a brother: that's quite a burden for a sister who's no saint at all.

But I've never been interested in designing a eulogy-garden, building a celebration-garden, or erecting a monument-garden. The only monument I'm interested in is the monument to my own obsessions; the only celebration that of my own fixations; the only eulogy, for my own visions. The only things that fascinate me are the ideas running through my head. (I say "running" but in fact some of them drag themselves along like soldiers with wounded legs, searching for shelter before the next barrage; and even that's not a good example because it still gives a sense of anxiety and urgency and mortal peril, while in fact some of my ideas simply haul themselves through the long corridors of my head like chronic depressives, dim in the leaden light seeping through the tall arched windows.) The only thing that fascinates me is myself.

But I force myself to look at the photos, to register a few details I can report to Carlo. The pictures all focus on Alfredo Renal's smile: he was always smiling, and his smile was tactful, affable, docile. He smiled at the camera with the look of someone relying on a friend while faced with a difficult choice; you couldn't disappoint him, you couldn't betray him: his smile said, "I'm an optimist," "The good will triumph," "Life is a gift" (I'm exaggerating, so I'm not registering anything; but those smiles irritate me). Renal's hands are another focal point: they're never out of place; I page back to check, and in picture after picture his hands are always resting lightly on his neighbor's shoulder, or hanging at his sides, or laid on the arms of a chair, half open or turned slightly toward the photographer; no fists, no fingers laced together on his knee, no hands supporting his head—they're resting, and they hide nothing. (But after a moment I realize that I'm looking again at that smile: it's not just irritating, it's disgusting, it's a terrible smile, an unctuous sore.)

Rossi scrutinizes me, savoring the sight of someone being won over by the photos of Alfredo Renal—he's won over by my interest. He is not in any of the photos. Elisabetta Renal isn't in any of them either. In fact, only a few elect personages are pictured with the saint. Just men—and sometimes a child. And there's no panorama around, no scenery, no stage. You can't tell where these pictures were taken; there's not even a faded little lemon tree or a boxwood hedge or a hornbeam to look at, so I keep going back to that smile, the ever-present smile on those dead lips.

It's 9:30 when we go into the dining room, and Rossi hasn't made any reference to his wife's being late; the table is set for four, but there are only three chairs, and at Rossi's place the edges of the tablecloth hang open, making a white archway around the darkness beneath the table, like the mouth of a tunnel or a maxilla waiting for its mandible to slip in below. I'm hungry enough to eat a chair, but I'm distracted by the arrival of Elisabetta Renal.

She appears just as I'm approaching the table and taking hold of the back of my seat and the gardener is slotting Rossi into his spot; she comes in greeting me and greeting her husband—it's the first time I've seen them together—she calls him "dear" but doesn't kiss him and doesn't look at him. She gazes at me and immediately sees my shameful bulging button.

She's wearing a light blue dress that makes her look younger — maybe even too young. Her round collar is a half-moon rising on the horizon of her neckline and sealing it shut from one clavicle to the other. My first thought is that she chose it because last time she noticed me peeking down her shirt. As she moves from the door to the table, her pleated skirt ripples and lifts and falls, covering and uncovering her knees until the skirt disappears under the tablecloth along with her naked legs (Elisabetta Renal also never gets cold). I throw her a few quick glances and then immediately check to see whether her husband has caught me out, if he's understood how I look at her, what I see in her.

We sit down, and I caress the little dinner roll set near my silverware; I don't know how long I can hold out. I can't hold out anymore: I pick it up, break it in half, and eat it. First one half, and then the other. Rossi and Elisabetta watch me in silence. I look at their rolls. And at the empty spot to my left, to Rossi's right, across from Elisabetta. At the roll set near the empty spot's silverware. I think, absurdly, that the servant is going to sit there. I have a strong sense that my hosts fear I'm going to reach for the other roll. These glances last no more than ten seconds altogether, but the silence and the awkwardness of the moment would be enough to mute the most enthusiastic conversationalists.

Rossi asks Elisabetta if we can begin. She looks stunned. "Of course," she says. "Are we expecting someone else?"

Rossi doesn't answer, he just raises one hand. The servant comes in carrying a steaming bowl and sets it down in front of Elisabetta Renal.

"Tortellini in brodo!" she exclaims, and I don't know whether she's being ironic or truly enthusiastic.

Another trip from the kitchen, another bowl. It's for me. It's quick work counting the tortellini: I get just ten of them. I try to suppress a sarcastic thought as I consider this other upper-class custom, which goes along with the hand washing in the basement. Instead of a tureen brought to the table, bowls are filled and then served with the items already apportioned. That's all you get, unless you're permitted to grab the daisies and poppies from the centerpiece and add them to the broth. I still have two or three hours ahead of me before I can leave here and stop in a pub and eat three burgers, and the realization stuns me; I put a tortellino in my mouth, and a flood of gastric juices doubles me over.

"Careful, it's hot," says Rossi.

After a bit, Elisabetta Renal asked whether we had already talked about the garden.

"Mr. Fratta presented some ideas to me," Rossi lied without looking at me. I was on my third tortellino, and he hadn't even shot me a conspiratorial look.

"Just random ideas," I said, to make it seem less concrete.

"Please tell them to me too—otherwise I'll feel left out."

I talked about some ideas I'd sketched for the bank's data center; they were structures and designs that couldn't easily be adapted for the site at the Villa Renal, but my two tablemates wouldn't have been able to figure that out. I spoke of steel and Plexiglas, fountains and topiaries, mosaics and mirrors and lights. They nodded without asking questions, and as I talked I went on eating; there was no risk of chewing with my mouth open because, as soon as a tortellino reached my tongue, it melted away into its broth—they were not only scant but overcooked, so I just drank them down instead of chewing. I tried to make them last, but there were only ten . . . such a perfect number: it must have been intentional.

The gardener-hunter comes in to take the plates, then goes back out and returns with the second course, a little coin of meat with three chunks of roasted potato. I feel a deep pain, along with deep shame over my hunger and my inability to hide it, to tame it. I'm pained by this

evening: by Rossi paralyzed in a wheelchair; by Alfredo Renal, the philanthropist with the ambiguous smile; by Elisabetta, who didn't finish
her tortellini (she ate only six or seven). Shamed by the thoughts piling
up in the ignoble corner of my mind (I should ask for guarantees; I
should be paid in advance; maybe they're not so flush right now; or
maybe they'll just be stingy and try to skimp on plants and not grant me
carte blanche with the materials), pained by the glances that build fragile suspension bridges from my eyes to hers and his (I think, I'm still in
time to walk out of here forever, all I have to do is speak up, they have
no power over me, today is April Fools' Day; then I immediately think,
They've got me, I'm caught).

Rossi's eyes are like those of a blind man, shifting from me to his
wife without seeing us; he molds his ideal world, wearing a saintly expression of obligatory kindness (as in the photos of Alfredo Renal: I
imagine that Rossi doesn't see the background, and the foreground figures he does see are clearly just posing, retouched by his own hand).
Elisabetta Renal doesn't ever look at her husband, as if she has ampu-
tated his whole corner of the table: she slices her scissor-eyes toward her
right side, and—snip!—the man in the wheelchair never existed.

When she looks at me, she keeps her eyes locked on mine until I
give in and look down. It's a game, I understand it perfectly, but I'm too
tired and disheartened, too floored by pain and shame, to hold her gaze,
and I'm also afraid that once again she'll use her eyes to transmit her
chill to me. I look at Rossi, shut up in a glass reliquary like a saintly relic;
he misunderstands my glance and calls the servant, who brings me a
miniature roll. Tired and depressed, I devour it in less than a second.

Who was the fourth place set for? Were we waiting for someone
who didn't come? Or was it Alfredo Renal's spot? I thought, They're
crazy, they scare me, but it wasn't true. Every now and then a fly fell into
the halogen lamp that opened toward the ceiling like a brazier, letting
off a sizzle and a foul-smelling plume of smoke.

It was as if something terrible was about to happen, some grotesque and terrible event. When the servant twin carried in the dessert, he'd suddenly be completely nude, or dressed as the big bad wolf, chased by the hunter twin. One of Momo's favorite fables was "The Wolf and the Seven Little Goats," because he identified with the little white goat, the one who saves himself by hiding inside the grandfather clock, and he always liked to claim that role before I began telling the story. I felt like scuttling under the table and hiding there for a while by myself.

"Alberto, you won't believe what happened to me today," says Elisabetta Renal suddenly.

She says that she ran into an old classmate and could hardly recognize her because the woman had gotten so old, fat, and sloppy—"she probably drinks"—but the amazing thing is that a few minutes later she ran into that woman's old boyfriend, who happened to be in the city just by chance, since he moved abroad ten years ago—and even though he came back to Italy occasionally, he hadn't been *here* in six years—but that's not all: he was with his wife, who was young and beautiful and Spanish, and the two of them were radiant, the very picture of happiness, and what made the story even more bizarre was that ten years ago the old classmate—the woman who's so fat and ugly now—had dumped that boyfriend and hooked up with another guy (the son of an industrialist, who married her and cheated on her and made her miserable), and—just think—her old boyfriend, the one who lives abroad, had tried to kill himself, in despair, when she'd left him.

"Isn't it incredible that I ran into them, and that they don't know anything about each other's lives, and that I'm the only one who knows how it all ended?"

"That *is* incredible, dear," said Rossi. "A classmate from which school?"

Elisabetta flushed and shook her head as if she didn't recall. She glanced around miserably and seemed to be on the verge of tears.

I didn't know what expression to put on.

We were silent again.

I cleaned my plate (wondering only whether the half teaspoonful of green sauce was merely decorative garnish) while Rossi struggled along with the slice of meat as if it were a whole shank of pork; Elisabetta hadn't even picked up her fork.

I can't take the tension, so I say, "You two haven't told me anything, though; do you have some idea for the new garden? Do you want something in particular?"

"I was afraid you'd ask me that," says Elisabetta, smiling gratefully just because I'd spoken.

"Afraid? Why afraid?" I smile too.

Rossi does not smile.

"Because I don't have a clear idea."

"There's nothing wrong with that," I say, and another of my famous phrases pops into my head: "It's not the client's job to have a clear idea."

Rossi doesn't react. Elisabetta would like to react, but she's afraid of making a mistake. So I speak—I have to.

"Please at least tell me what you *don't* want. What you don't like in a garden."

She shakes her head and smiles.

I press her: "There are gardens that are like objects for contemplation, beautiful and a bit chilly, a bit fake, like a seventeenth-century painting. Would you like a garden like that?"

She looks at me as if she's seeking a hint. But I didn't pose a difficult question. "Oh no," she says, "no."

"Beautiful things get boring after a while," I add. "At least for me . . . I mean . . . often it seems to me it's in bad taste . . . to go for beauty alone . . ."

She looks at me to see whether I'm making fun of her, to see where I'm going with this.

"Then there are theatrical gardens . . . built as stage sets: the backdrops, the wings . . . Is that what you want?"

Now she understands how it works. "No, I think not." But she's less sure than she was before.

"Quite right," I say. "Nowadays there's not . . . there aren't the right people or occasions anymore . . . for filling a stage. The garden itself has to be the show . . . but it needn't necessarily be showy . . ."

I've started talking like her, limping, accelerating, and slowing down; at first I can't find the right words, and then they all come in a rush. An uncertain anger compels me as I speak.

Elisabetta keeps her hands in her lap, twisting her napkin. Rossi seems distracted, staring at the wall behind me.

"Then there's the tranquil, peaceful retreat . . . the place to pull away and meditate . . . the silent refuge . . . an orderly, symmetrical, unchanging, perfect garden . . . Do you want a garden like that?"

"No."

"Good," I say. "I wouldn't have designed it for you."

At this point they don't know whether they should wipe away their smiles and just feel awkward.

"Then there are the gardens made for walking . . . I don't mean just mazes . . . but gardens in motion, musical gardens . . ."

"My wife loves to listen to music while driving," Rossi says suddenly. "She often takes a drive in the middle of the night when she can't sleep, and comes back after an hour or two."

Elisabetta picks up her glass full of water and very calmly stretches out her arm and empties the glass onto the carpet. As she puts it back down on the table, Rossi smiles slightly, just as calm as she is. I'm not exactly petrified, because everything happened so fast that the gesture didn't even surprise me—maybe I'm just slow to react. Now Elisabetta's looking down at her plate, at the untouched roast and potatoes.

I almost don't notice that Rossi has begun to talk again:

". . . Yes, she likes to drive at night . . . I used to go with her my-self . . . the movement of the car, the music, moving through the towns and the countryside . . . even without music, there's a kind of deafening silence . . . and there's no risk of seeing too much, of getting caught up in some detail . . . you just want to keep going forward . . . things sud-denly appear out of the night, for an instant, as if they're going to be there forever . . . and even the most banal things—the ugliest things—look marvelous when they appear and disappear immediately . . . Mr. Fratta, have you ever thought that, before the invention of the car, no-body could experience such a thing?"

"No . . . actually . . . But how would one make a garden for—" I stop short: I've already had an idea.

"Maybe we're asking too much of you." Rossi smiles.

"No," I say, and before I can stop myself I've invented another phrase: "There's no such thing as asking too much."

There's no such thing as asking too much? Wrong: people always ask too much.

"Listen," Elisabetta Renal said then. "Maybe I really don't know what kind of garden I want. But I'm sure about one thing: whatever it is, you'll know how to make it."

And without giving me any time to thank her for her faith in me, without checking to see whether her husband was watching or whether the servant was nearby, she held her plate out to me: the slice of meat and the three chunks of potato, all intact though probably cold. The plate slowly skimmed over the centerpiece and hovered in midair for five seconds. I felt myself blush with shame; my arm weighed two tons—I couldn't lift it. Finally I managed to take the plate, in silence; I laid it on top of my own and started eating again, with down-cast eyes.

• • •

Carlo never found himself a girl who liked cooking, a girl who deliberately used the age-old strategy of getting to a man's heart through his stomach; indeed, he was never really satisfied with any woman. Occasionally I thought that if he'd found such a girl he would have ended up differently: if he'd found a woman who was simple in every way but had an incredible gift for inventing a complicated dish every night that would make him forget everything else; a short, ugly wife with no tits or ass, an exceptional cook whose dinners would leave him speechless and untormented by desire—because that was more or less the problem. His first serious girlfriend didn't even know how to mix mint syrup into water: I clearly remember that she put too much mint in her drinks. Cecilia belongs to an even more dangerous category—she's an experimenter: she thinks that cooking should be inventive, and she pairs flavors that are irreconcilable and tastes that clash, and then expects everyone to applaud the audacity of the inedible results. But that's not to say she doesn't have other virtues.

Now I myself filled that ideal feminine role during the weekends when my brother and the kids came to stay with me, because I would spend long hours developing meals for them. They arrived on the evening after my dinner at the Renals' (Carlo had the kids over Easter weekend) and stayed until Monday; we even saw their grandmother on Sunday—she didn't cry in front of them. I made a prosciutto foam, an oven-baked pasta gratin, and turkey breast cooked in milk and pancetta. Except at mealtime, Carlo spent all three days in front of the TV, watching the news updates and the special reports and the written crawl of the teletext, and even asked me if he could go online to look for more news. Better than nothing, I thought: at least he's interested in something, even though he seemed as inanimate as before. Two or three times I came close to asking him if he had ever heard of someone named Alfredo Renal, but I didn't want to break the spell of his wan curiosity about the world that began when the bombing did—and maybe I wasn't sure I wanted to know anything more about Renal.

So I play war games with the kids and take them to see Malik's dogs; Durga has recovered and is in great shape: I've been hearing her barking again in the last few days, and burbling with happiness, especially late at night, as if she's glad it's nighttime and she's expecting some male dog to hear her and hurry over to keep her company. We also see one of the two new dachshund puppies—Malik holds it in his arms; it should be striped like its parents, but the markings aren't visible yet. Filippo doesn't buy it, though; things in his universe are divided into groups— big (fathers), medium-sized (mothers), and small and insignificant (children). For example, there are cars, motorcycles, and bicycles. Soccer balls, baseballs, and marbles. So the puppies will never have stripes, he says, until they themselves become fathers and mothers. Malik starts to ask for an explanation, but I signal him to let it drop.

As usual, though, Durga was the highlight of the visit; she can always hypnotize the kids. On our way home we stopped again to look at her, in her pen, from above. The path that runs up diagonally through the chestnut woods and ends at my back door starts here, on the property where the famous photographer built his breeding farm. I cordially dislike the famous photographer, and I think he dislikes me; we're nothing more than civil to each other . . . maybe he's annoyed that I'm friendly with Malik and not with him; the problem is that I don't like his obsession with breeding stripes into all kinds of dogs, his absurd quest for the perfect mix—the striped Doberman, the striped dachshund, the striped Shar-Pei (that experiment was a failure). But I do have to admit that he treats them very well: the pens are immense, and for Malik it's a sort of paradise on earth (until two years ago he was working in a barn somewhere, looking after thirty cows), and coming here with the kids has become indispensable for me—I couldn't possibly invent anything better to engage them, especially when they're with me for three days.

I made Filippo promise that he would never venture alone into the woods to come look down on Durga's pen like this; I don't think he has the courage for it, but one time even I nearly rolled down the bluff—despite my knowing this underbrush like the back of my hand, because I've gone back and forth so often (sometimes, instead of eating, I've tramped around in the weeds to keep myself from thinking too much). We stood and watched Durga trot frenetically and yet somehow phleg-matically along the horseshoe curve of reinforced glass, swinging back and forth like a living pendulum. The limestone overhang where we were standing acts as the fourth wall of the enclosure; the dog can't climb it, since even the feline hadn't been able to. Durga's pen had orig-inally been built for Julio, a beautiful, arrogant ocelot, when the photog-rapher had a passion for actual tigers (before moving on to tiger-striped dogs) and was trying to set up a small zoo. But Julio died of boredom af-ter a year—boredom or loneliness.

"How can you stand being here alone all the time?" Before Carlo met Cecilia, he had lived with me in the farmhouse for two years. He wasn't a guest: he paid the bills, so to speak. I remembered the feeling of being in the house and hearing someone else moving from room to room, opening drawers, turning on faucets; the feeling of coming home and finding someone there; it was a pleasant feeling, and sometimes I wondered if it was always pleasant, no matter who your housemate was, and each time I'd tell myself, No, of course not . . . But then, after a few days, I'd be asking myself the same question again, or some variation on it. Like: when my father came home, was he happy to find my mother there (and vice versa)? That was ten years ago, and when Carlo lived with me I was someone else—I worked as a gardener, our father had re-cently died—and physically I was someone else too: a stranger, an un-known. Thin.

The week after Easter, I met with the bank directors to turn down their job, but they wouldn't hear of it: they said they didn't intend to make do with a "second best" designer, and they were willing to wait three or four months until I had finished the Renal garden. I pretended not to be happy about this, but I was happy—and how!—and, when I told Witold, I could see that he, too, was very pleased; he imagines that working for people who handle a lot of money will be to our advantage somehow, but I wouldn't be so sure.

After a couple of weeks I presented Rossi with a project that was essentially the project for the data center, simply lifted and dragged into the perimeter of the Renal garden, stuffed into the outline there; it's the kind of thing you can do only with a computer, and I'll have to redesign it completely, but there's plenty of time for that. Not that I didn't already try, but I kept going back to what Rossi had said, the thing about the deafening silence and the car moving through the night, which in itself is a banal and senseless idea, a definition that could easily suit two opposite kinds of gardens, but I wasn't willing to admit that, and so I was racking my brain to wring some deep meaning from it, with logic like "Deafening means it eliminates other sounds, it covers the whole aural field, the inside of the car is a closed space, separated from the outside, and yet open to the outside, but the windows act as frames, so your point of view is restricted, as it is by a photograph, and music does something similar, it erases sounds and substitutes melody for random noise, and the most important thing is the idea of the continuity of sound, but there's also the idea of the fragmentation of images . . ." And I went on like this for hours, getting tangled up in my thoughts.

In mid-April we began the job. We had to prepare the terrain, saving some plants and the hedges, which I had no intention of uprooting, and sweeping away everything else. Witold, Jan, and I couldn't do it alone; we always asked other people for help with the first part, and this time the others were two Moroccans who usually helped Witold's bricklayer brother. We worked hard for ten days; the weather was good, and I wanted to finish the preparations before the beginning of May; we got to the Villa Renal at seven, and we would find the twins already waiting for us; during the day, when we least expected it, they would pop out of the bushes like the twins in *Alice's Adventures in Wonderland*; we would stop promptly at midday and eat lunch in the shade of a pair of linden trees, talking and laughing; the Moroccans added a merry spirit, and they had funny stories to tell (some of them dirty); without them the two Poles can be lethal—depression and sulky faces—but when egged on in the right way, the Poles can also come up with funny stories, and even Witold made us laugh; at one o'clock every day I went up the slope to where Rossi awaited me, sitting at a table under one of the big umbrellas; then I'd eat a second time (at his table there was no chance of overeating); I never figured out whether he was putting on a show just for me—hadn't he said that he didn't eat at lunchtime? He told me about his commitment to the Renal Foundation; the charity projects, which needed tending and expanding, and then there were Alfredo's writings to edit.

Often we were joined at the table by the assistant whom I'd met the first day; it felt like a century ago—everything had changed—but the impression she made on me hadn't changed; sometimes your first impression is diabolically on target, and it's almost worse, later, when it turns out you were right, when you have to recognize the terrible truth that you grasped the essence of another human being at first glance. Fortunately, though, I had completely misunderstood Rossi: he was not at all a shy recluse, cut off from daily life, as I'd thought; he seemed to be busy with all kinds of commitments, and he certainly knew more people than I did. From what I could tell, they were organizing a party to present a book by Alfredo Renal. The assistant was almost always walking around the terrace and talking on her cell phone, and she would come back to sit with us for just a few minutes, passing coded, allusive messages to Rossi, referring to people by their titles or professions. I made it a point of pride to ignore her, and I would slip into the silences in their conversation with my talk of plants and materials. She ignored me too, naturally, and I believe she was quite irritated by my presence at that little table, day after day. But she didn't show it: she didn't seem to notice me—it appeared that she didn't even see me.

It's terrible to think that people don't see you. It was as if I'd become invisible when I grew fat. Women especially, it seemed, didn't notice that I was around. Naturally I thought it could be my fault: maybe I was the one not noticing them when they noticed me. As if you win a woman not because she likes you—as if charm weren't important, or any other virtue—as if it were actually a question only of intuition, of seizing the moment when her guard is down. It might have been true, but more likely it was just an excuse to justify my loneliness. All the same, I went on gazing at women, and every now and then I noticed one looking annoyed, which means that she'd noticed, maybe. Elisabetta Renal seemed to see me, but she had her own reasons.

In those early days working at the Villa Renal, I saw her rarely and only in passing. She wore different masks depending on the circumstances, but mostly she avoided me. When I ran into her by myself, she usually wore the frightened expression she'd had the night she appeared in my courtyard. When I was with the workers, she had an empty, lifeless expression, exactly like a plaster mask. When her husband was around, she was falsely cordial. She never gave me more than five minutes of her time, and after a few days I thought that maybe I'd finish the job and go back to my usual life and never see her again. Such an idea was completely intolerable, especially if it bubbled up late at night, when I was already feeling impatient and my muscles were tense. Wine alone wasn't enough to chase it away; I needed a stronger antidote. Then Elisabetta would come back to me and get undressed and straddle me on the guest's sofa.

One time I came across her by surprise on the terrace with her husband; they didn't see me, and I couldn't resist the temptation to spy on them: I hid behind the balustrade with my face wedged between two of the little columns. The scene troubled me because by this point I'd convinced myself, for my own pitiful personal reasons, that there was nothing between them anymore, that the dinner on April first had revealed the true status of their marriage, which was nothing more than a chilly, impatient cohabitation, and that at best they ignored each other, while at worst they poured glasses of water on the floor. But that day I saw Elisabetta Renal stroking Rossi's hand tenderly, cradling it in her own hands almost as if it were a kitten. I was spellbound by his closed eyes, by the light kisses she scattered over the back of his hand.

When Rossi invited me, on one of the last days in April, to visit Alfredo Renal's study, which he now used as his own, I didn't imagine that he wanted to talk to me about his wife. I accepted out of mere courtesy, but he acted as if he were granting me some great privilege. An elevator rose up along the shady side of the house, within a glass cage; we went into the attic. The study was overrun with filing cabinets and shelves packed with books, and photographs and prints hung on every square inch of the walls. There was a faint scent of eucalyptus, probably from a humidifier that ran all winter. Hanging conspicuously above a broad walnut desk overflowing with papers was a map of Italy, with an odd distribution of the colors that usually differentiate the regions.

"I knew you would notice it," Rossi said. "It's not easy to overlook it."

He explained that this was one of Alfredo's many prophetic visions. Thirty years ago, Renal had thought that our country could no longer hope for peace. It would be best to divide it up, but it had to be done on a profound level; secession wasn't enough. We would have to give up our sovereignty and have other countries teach us good government, because we weren't able to develop it by ourselves. Thus the North was to be annexed by Switzerland, creating five or six more Swiss cantons, which would be a good deal for the Helvetic Confederation too. Central Italy would be given back to the pope to deal with. And the South could choose to form a federation with the Arab states of Tunisia and Libya, or go back to the Bourbons to make a Mediterranean monarchy, maybe a tax haven, like a gigantic Principality of Monaco. It wouldn't be a downsizing or layoff: actually, everybody stood to gain a lot. The North in particular, if it accepted management by the Swiss, would finally learn the secrets of good public administration. And later generations would only benefit from this new culture, acquired—as it were—for free.

"It sounds like a crazy idea," Rossi said. "But, after all, something like it is happening right now. We're giving up our sovereignty to Europe, to America—we're the ward of other governments."

"I'm sorry, I don't know about politics," I said.

"Yes, I know," he said unexpectedly. "Actually, there was a different reason why I asked you to come up here with me."

He gestured to a little red sofa, and I sat down.

"I'm very worried about my wife," he said.

I nodded without showing any curiosity, as if we were talking about a natural event (I'm very worried about the hail) or a topic in the news (I'm very worried about juvenile delinquency).

"As you can imagine, in my condition I can't keep an eye on her." He smiled sadly. "I don't know where she goes, who she goes with; I'm afraid she gets herself into trouble." A square of sunlight was sliding up his lifeless legs; he smoothed the wrinkles in his thin blanket as if he wanted to brush away the light. "Look, I know perfectly well she has every right to have a life of her own, she's not obliged to spend her days with an invalid, but that's not what worries me." There was no telephone in the room, no computer, no fax machine or radio. Only papers and books, and old photos hanging on the wall. "I don't know who she spends time with, and in my position I can't even have a private investigator tail her; you understand, yes?"

I nodded again. The door we had come in through was still half open.

We sat in silence. Rossi looked at his hands lying inert in his lap.

"I have to get back to my men," I said after a bit. "Today I took too long a lunch break." I stood up. "I envy you, working in such a peaceful study."

This time he was the one who nodded.

3

BY NOW I WAS SPENDING MY EVENINGS AND WHOLE STRETCHES OF THE NIGHT AT MY table developing new ideas for the garden of the villa and sketching them out; what little Rossi had said that evening, almost a month earlier, had taken root inside me and grown and matured and produced a twilit—or nighttime—vision of shapes picked out of the gloom by a light sweeping across them, then quickly swallowed by darkness; the idea was a closed garden, with no eyes looking outward, soft and fluid, changeable, restless; a garden that was as warm and sweet as a dream but not suffocating, with a dream's deafening silence; and so I had to forget the park, and the house, and that wasn't easy. Especially in the mornings, as I shaped the entrance to the garden with Witold and Jan, I couldn't tear my mind away from the topography of the house, where I had figured out which room was Elisabetta's; I imagined her waking up when we had already been at work for two hours, I imagined her in the shower, then in her bathrobe, then dressing (I imagined the shape of her bra clasp and her swift, automatic gesture as she hooked it shut, her spine arching). If I heard the distant sound of her Ka driving off, I would calm down somewhat and go back to concentrating on the seven aluminum channels that were to reflect the lamb's ear foliage, and that would serve as the membranes, the gills for penetrating the garden.

At the beginning of May, I got two phone calls from my brother. The first time Carlo asked for more details about the location of "the Renal estate"; he wanted to know the people's exact names, and he made me repeat them twice, and he said, "Are you sure?" about every piece of information I gave him; without actually doubting my words, he gave me the impression that something didn't quite add up. I was disconcerted by his call because I had absolutely no recollection of having talked to him about any of it. I knew I had meant to ask him, but I didn't remember when I had done so. So I couldn't even say *what* I'd asked him; in the course of some other conversation, I'd probably asked whether he knew someone named Alfredo Renal. But the name had stuck in his mind, and piqued his curiosity—which in itself made me happy: I had managed to distract him.

A week later he called me again and reported what he had found out.

"So: these Renals you know are the ones that run the Renal Foundation, right?"

"Right."

"So why didn't you tell me that earlier?"

"Because you didn't ask."

"So Alfredo Renal is the *famous* Alfredo Renal—"

"I didn't know who he was."

"You don't know anyone. But tell me now: did you ever *see* him?"

"No, he's dead."

"Exactly. Couldn't you have told me that?"

"It didn't occur to me. Why is he famous?"

"Because he was a professional philanthropist." He sighed. "Have you seen his picture?"

"Yes."

I wait for a comment that doesn't come.

"And the money?" I ask.

"The money?"

"Why was he so rich?"

"Patents, chemical stuff. Flavorings and scents."

He stops. Then, after a moment, he starts again. "Did you know that philanthropy isn't the only thing they do?"

"What do you mean?"

"If you do an Internet search for 'Renal Foundation,' you get dozens of associations, conferences, and periodicals that thank the foundation for its sponsorships and donations . . ."

"What's wrong with that?"

"Wrong? There's nothing *wrong* with it. But if you look more closely, you can see what their politics are."

Silence.

"Did you expect them to be bankrolling the global revolution?"

"No, *I* didn't. I'm not the one working with these people. These people make me *sick*."

"Don't get angry."

"For you it's a job, but to me it's *pure shit*."

"Well, at least it's 'pure.'"

"Because now the pope himself is getting involved . . ."

"Pardon me?"

"The pope has given his blessing to Andreotti."

"What does that have to do with the Renals?"

"Completely coincidentally, he blessed Andreotti two days after a magistrate requested life in prison for the guy."

"I don't follow you."

"Let's say an investigative journalist was bothering Andreotti—"

"No, wait, we were talking about the Renals—"

"If you don't understand this story, you can't understand the rest of it."

"The rest of it?"

"You ought to read the papers every now and then. Do you know there's a war going on?"

"Yeah, I know, but what does Andreotti have to do with the Renals?"

"Everything! *Everything* is connected to everything else; people like that, who don't do anything, people who let themselves be manipulated—"

I interrupt him: "No, wait. Renal's ideas were weirder than you think. He wrote books."

"He never published any books."

"But he did write stuff. Now Rossi has made a book out of Renal's stuff, and he's throwing a book party two weeks from now."

"And you're invited?"

"Yes."

"So you'll see them with your own eyes."

"Who?"

"The people who hang around the foundation."

"Okay. Then I'll tell you all about it."

"Yeah, right; you tell me things only once I've already discovered them. You ask questions without telling me anything, and then it turns out that you already knew everything . . . And you could have found this stuff for yourself: all you have to do is search online."

"I thought you had other sources—"

"What kinds of sources do you expect me to have? Are you fucking with me?"

"No way."

But now the silence is heavier. I wait and let him be the one to break it.

"Who is Rossi?"

"He's the husband of Elisabetta Renal."

"Are you hiding anyone else from me?"

"I haven't hid anything from you; we talked about Rossi—"

"I thought he was a Renal too."

"If his name is Rossi, then he can't be a Renal."

"Do you know about the massacre?"

"Yes, I know about it. In the War of Independence, in the 1840s."

"Well, then there was another one too."

"When?"

"In 1945, right after the war ended. People assassinated the owners of the estate, and their peasants. Fourteen people in all—ten adults and four children. Taken into the stables one by one to have their throats slit. The kids too. The killers were never caught."

"It seems odd to me that there were *two* massacres . . . Do me a favor, look for—"

He interrupts me: "Okay, I'll look, but then you have to tell me why you're so interested—"

"I'm interested because they're my clients."

"So why is it that you've never asked me to do searches like this before?"

Finally he's using a different tone. I laugh. "This time I'm more interested."

"Does it have something to do with a black Ka?"

Pause. "Maybe."

Pause. "And what if I discover that the Renals were complete fascists? What will you do—drop the job?"

I don't answer.

Carlo sighs and says, "Okay, I'll let you know."

I put down the phone, thinking that I'd like to hug my brother. But if he were here, I wouldn't hug him. There are some things brothers don't do anymore, at our age.

I think about it again, a few days before the Renals' party, when I'm in the city trying on a dark gray suit in a men's shop downtown; the salesman marks it with pins beneath the collar, on the sleeves, at the waist, and the hem of the pants: it needs tailoring all over because I'm not a standard size. Every inch of the shop is lined with fake walnut paneling. I haven't been in a store like this since Carlo's wedding, when the bride's parents insisted that at least the family members all wear jacket and tie, and I ended up buying a beige suit, which later went to the basement and was devoured by mice.

"Before offering you a selection of shirts, I'll need to know something more about the occasion. Is it a wedding?"

"No, a party."

"Then I'd opt for a stripe. A wide stripe or a narrow one—you could go either way. Would you like people to notice you?"

I look at him in the mirror to see whether he's joking. No, he's quite serious.

"Certainly," I answer.

Statuesque and immobile in the mirror, I admire the profile of my belly in the three-button suit while the salesman flutters around me. When I walked into the shop and told him that I needed to be completely re-outfitted, top to toe, his face lit up; he's a young guy, completely bald, with a knot in his tie more than four inches across. I'd suggested a double-breasted jacket at first, but he argued against it fervently, and he turned out to be right: the three-button model does me quite nicely.

The black shoes: the toe looks too square to me. I point it out, but he mishears me and gets it backward.

"I have a shoe that is even squarer. Shall I bring it out?"

Obviously not. I try this pair on and find that it's very comfortable. I say so: "These are also very comfortable." He doesn't comment.

The tie: he explains how to make a knot like his. Is it necessary? Not only necessary, apparently, but crucial. It's the most important thing.

He wants me to look in the mirror to see the overall effect. The overall effect is pure shit, in other words good. Would I like people to notice me? Certainly. Does it have something to do with a black Ka? Certainly. Because I actually have followed Elisabetta Renal. I know who she spends time with, I know the kind of clothes worn by the men she spends time with. I know who she sees in the evening, at night. But I don't think I'll go tell Rossi.

The first time, I didn't have to lie in wait for her, I didn't even mean to follow her, not in the morning, anyway, but we needed some fertilizer, and I heard the Ka driving away and I told Witold that I'd go buy it. She had a five-minute advantage; when I got out to the road I turned right, toward the plant nursery, and if she had gone the other way I would already have lost her. I sped up to catch her before she got to the other fork in the road, the one in front of the abandoned factory, and I was just in time to see her turn left; she was behind a blue van that must have slowed her down, helping me out. After half an hour, we were still on the same main road; there were three cars between us, and Elisabetta didn't seem in a hurry: she didn't try to pass but simply kept to her place in the line of cars, behind a Fiat Panda, like a well-behaved carriage in a train. Was she also reading the wooden billboards along the road—those affable and inoffensive wayfarers from another era that rose on the dusty shoulder to advertise Morpheus Mattresses and Beta Tools? And what was she thinking, what ideas was she spinning? In any case, I decided to phone Witold: I told him that I'd gotten a call from my mother, that she needed me, that I didn't know if I'd get back to the villa before late afternoon. He stuttered something confusing, and it took me a second to realize that it was a famous quote for me to identify ("Be careful not to get mixed up in riots and not to raise your elbow too often"); I said I had a weak cell-phone signal, I couldn't hear, I'd call him later.

Three times I was tempted to stop following her, and three times I ignored the temptation; my eyes were attached to the Ka with elastic bands, and I hadn't felt so peaceful and relaxed in days—all I had to do was follow a woman who was cheating on her husband, maybe, and if at times I felt like turning around and going back (stopping off to see my mother for real, perhaps), it was only a reflection of the boredom of driving on a flat, straight road without any hope, at fifty miles an hour, when even the sky was cloudy, like a great curtain of pale gray flannel. I listened to the *Trovatore* that Witold had left—maybe on purpose—in the Mercedes. The landscape of the plain seemed even greener in that milky light; the leaves above the road whirled in the wake of each passing car, but the trees themselves didn't get involved, and the whirling died down right away.

By the end of the hour-long drive, she had led me into the city; I smiled about the time I'd wasted, childlike, and I had the same feeling I'd had on the days I played hooky from school. I waited with my motor running beneath a row of horse-chestnut trees while Elisabetta parked her car, paid the attendant, and displayed the receipt on her dashboard. Then she headed for a building that had a dark wood door with shining brass knobs, pushed a buzzer, and went in. This, I thought, will be the first and last time I follow her.

I parked too. I walked past the dark wood door, slowing down and examining the panel of buzzers long enough to see "Renal" amid a crowd of strangers' names: Renal, third floor on the right. I didn't know what to do, what a professional detective would have done in this case; maybe he'd have waited all day—but his business would have been tailing people, not designing gardens. In any case, I needed to call some suppliers, and the bar across the avenue didn't look too smoky. I sat down at a table by the window and ordered a cappuccino and two croissants. I made my calls while running my eyes over the imposing 1920s building: some windows were plain, but others were French doors opening onto balconies; bow windows ran up each corner of the building; and in the hierarchy of the apartments, the best ones were clearly on the lower floors. I stared so long at the façade that suddenly it seemed to move, to expand and stretch and swell as if something were pushing to get out, like an enormous sigh that would shatter the window glass and scatter transparent debris along the avenue.

After an hour I got bored: the building didn't get a lot of visitors; in fact, no one had gone in or out, and wasting a day like this didn't seem childish anymore—it seemed just moronic. I paid and abandoned my post. As I crossed the avenue, I noticed that the sky was clearing, and I pictured the woods and the pond and the slope of the meadow, and Witold and the others at work, and the details of the project, the little mistakes that were surely piling up in my absence. When I got to the car, I picked a flyer off my windshield, and it suddenly hit me that Elisabetta Renal could have come out during my brief stop in the bar's bathroom. The flyer promised "Easy Financing!—Full-time employees: get a cash advance on your paycheck—Small-business owners: money-order financing available—5 million lire in 120 payments of 69,000 lire each, at only 6.5%—Only one signature needed (even for married applicants)—Don't worry if you have a poor credit rating or outstanding liens—No matter what other loans you already have—Even if you already have a paycheck advance—Let us come to your home and tell you how." A wastepaper basket stood at the corner, a few yards beyond the building's entrance.

I went past the buzzers, and on a sudden impulse I pressed a buzzer at the top left. A man's voice answered, said "Who is it?" a few times, but he didn't open the door. I pressed another buzzer, a few buttons down, and the people buzzed me in without saying a word. The dark lobby opened onto a narrow courtyard lined with green climbers that absorbed all the light. The stairs were made of black stone, the railing of hammered iron. I went up to the third floor, but the plaque on the door was as vague as the buzzer: RENAL. Before I could turn and go back downstairs, one side of the double doors opened up.

An old woman appeared: metallic blue hair, camel coat with enormous buttons. She had keys in her hand: she was going out. I stepped back into the shadows on the landing and stood silently. The woman studied me without interest, waiting for me to speak. I hesitated five seconds, and then I held out the flyer I had in my pocket. Suddenly she sprang to life. "No, no—there's a big sign downstairs, didn't you see it? No flyers allowed in this building." And she shook her withered finger in my face, taking me for a deaf-mute. I nodded and shrugged and even produced a disappointed whimper. Then from inside the apartment I heard Elisabetta's voice, very nearby, saying, "Did you take the letters to be mailed?" The woman turned around. I was paralyzed. "Did he offend you?" Elisabetta continued. "No," the woman answered, "I know him pretty well by now."

At this point I managed to tear myself away from the landing and flee down the stairs. Out in the street, I hugged the wall to keep from being seen, just in case Elisabetta Renal came to the window. When I reached the corner, I turned left so I could get to my car by going all the way around the block, and that was when I discovered the clothing shop, the same shop I would go back to a few days later; I studied the display windows, trying to act nonchalant, pretending that I'd just been passing by, but I hadn't yet decided to redo my wardrobe; no, I was actually thinking of Fabio.

It's incredible that it took so many hours for Fabio to come to mind: Elisabetta Renal and Conti were not the only two people I'd tailed in my life, and that other time, too, someone had asked me to do it, and that other time, too, I had refused at first but then secretly obeyed. "Go and see where he goes," my mother had said to me. I couldn't do that— it wasn't right. I had turned her down. And then I followed him. I didn't tell my mother where he went—she already knew anyway, we all knew . . . what was there to discover? But of course my mother was actually asking for something else. She said "Go and see where he goes," but clearly she meant "Do something, save him"—how absurd that she asked it of me: I didn't even know how to save my dog from his insane passion for the woods, and now he was gone. Why me? Why not Carlo? Just because Carlo was far away, studying in another city? Or to avoid distracting him, because it was important not to worry him? So it fell to me: "Go and see where he goes." As if nothing bad could happen to him as long as I was following him. But it seemed that the opposite was true: when I followed people, I hurried them toward their deaths.

I watched the movements of the bald salesman through the reflections on the glass. No wonder I'd felt so good, no wonder I'd thought of the word "peaceful" that morning when I began following Elisabetta. It was because I was going back to what I did in the old days, and it never matters whether the old days were good or bad. "And yet remembering gladdens you, as does the fresh return of the time of your unhappiness" (Witold Witkiewicz).

I got the first phone call from my brother after that trip to the city, and on the following nights I couldn't stand being home when it got late—I needed to do something. Elisabetta Renal was still ignoring me, as if nothing had happened, and I was gripped by an urge to find out everything about her life. Each night I would stand guard in front of the abandoned factory, which seemed more and more—especially in the dark—like the giant skull of a beast that had been dead for millions of years, thrust into view now by the erosion of the land around it. Regularly at around eleven ("in the middle of the night," as Rossi had said), the Ka would appear at the fork and turn left. For a few nights she drove around without stopping, as Rossi had said, and her meandering seemed to trace a series of spirals around the villa, as if she were trying to say that she wanted to get away, or that getting away was impossible.

One night she stopped in front of a club that has had three different names over the past three years: Blue Nightclub, The Flower Piano Bar, and Blue Dahlia—A Members-Only Club. The name was written with a complicated twist of blue neon tubing molded into softly looping script. She waited until a metallic gray Audi A8 drove up and two men got out. She went into the club with them. I had brought along a thermos full of coffee, and I immediately poured myself a cup, turned on the interior light, and began reading the newspaper I'd bought that morning with the idea of whiling away the time during my long wait.

I was parked in front of the window of a furniture store, reading about hails of bombs, rivers of fire, ten thousand refugees, ethnic cleansing, and atrocities; about age-old vendettas, innocent women and children, outdated maps, and Chinese embassies targeted by mistake. Every now and then I looked up at the living room displayed behind the plate-glass window: a sofa and two armchairs upholstered in zebra-striped Ultrasuede, a colonial-style rattan chaise longue, a fake kilim rug, twin towers of metal for storing CDs and videos; the TV was on and running the late news, the glass-fronted bookcase was bare, the shelves enlivened by vases of fake flowers; there was no one in the living room, naturally, but the couple of times that I raised my eyes to look, the emptiness seemed absurd and incongruous. I thought maybe they could have found someone willing to spend the night in that living room. I imagined myself sitting there comfortably, nestled in an armchair, chatting with another stand-in; but I would have preferred the sofa to be tiger-striped, to please the kids (Carlo could bring them to visit me there).

And as if by magic, as if they'd survived the bombing of their embassy in Belgrade, ten Chinese men filed silently past the illuminated living room display; their hands were thrust into their pockets, and looped around their wrists were plastic bags holding soda cans and sandwiches. It was an important coincidence—or maybe not, maybe it was a normal event. But it wasn't totally normal: ten minutes later another ten Chinese came by, just like the others, with the same weary and determined expressions. I tried to follow a news item about Mallory's corpse, which had been found on Mount Everest, and to spin a fantasy about the rock-hard cadaver marooned up there, in a snowy armchair, looking peacefully down on the world. But I was too distracted. And when the third platoon of Chinese went by, I gave up on the newspaper, got out of the E270, and followed them.

Strange sidewalks spring up wherever a stretch of no-man's-land suddenly tries to redeem itself and turn user-friendly, like certain computer systems. The sidewalks flank the buildings and run along the streets and generally make a show of being functional, but they really can't hope to, because they're useless. No one walks on them: around here a car can always drive up to within five yards of its destination, and there's always ample parking.

But here were people using the sidewalks: the Chinese (though they were using them at night). Where were they going? Parked in front of the Shoe Warehouse, a hundred yards beyond the Blue Dahlia, three Nissan vans were waiting to take them to work somewhere. The condensed vapor on the vans' windows shone beneath the streetlights, and the pale faces behind the clouded windows looked like hooded paper masks against the headrests. I thought I would return to the Blue Dahlia the back way, passing behind the stage set of shops and clubs facing the main road. But it was too dark, and the terrain was strewn with garbage and pieces of rotted wood and rusty metal, so as soon as I could I slipped between two buildings to get back to the light. And halfway up the shadowy alley I tripped over a leg; I didn't understand what it was until the two guys began talking, asking me for 10,000 lire for a sandwich. I couldn't see their faces, which merged into the wall behind them, but they both had their legs spread across the concrete, as if they were stretching. I didn't answer; rage welling up inside, I ran off, heading into the Blue Dahlia to hide.

It was half past midnight, and just inside the red door Elisabetta Renal was retrieving her rainproof cape from the coat check, watched by the two men she'd come in with. A sort of maître d' came toward me from the back of the bar; Elisabetta turned around, saw me, and came over to me before he did. She was agitated in her normal way, and her eyes were red, but she was cordial, even though she didn't introduce me to her friends; one was taller than I am, with gray hair and a receding hairline; he had an imposing aquiline nose that didn't ruin his looks, and very pale white-blue eyes that balanced out his face; he wore a dark gray suit, a dark blue tie, and a striped shirt (I couldn't see his shoes). The other guy was short, lean, and older, and had bovine eyes and a boxer's squashed nose; he too was impeccably dressed, in a light-colored suit and a regimental stripe tie, but he stood apart, behind the first man. We lingered inside the entrance for three or four minutes while the maître d', smiling professionally, waited for the situation in front of his coat check station to develop one way or another (was I a chauffeur coming to pick up one of his clients?), and while Receding Hairline scrutinized me. He didn't understand who I was or what I was doing there. Elisabetta said: "So you're a night owl too," and we joked a bit about insomnia and driving around at night to get rid of it. I promised her that I would be at work the next day at seven as usual, and she laid a hand on my arm, saying with a laugh that she wouldn't notice if I was late. We both gave very convincing performances.

"You've got to be the most efficient and early-to-work garden designer in the whole country. Did I ever tell you that we consulted with a colleague of yours a few years back?"

"A garden designer?"

"Yes, a really odd guy—he refused to drive a car, or use any vehicle, actually, even a bike; he always walked everywhere, in these worn-out sandals. He came every morning—not at seven like you, but around noon—and spent a few hours conferring orders on his Senegalese assistant. He wanted to make a minimal garden—or at least that's what he said. He spent most of his day traveling from one place to another, but he maintained that he came up with his ideas while walking. He was like one of those little creatures that live inside shells, at the beach . . . what are they called?"

"Hermit crabs," says Receding Hairline icily.

"Right, exactly, a hermit crab. Because he carried an enormous backpack that he never put down."

"I've heard about him," I say. "His name is Astoldi, right?"

"That's the guy. And the oddest thing is that before becoming a garden designer he was a doctor."

"A doctor? I didn't know that."

"An orthopedist, I think. He said he was fed up with looking after animals, and that plants were more interesting." She snickers.

"Why didn't he finish the garden?"

"Well, after two weeks the Senegalese guy dumped him and found a nursing job in the city."

Receding Hairline looks down toward his shoes and shakes his head.

Her face goes dark. "Now we really should go," she says.

After they went out, the maître d' stepped forward, and I asked to use the bathroom; usually the toilets are reserved for customers, but I didn't care whether he said yes or no. Anxiety and torment showed in his eyes: I could see that years of experience had taught him to refuse, but he was trying to smother his objections. Maybe he couldn't say no to me—apparently I was friendly with the regular customers. With a look of defeat, he directed me to a corridor lined in red: "Last door on the left." Then he had a flash of inspiration: "Can I prepare a table for you? At this time of night we can offer a nice plate of linguine alla puttanesca . . ."

I admire people who really know how to do their jobs. I looked him in the eye to let him know that he had me pegged, that I would rise to his bait: "Of course, the linguine will be fine," I murmured.

The only other time I had come to the Renals' in the dark had been more than a month previously, the night they'd invited me to dinner.

This time the scene was already different at the entry arch: two great torches were hooked to the pilasters, and three attendants, new faces, were checking the guests' names against a list. The whole driveway was studded with torches, and before you got to the plane-tree tunnel, two other attendants had you park in a field where other guests' cars were already slumbering beneath the starry sky. The parking area was tightly packed, and lingering between the Mercedeses and BMWs were shadowy figures in jackets and ties—chauffeurs; the occasional cigarette lighter flared up to illuminate their lips and nostrils. As I walked through the darkness, I kicked a little white terrier by mistake, and he ran off yelping. I was reminded of the story about wild dogs invading the estate; during the whole month of work we hadn't seen any dogs, and Rossi hadn't spoken to me about it again, but maybe he was concerned about his guests' safety: he had an army of attendants on duty.

Anticipating that not everyone would want to make the long walk up the driveway to the villa, they had provided vehicles: a pair of funny little three-wheel cars with wicker seats for the ladies, the elderly, the lazy, and the obese. I rode in one with a middle-aged couple; we joked about riding in it, and then we traded wisecracks with two other groups who were going up on foot—the men proud of their strength, the women wobbling on their heels and regretting that they hadn't accepted a ride. We got out by the greenhouse. The villa seemed less austere, its lines softened. Its spikiness was masked by the night and by the torch flames that cast leaping curves and spirals onto the walls.

I head up the knoll to look for Rossi and thank him for inviting me, but when I get to the top, I instantly wish I were elsewhere. Many faces turn toward me and look me up and down, and many backs of heads remain indifferent to my arrival; there are too many people here crowded together, and I feel like roaring and tearing someone to shreds. Like this waitress, for example, who approaches with a tray of champagne flutes but no intention of offering one to me. She asks me if I need anything, because otherwise I should wait down below. At first I don't understand, and some guests look at me blankly, neutrally. "There is a possible upside, though," remarks someone behind me, "the man is solid, he's there."

I say that I'm looking for Mr. Rossi so I can thank him for inviting me, that I'm Claudio Fratta and I designed the new garden (gesturing toward the far side of the house).

The waitress flushes, blurts an apology, and flees. I'm left without any champagne. For a moment the crowd looks like a gigantic tree full of forking branches, and you think that the only way to explore it is by passing from one person to another, from one conversation to another, mapping it with the agility of a clever monkey—not like the elephant you are, with great gray cylindrical legs, unbudgeable blocks of reinforced concrete. "We have to be realistic about it: he's not completely on the right side," says a guest. Someone has attached two halogen floodlights near the second-floor windows, and the blinding white beam flattens all the guests to the ground, making halos of their hair and casting dark shadows across their eyes.

I go around to the back of the house, slalom between the flaming terra-cotta pots of citronella, brush past the buffet—this time they pulled out all the stops, but I ate dinner anyway before coming, to be on the safe side. At the far end of the terrace are a bunch of heads standing high above the rest, and for an instant I wonder whether they're all members of a very tall family, but that's because I forgot about the dais set up for the presentation of the book: the twins built it over the last few days. And I finally see Rossi, signing copies of Alfredo Renal's book; I've already been given a complimentary copy. I don't approach; Elisabetta must be next to him, blocked by some guests' backs: I see only her hand resting on her husband's shoulder.

After the longest five minutes of the evening, Elisabetta steps away, and I manage to approach. Rossi greets me, smiling. "How elegant!"

I just look at him.

"Why are you making that face?" He says that he wasn't poking fun at me, that I'm the other star of the evening, apart from the book itself. "Do you know how many guests have already told me they want to meet you?"

No, I don't know.

"I took the liberty of displaying your project, down there—"

I turn around, incredulous, and see a cluster of people studying the blueprint for the garden I designed for the bank's data center: it's standing on a large easel like a painter's unfinished picture.

Strengthened by a few Bellinis mixed by the bartender, I spent half an hour describing the details of the plantings and paving and rocks and lighting; I don't generally like to talk about my ideas, not even with clients, but I would have revealed my most important professional secrets if these people had asked me to. I went on talking and drinking, casually reaching out to take a glass from the tray each time a waitress came near; I must have had ten or twelve. I was beginning to feel like a mangy old bear performing at a town fair (in his childhood, my grandfather looked forward to the moment when the itinerant bear tamer would say, "Do what the mountain bears do," and the beast would obediently, wearily stand upright) when Elisabetta Renal appeared before me, shining like a figure in a dream, like Cinderella at the ball—wearing a dress of red silk I would never forget, with a black shawl covering her bare back and shoulders—and took me by the hand, saying she was rescuing me from the curious throng because the risotto was being served.

Before the alcohol suddenly wore off, I staggered around the party, letting myself be towed by the hostess, mumbling some blather in response to questions that seemed to me to be (and perhaps actually were) increasingly stupid. ("But how do you come up with your ideas?" I don't come up with ideas: ideas live in my brain, they've pitched their tents inside me like nomads on the steppes of the Caucasus; I don't summon them, they're already there, and they bounce around without paying me any attention, they live their primitive life and I watch them from afar.)

People looked at me and smiled, for some reason; I could no longer pronounce certain consonants, my tongue refused to tap against my palate or my teeth, and my voice was drowning in a dull, distant buzz. But Elisabetta Renal was laughing and looking at me merrily: I made her forget her fear, and that was what kept me standing; otherwise I would have let go and shut my eyes and dropped to the ground in the crowd, curling up to sleep in a flower bed. Actually, there was one specific spot that I wanted to disappear into, and it was a square inch of Elisabetta's skin, a soft, white, tender spot.

I didn't make a good impression. Thinking back on it, I realized I could have signed up some new clients (Witold would criticize me for that later), and the client that I picked up shortly afterward didn't count, because it wasn't my doing. At a certain point Elisabetta grasped my necktie, tugging on it like the pull chain of an old toilet so that I had to lean toward her, and murmured in my ear that the knot was dreadful; I didn't need to be told twice—I felt as if I had a cowbell hanging from my neck—so I undid the knot and slipped the tie into my pocket. I began to moo, and, since that made Elisabetta laugh, I went on to bark at a woman's back, and then I growled and startled another woman. I can't establish exactly the order of the events that followed the animal noises. I know only that I spilled a Bellini on my shirt, and right after that I overturned a plate of risotto on my hostess's arm, and that she laughed, her eyes tearing up (maybe partly because she was scalded). We went into the house to clean up.

The kitchen was bustling. She must have been drinking too—I hadn't noticed—or maybe it was her laughter that destabilized her: she leaned against my arm while I cleaned my shirt with a wet towel, and my own knees were out of control, so I had to find something solid to hold on to. Talking about animals made me think of the twins; I hadn't seen them all evening, and I did an imitation of their usual look, a stunned and perplexed expression—the kind of imitation that's terribly difficult unless you're drunk.

Elisabetta asked me if I'd ever seen where they slept.

"Are they somewhere else tonight?"

She shook her head. "They're here."

"Then I don't want to see," I told her. Even drunk, I thought that would be too much, but she had taken my hand and I didn't have the strength to resist that pressure, to resist the red silk dress and what it hid. We went down the stairs to the ground floor, behind the greenhouse, Elisabetta leading the way to the twins' apartment, and I following her naked back above all, the movement of her hips, and the tiny toes that peeked out, rosy and perfect, from her sandals. At that moment, if I had a choice, I would have taken her feet instead of her décolleté as my pillow.

She threw open a door and turned on the lights, and I saw a big brass double bed, two marble-topped night tables, a crucifix centered over the bed, and blue-striped pajamas folded on each of the two pillows. I wasn't laughing anymore. Elisabetta watched me with a bright look.

I took two steps toward the bed. When I heard her shut the door, I turned to see what she intended to do.

"Why did you follow me?"

It was the first time she used the familiar *tu* with me. She wasn't talking about this evening: she wasn't asking why I'd followed her into the twins' room. She wouldn't have used that tone.

"Tell me why," she repeated.

"No."

Maybe she expected me to account for it, or to make up some story.

She stiffened. Then she smiled. She approached the pillows, picked up one of the pairs of pajamas, and rumpled it.

"Just one. It'll drive them crazy."

"Come," she added after a moment.

She took me into a little room where there was a character dressed like me, sitting on a swivel chair in front of a pyramid of small TV monitors; Elisabetta completely ignored him. "Alberto had these cameras installed for our security," she said. She pointed to a screen. In the greenish aquarium of the infrared picture, one of the twins could be seen, dressed as a hunter, patrolling around the cistern. On other monitors, I recognized the garden we were building, seen from various angles, and some stretches of the entrance driveway: more or less the spot where I ran over the dog the first day and, yes, the spot where I had pissed that evening when I came to dinner.

I said I understood. The security guard shot me a suspicious look.

Elisabetta was hypnotized by the monitors. They must have spoken to her somehow, spoken of a prison that she had to flee from—or maybe not, maybe that was just what I'd hoped.

"We have to go back up," she said finally.

As soon as we got outside she abandoned me, and I found myself standing with Receding Hairline and his aquiline nose and pale eyes, along with the small, solid type I'd also met at the Blue Dahlia. Elisabetta was leaving me in good hands, she said, while she had to go sit in the front row. Receding Hairline was Mr. Mosca, and the other was named Giletti, but Giletti was a sort of shadow: he always stood silent and half hidden behind Mosca. We three sat down near the balustrade, waiting for Rossi and an eminent mustachioed historian to take their places on the dais to talk about Alfredo Renal's book. The atmosphere had changed: the guests were whispering now instead of chattering loudly, and they'd put down their plates and glasses and composed their expressions as if at a funeral.

At first I hardly listened to Mosca, because I was so offended that Elisabetta had left me in the lurch this way: I'd been having fun like a little kid when she suddenly shattered the toy, and then, to top it all off, she had left me with her lover, if that was what he was—if not, who was he? He was a guy who talked like Rossi, and I could have listened to him, too, for days without registering a word, just for the pleasure of hearing him talk, watching his gestures, admiring the confidence they expressed. I think he was asking me to design a hanging garden for him, for his penthouse in the city, or else he asked me later—maybe early on in the conversation he was just telling me how much he loved plants, and I was nodding, trying hard to stay pinned to the center of my seat instead of slumping over.

At a certain point he begs my pardon and says that he didn't catch my name. I pull out a business card, and he begins to mutter, "Fratta, Fratta, Fratta," as if he's praying, fingering the beads on a rosary. I feel a warm breeze stroking my face, like when you're driving with the window open, in summer, and you slow down for a red light and a backwash of warm air floods the car and envelops you. Everything around us slows down, we brake, the temperature rises.

"Did you used to be an interior designer? For some reason I associate your name with furniture."

His heavy words drop into the pond of my attention and sink quickly; I hear the thud and the splash, and I feel the concentric waves that fan out and break against my temples, the stab of a migraine.

Now I'm perfectly sober. I straighten my spine and turn toward him slightly. I smile at him.

"No, I've never done interior design. Always only plants and gardens."

I consider asking him right away whether he knew my father, if he remembers Fratta Furniture. Instead I say, "And what do you do?"

"I've done a lot of different things . . . I went from finance to politics, but I got fed up with that—it was too difficult, and now I do market research. And in my free time I help out the Renal Foundation."

"What kind of research?"

"Mainly for credit card companies."

"So you're still dealing with money after all . . ."

He smiles. "Yes, you're right; I pretend that I've changed fields, but it's still about money. I used to deal with it in the traditional way—bringing it together, moving it around, making interest on it. Now I report on people's buying habits, I sell databases . . ."

"And are those databases reliable?"

"Shh," he said, and gestured to say that the conversation could continue later.

The eminent historian tapped the microphone twice with his finger, shot a sardonic look at the audience—an expression of deep hatred mixed with a comedian's grimace—and began to read his text. Giletti pulled a microscopic video camera from his pocket to film it all.

I wasn't able to pay attention because I had too much new information to file away, a jumbled mass of clues in my head that needed cataloging.

And anyway I knew what we were about to be told, since the speech more or less followed the introduction to the book written by the same eminence, which I had read. This collection of Alfredo Renal's essays was only the first volume in a series. It was a selection of his writings on urbanism and sociology.

"—but the great cancer devouring the flatlands, the scattered 'exurban city,' is a mixed-up sprawl of residential, industrial, and agricultural areas, a structure with no beauty, no order, and no hierarchy—"

Hierarchy was the saintly Alfredo's real fixation. But I was thinking about another hierarchy, about a hierarchy that might exist; I was thinking things like: What if one person had another behind him, and that person had another one behind him, and so on into infinity? Then the remembering would never stop—there would be no end to the effort required of the people who have to do the remembering, even if they preferred to forget.

"—and without hierarchy, space is simply anarchic, and anarchy is above all an absence of civility: consumer culture devours our souls— our Western culture is based on Greek philosophy and Christian religion, but consumer culture rocks our environment first, erasing our traditions, our style, our roots—"

And I was thinking about how far I had come with my memories weighing me down, how far I'd walked on the earth, in the mud, over the dry leaves in the woods, even when I spent hours walking in order not to think, even then, my boots sank half an inch deeper; even though I wasn't as fat as I am now, I sank under the weight of those memories, my past like heavy ballast in my head.

"—the old town centers, full of charm and history, are disappearing, our lovely countryside is being blotted out by suburbs, getting mixed up and patchy like the hide of a sick animal . . . the villages and the crops of our beautiful Italy . . . and the flatlands turn into a headless body, where, instead of town centers, we have only 'shopping centers,' 'exercise centers,' 'meat centers,' 'used-car centers'—centers for nomadic communities, centers for consumers, for people without any history and without any joy—"

My thoughts were winding like long, voracious snakes, tangled and sinuous but running only one way, like the garden mazes you can't get lost in because they've got only one entrance and one exit and no forking paths: I knew where my life began and ended, and I knew the flavor of the poison.

"—because supermarkets were first conceived as miniaturizations of the old town center, and then they became the model for the exurban city. The exurban city is a dissemination of the metaphor of the supermarket . . . and it's a model imposed on us from outside, there's nothing Italian about it—"

Two for the price of one . . . Why hadn't I ever thought of that? I knew perfectly well why. Because one was more than enough. But it turned out that there were at least two of them, if not more—did I have to discover them all? Or was there a limit to remembering? Three, four—how many names were required to make sure the memory was saved, to make sure it was left in good hands?

"—we move through the world as if we're walking the aisles of a su-permarket, we pick things off the shelf—life and people and human bargains—as if everything had a price and we could appropriate any-thing just by paying for it at the cash register. What a terrible moral les-son Alfredo Renal teaches us!"

Everyone's head was nodding: some agreeing, some drowsing. I've always liked supermarkets, but I know some people hate them. Carlo, for one, even though he hasn't got much in common with Renal. He doesn't like me to take the kids to the mall too often, though they have as much fun there as they do at the amusement park.

After twenty minutes I leaned toward Mosca and asked him what he thought.

"A genius," he whispered. "Renal was a genius."

It didn't seem like he was joking.

I went on observing him from the corner of my eye.

When I drove around with my father and he told me (not at any length, but with brief references and gestures, without wasting any words, with-out repeating himself) how places had changed, what old factories had been replaced by new ones, who had sold their businesses and who had bought them, it felt like he was talking about a friend or some other living organism; he talked about these flatlands as if he were talking about a person he'd observed since childhood, and even now he saw the traces of the child in the grown man, he knew all its virtues and defects and accepted them all. Remembering was actually a pleasure for him, not just a pastime: preserving the traces of the metamorphosis, reconstructing the small-scale history of the land through the genealogy of names and things. The land was an animal that sloughed off its skin every season, but it couldn't turn into an entirely different beast: the limit to its mutation was written into its genetic code. And being a citizen of the plain meant knowing that code (which could never be taught; even if you had a more loquacious father, you had to learn it yourself).

After his accident, he lost all his curiosity. Coming home at night, I would tell him that I'd noticed work being done on some road, or a For Sale sign on some villa, but he didn't listen to me—he no longer cared. Now it was my turn to point to places and say, "Do you remember?" when I took him to the hospital for a checkup, or to visit my uncle and aunt, or to the city to see Carlo. I would show him a building being demolished and say, "This was the place where that guy made cabinet handles for you, right?" or "Am I crazy, or did this road use to run behind the town, on the other side of the canal?" He would shake his head and not answer.

"Maybe it happens to everyone when they get old," I said to Carlo.

Carlo got angry. "It doesn't happen to everyone when they get old, the old people figured it out a while ago, but Papa has always been slow." He maintained that at some point the changes in the landscape got too frenetic for his memory to keep up with. Places had always preserved their identities despite all the changes, but at a certain point this had failed. Now places did their best to be unrecognizable; they camouflaged themselves as if to confuse an invading army. Nowadays people fished for their dreams in a different imaginative pool; there were spores free-falling to earth from distant planets; there were sponges that could absorb any current.

One time Carlo explained to me why our father had lost his factory. "The idea that someone, some *bad person*, ruined him isn't important—that's just a fairy tale circulated in the family to preserve the *patriarch's* honor; it could even be true, maybe someone made him fail intentionally, and if so, so what? Why should the world have been more generous with our father? Just because he was a serious and sober person, just because he was a fair-minded and energetic entrepreneur? Come on, no one gets a break if he screws up; that's been true since the dawn of humankind. Filippo Fratta paid the price for his own mistake—and what was his mistake? He didn't grasp that between 1965 and 1975 the concept of quality was turned upside down—" (At this point Carlo's explanation becomes very technical and I'm not sure I can render it exactly; I'll try to reconstruct it from memory, based on where we were standing and why we had begun this conversation.)

This is how it went: in the basement a while ago we found some brochures that our father had had printed at the beginning of the 1970s, and we started leafing through them, joking about the photographs and the copy put together by an advertising agency that then tendered an outrageously high bill, which led to weeks of (silent) recrimination from my mother. Here again was the unmistakable furniture that perfectly matched the personality of its maker; we always knew the pieces looked like him, but what's incredible is that our father was able to give such a personal briefing to the advertising agency ("who were absolutely genius mind readers," according to Carlo) that even the room settings and the captions were completely Fratta-esque. "What did he *say*, what *silences* did he use, to make himself clear? These must have been the most perceptive advertising men ever—they must be millionaires by now."

Whether or not he said them out loud, his words must have been "functional" and "modular." The furniture had simple, modern, clean lines, the materials were solid, the details spare, the composition rational. The room settings were subtle, neither loud nor dull (a vase of flowers here, a table lamp there). The colors were natural; the dominant note was of wood finishes, such as birch and cherry. Only one clashing element leapt out at us: the rugs, which were thick and furry, in white, gray, or brown, and even a bottle green as luxuriant as a rich, fertile American prairie. Not at all a Fratta Furniture type of thing; but it was a masterly tribute to the taste of the period (we laughed when we imagined how the art director must have insisted on it). And the captions! "Door fronts with contrasting trim highlight the elegance of this suite of furniture," "The corner night tables extend the lines of this charming combination," "Beautiful lines and spare styling make this the perfect bedroom set." Our father himself couldn't have written them any better, even if he had been able to express his feelings in words.

So why did people stop wanting this stuff in the mid-1970s? Why did Filippo Fratta get into trouble? Because, according to Carlo, quality ceased to be an *internal* attribute (and not only for furniture). Quality became external; in other words, it was nothing but the image that the product managed to project into the consumer's mind. "Don't get me wrong: it's not as if customers used to buy an armoire only for its use-value; objects have *always* represented something else *too*. But at a certain point the process swung to the extreme: image became *everything*. The image of our father's furniture *never fucking changed*: it was solid, robust, reliable—but who the hell cares about things being robust? Who the hell cares about things being reliable? People buy new things because they want to live a different life, because they want to *dream* . . . There's no reason to make a face like that. It benefits you too."

I didn't realize I was making any face. "Me?" I said.

"Yes, *you*, with your innocent look. What do you think you're doing? All you do is sell dreams too."

Selling dreams. That didn't seem so bad. I just smiled; ultimately, no matter what he said, Carlo couldn't be really harsh with me, he couldn't help loving me (that's how it seemed to me).

Anyway, I think it's a professional liability of his. This is the way Carlo explains everything, or almost everything. There's no such thing as individual responsibility, or if there is, it's only minimal: we're crushed by things that are bigger than we are, we're tossed on the waves. The course of our lives is shaped by great historical forces.

Marriage, for example: it's an anachronistic institution, based on social controls that no longer exist, on traditional values that were completely swept away at least half a century ago, not only swept away but forgotten, suppressed, or—worse yet—served up again in a kitschy version; anyway, everything is supposed to be more flexible nowadays, so why not values too? Such as fidelity: it's not his fault that he couldn't be faithful, it's society's fault (and is it really a fault at all?).

Carlo and Cecilia met at university; they were both getting advanced degrees in modern history. They were thirty. They lived together for five years. They got married. They had no children for another six years. In the meantime, she became a full professor. Carlo remained an assistant professor (the fault of the university system). At forty they decided they wanted children. They had them. Last year Cecilia walked in on Carlo kissing a student during his office hours in a room in the History Department. Carlo made the following series of declarations: (1) it was the first time it ever happened; (2) it was the third or fourth time; (3) she wasn't the first girl he'd kissed; (4) he did more than just kiss them; (5) there had also been some fellow teachers; (6) and some friends; (7) and some strangers; (8) even before they had the kids; (9) even before they were married; (10) anyway he was still in love with Cecilia. This episodic series of confessions took five months, and at the end of it Carlo was invited to hit the road.

What fascinates me about Cecilia is her tenacity. She was as persis-

tent as a Los Angeles Police Department detective with a suspected se-
rial killer; she shined the interrogation light in his eyes and she waited.
She staged scenes: jealous rage, then indifference, then suicide attempts, then a polar freeze, then a fake attempt at getting back together,
then a famous biting episode ("I bit his thing—it was in my mouth and
I bit it," she told me. "Thing?" "Thing, cock, penis, what do you men
call it?"); then she feigned forgiveness (which led to the most important
confessions); then came the suitcases on the landing outside the door
and a changed set of locks.

That's how history punished my brother, while he was studying history to make some sense of it.

"Papa moved out because his keys didn't work anymore," Filippo
told me on the phone a few days later.

At 1:00 a.m. I'm waiting near the abandoned factory; I would stay here
until tomorrow morning just to catch sight of Elisabetta again, even
from far away, while she gets out of a car holding up her long red dress
to walk, like a bride. One by one, the big sedans that were parked in the
field go past, and by the light of the streetlamp at the intersection I
count the gigantic knots of the chauffeurs' ties: thirty-six. To kill some
time I try making a more discreet knot for myself—I'd like to reuse the
tie, at least, but I can give the shoes to Witold, if he needs them for going to church on Sunday. At two o'clock I decide there's no middle
ground: it's either a gigantic knot or a skinny, constipated one that
makes the tie into a noose. I could ignore the notion, but I follow it all
the way to its logical conclusion: it's too late, I'll never learn to craft a
proper, balanced knot.

It's Saturday night in the exurban city (actually, Sunday morning),
and no one wants to go to sleep. The stars have disappeared, there's too
much brightness down here; the sky is purplish and there's no moon,

but it must be clear . . . there's no humidity, I have my windows rolled halfway down. I should know this intersection by heart now, but, apart from the factory (I've grown as fond of it as if it were my own house), I've never really observed the other structures: the gravel area where I'm parked, next to the yellow arrow pointing to the Renal estate, is ringed by a white railing that's almost completely swallowed up by the bushes of forsythia and ceanothus lilac growing behind it. There must be a house back there, though I can't see it. But I can see the house on the other side of the road, and, while I try to figure out why it never caught my attention before (because it's like all the others, because it's not noticeable), the silver Audi A8 turns out of the driveway and flies down the main road.

I turn my engine on instantly; I didn't see whether the Ka was in front of it, I didn't see who was sitting next to the driver, but it seems to me that, if Elisabetta Renal isn't already asleep, she must be in that car. It's not easy to follow Mosca, though, and I make some fresh enemies by passing on the right side of a truck and failing to yield while merging into a traffic rotary. No matter what I do, the A8 keeps getting farther away, and, seeing it accelerate like that, I wonder whether it's escaping someone—me, for instance. Maybe Mosca saw me, or maybe Elisabetta did, or Giletti, posted as a sentry in the backseat. So I let them get even farther ahead, for fear they'll get mad and stop to ask me for an explanation. For fear they'll jump me and beat me bloody—with that snub nose, Giletti is like a gorilla, or one of those superstrong dwarves out of a fairy tale.

For ten minutes I followed their two red lights, losing sight of them at every curve and then catching up again, until I thought I saw them blink off to the right at a fork, so I very carefully turned right myself. The road ran through ghostly poplar forests and anonymous industrial sheds of reinforced cement, and I began to imagine that up ahead was an enormous tuft of black cotton, which I would plunge into and get swaddled up in and be smothered to death. I didn't know where I was going and didn't see any lights up ahead or in back of me; if they were hiding in some excavation, I would lose them completely and forever . . . shouldn't I just go home and slip into bed or do something else more interesting than this? After a mile or so I stopped, with my motor running, in the middle of the road. All I needed was to see her for an instant, but that wasn't possible. So okay. I turned back.

When I get back to the intersection with the main road, the first thing I see is a gray Clio with my brother at the wheel; he drives by without turning his head and disappears into the night. What's he doing out here—maybe he's looking for me—something happened to the kids—but why didn't he call my cell phone—after all, I switched it back on after the book presentation. While turning onto the main road to follow him, I check the phone's screen to see if there are any messages that I didn't hear coming in; I bring his number up, and I'm about to call him, but then I stop dialing and begin to brake. Maybe he's not looking for me, maybe he wouldn't want to know that I saw him here. And I start to doubt it's even him . . . after all, I couldn't read the license plate.

I keep following him, but more carefully, and slowly I come to understand where he's going (or maybe I'd grasped it right away).

The girls gather around the campfires on the turnouts that open up along the shoulder of the highway, little groups of three or four; at this time of year the flames serve not so much for warmth as to let them be seen, especially the Nigerians, who occupy the area just before the railroad bridge: on moonless nights they're almost invisible. And in every group, behind the exhibitionists who bare their breasts at you or gesture obscenely, you can glimpse the shadowy figures who wish they weren't there, sitting off to the side on a curb, the ones who never step up to the cars that halt, who never bend down to talk through the rolled-down windows, never, unless they're the last ones left at the fireside. The closer I get to the bridge, the bigger the groups get, and the traffic chokes up in honking lines with flashing rear lights: it's like a wedding party. It's market day under the bridge, and on the far side are the Albanians, the Macedonians, the Bosnians, the Kosovars: the white girls.

I slow down to examine the girls in their thigh-high white boots, see-through white lace, nearly white bleached hair; the blacks dress in black, and the whites dress in white: maybe Carlo has a ready explanation for prostitute fashions too. But he can't explain it to me now, because he's disappeared: I lost him . . . surely he wasn't coming here, that was only my idea—it's not like him to have to pay. But now that I've begun, I continue my rounds, and even stop a few times to look more closely at the girls who knock on my window, trying to make me roll it down. Cute, young.

After accumulating a strong enough dose of excitement and despondency, I decided it was time to go home, and I wheeled onto a deserted-looking stretch of roadside so that I could back up and turn around. Framed in my rear window, in the white glow of my backup lights, I saw a threesome that looked like two women sitting and one standing. But the sitting ones' heads were too small for grown women; they were actually kids, a boy and a girl, and they weren't seated. I rolled down my window and leaned out to see them better: the woman wasn't dressed as a hooker, and she couldn't possibly have brought the children along while she worked; their car must have broken down . . . maybe they needed help.

She came over to me smiling, holding the children by the hand. She wasn't wearing makeup, she wasn't pretty.

"Let's make a family?" she asked with a Slavic accent.

I didn't understand. I kept following my own line of reasoning, completely autistically.

"Do you need a ride? Where do you have to go?"

She shook her head.

"Let's make a family," she declared.

"What does that mean?" I murmured.

She shrugged her shoulders, and her smile vanished; she was disappointed I didn't understand. Other cars had stopped; wide-open eyes observed us through the windshields. They stopped because they'd seen someone else stop, and the more people pulled over, the more others would stop, for the same reason that no one goes into a deserted restaurant. Anyway, I couldn't leave the children on that road; I told her to get in.

She directed me to the outskirts of the nearest semiurban area, a few miles away. She didn't say a word, and the kids sitting in the back looked out the window. We stopped in front of a four-story apartment building, and we went into an apartment on the ground floor. It wasn't particularly bare; it didn't seem temporary. The rooms were all lit up, the table in the kitchen was set, and in the kids' room there were toys on the floor. The girl lay on one of the beds to read a Pokémon comic; the boy took my hand and gestured for me to sit down on the red rug.

He wanted me to drive a truck along an imaginary road while he bombed me from above with a fighter plane. I nodded—this was a role I knew well. Then the woman appeared at the door, saying "Hello?" as if she were answering the phone. She had me sit at the head of the table, where she had laid out a supper of fatty, spicy stew; it was tasty, and I had seconds. They sat at the table but didn't eat, and the kids muttered and looked at me, laughing. The wine was crummy. I didn't want coffee; it was 3:30 in the morning.

The whole performance wasn't as sad as it might have seemed, at least not until the last act. But I didn't even go into the bedroom, so I didn't leave in a bad mood. The woman made a slightly disappointed face, I don't know why; maybe she thought that without sex I wouldn't come back. She must have thought that I'd completely misunderstood, because she repeated it twice, she even asked me if I didn't want something quick. I paid her and said goodbye to the kids. They looked mortified too, as if I really was a father and had just announced that I was leaving forever.

He said that the marriage is the biggest mystery; it's hard to understand why a man of forty-five who has always lived with his mother suddenly decides to get married, unless he wants to start a family; the family is the thing that triggers it—certainly not the woman—because the aim is to have children and raise them with Christian values, to bring up an eager platoon of Christian soldiers.

I begged him to stop exaggerating and get to the point, but it was as if I hadn't spoken.

And, on the other hand, there's the mystery of a girl who falls in love with someone like Renal—what could a woman see in a man like that? If people were obligated to write something when they got married, if people had to explain why they were marrying, listing their noble and idealistic reasons along with their self-interested ones, or sketching their loved one's portrait, for example, describing the other person in black and white, describing their bride's or groom's irresistible aspects . . .

Now he was really annoying me.

I told him that it was impossible, that it made no sense. Elisabetta was the *sister* of Alfredo, and the *wife* of Rossi.

"Has she ever told you she was Renal's sister?"

"No. Why should she? I never asked her."

"Exactly. Why didn't you ever ask her?"

"Because it's obvious that she's the sister—she's a Renal."

"Yes, of course, the *widow* of Alberto Renal would naturally introduce herself as Elisabetta Renal. But explain to me why you never asked her. What would be wrong with it? You could have asked her in a thousand different ways—why would it be a problem? You didn't want to seem too curious?"

"Maybe."

"But then you come and ask me, and you don't believe what I tell you."

"No, that's not true. I believe you, but I don't know if I believe that professor of yours."

To find out more about the Renals, Carlo went to talk with an old teacher of his, Professor Pozzi. He's a widower of seventy-seven who lives alone in an enormous house, full of furniture and lace doilies and a gigantic TV with a gigantic armchair facing it. Carlo remembered vaguely that Pozzi knew a lot of lay Catholic volunteers and other charity activists, because his wife pushed or dragged him into it. And Pozzi naturally remembered Renal. He remembered that Renal had married a very young girl and that he was deeply attached to an old high school friend.

I didn't like my brother's smug way of telling me what he had discovered, as if he were showing me up for some incapacity of mine. His tone, too, was irritating. To dampen it, I asked him whether Pozzi was that old Communist who, according to Cecilia, pretended to help Carlo secure university positions while actually throwing obstacles in his way.

He didn't answer. He sighed and waved his hand to chase off an invisible fly.

He tells me that I have to concentrate on the story, that I have to imagine it as a melodrama, a passionate, violent struggle: it has all the right ingredients—love, jealousy, betrayal. And then he stares at me.

I don't react.

Alfredo Renal needed to take on a secretary to help manage his inheritance. But, as with all his other initiatives, he also wanted to help a friend in need. And Rossi repaid his generosity: he seemed to be born for the job—he was perfect in the role of the grand philanthropist. He came up with the idea for the foundation, according to Pozzi. Renal would have been happy just visiting the sick, organizing charity auctions, and occasionally accompanying the handicapped to Lourdes.

What annoys me most is that I have to admit he's right.

So Elisabetta married Alfredo Renal. So she wasn't the normal sister who had to deal with an exceptional brother. She had *chosen* Renal. And then she chose Rossi.

"So she's not necessarily married to Rossi."

"Pozzi says she's not. At least, not formally."

"Okay, but why is it a melodrama?"

"I was just saying that for effect. Picture it: your best friend, a man you trust completely, steals your wife . . . and not only that, he expects to go on living with you, as if nothing had happened. And if, after just a few months of marriage, your wife couldn't stand you, couldn't stand the sight of you—"

"But you're just making all this up!"

"No, I'm trying to understand. I'm hypothesizing."

"Don't try to tell me that the two of them killed Alfredo Renal."

"I don't think so. He died of cancer. He must have had a miserable time in his final years. Or maybe he didn't care. But just try to imagine one more thing: the three of them in the villa, the life they lived together. Can you imagine it?"

"No, I can't."

"Make an effort. Alfredo marries Elisabetta. But there's nothing between them. What could there be? Alfredo Renal isn't a man, he's a saint. Elisabetta is young, Alberto makes her laugh, he takes her places, he doesn't shut himself up in his room writing treatises for the good of mankind; he doesn't dedicate all his time to prisoners or sick people."

"But why would they all live together?"

"Alfredo needed both of them. Ultimately he chose to withdraw to the country and give up the active life, but he kept them both close by.

He became a philosopher, and meanwhile the two lovers stayed lovers. Until they'd had enough, and they stopped loving each other. Now, think about that moment: Renal sees that Elisabetta no longer loves Alberto. It's as if she's betraying him all over again."

"You're making all this up," I repeat, irritated.

"No, I'm building realistic hypotheses on the basis of known facts."

"If I knew this was what you'd do, I wouldn't have asked you anything. My fault."

"No, no, I enjoyed myself. You're the one without any imagination."

"It's true. I haven't." I don't mind not having any. "And what about Rossi: did she push him off a cliff?"

"You can joke if you want. But you're not far off the mark, anyway. It was an accident—the car drove off a bluff and flipped over; she got away with a few scratches, but Rossi was paralyzed from the waist down, his vertebrae were crushed."

"If he's the same person you're talking about," I say, "Rossi must have changed a lot. He's more like your portrait of Alfredo Renal."

"He probably began to imitate Renal, from being around him so long."

"It's strange, though. Sometimes they seem to ignore each other. At other times it seems like they're still in love."

He looks at me with half a smile, as if it's clear that I don't understand anything, that there's no hope I'll ever understand anything, as if the secrets of the human soul were suited only for finer minds than mine. So, out of spite, I ask him whether we should trust this professor, whether he might be losing his memory.

"He's got the memory of an elephant, that shithead."

When the war ended, my grandfather came to the village to open his "artisanal woodworking shop." He brought my grandmother, and my father, who was twenty-two. They came from the lake up north, almost at the Swiss border, where until 1940 they'd lived peacefully in a farmhouse with animals and a vineyard, and where my grandfather had a small carpentry shop with four workers. They owned some land, which they sold along with the house in order to move close to the city, which offered more job opportunities and fewer people looking to settle old scores. My father's situation was the most serious and urgent reason for their move: after Italy's 1943 armistice with the Allies, he had lain low to avoid further military duty; ten months of freezing guard duty in a regiment of Alpine troops had been enough. Everyone in his neighborhood knew him, and both the partisans and the Fascists swore they would get even with him for not joining their respective sides; after the Liberation in 1945, the partisans came looking for him, explaining to my grandfather that the boy's failure to join them meant he must have been spying for Mussolini's Republic. So my grandfather went down to the valley, where he found success. Each year his business got bigger, and when he turned the reins over to my father, ten years later, he had twenty workers and a well-established, thriving little company. I never saw the old house near the lake; I don't know when my grandparents got married; I know just a few details and some worn-out old anecdotes about them, and the same is true for my mother's family.

When we meet someone, we rarely wonder what path brought him to us—our curiosity never reaches very far back; with just a few bits of information we can sketch in his whole background and then file the issue away forever. We're hardly interested in our own history—forget about other people's. For example, I wondered what odd circumstances had brought me into the world of Alfredo Renal, a person I could never know now, who would never tell me his version of the facts, who maybe wouldn't even have spoken a word to me if we had met while he was alive: I was neither a derelict nor one of the elect, according to his criteria. And anyway, the real Alfredo surely wasn't the saint people said he was. In those final days of May, I was building a garden commissioned by two people about whom I knew almost nothing. I knew nothing about Alfredo's grandparents, who used to sip lemonade on a summer afternoon in the shade of a walnut tree in the middle of the meadow (we found the roots underground and the base of the trunk, and the twins confirmed that the tree had been chopped down ten years earlier; the lemonade is my own invention). I don't know much about the Pole who has been working with me for five years; only that he has a literature degree and adores nineteenth-century Italian writers, and couldn't find work in Poland.

I didn't see Rossi anymore; our regular lunches had stopped abruptly after the party. I was told that he couldn't stand the heat and preferred to eat indoors, but evidently guests weren't expected to follow him inside—maybe he couldn't stand guests either. If he was angry with me for some reason, I didn't care. All I needed was to see Elisabetta. She was the one who kept us company now, but from a distance. They were sunny, blue-sky days, and the air was laced with the fragrance of jasmine and lindens and early hay. Elisabetta would sit by the balustrade in a tank top and shorts and a big straw hat and watch us for half an hour every day, holding a glass of orange juice. Whenever she appeared, I would stop whatever I was doing and lift my eyes to her. I would stare at her until she waved at me cautiously. It was a game, like the glances we'd exchanged the first night at dinner, but this time I had the upper hand. I wanted to force her to wave to me, I wanted to put her embarrassment to the test, because the longer I stood still, the more my insistent gaze would be noticeable to Witold and Jan (and the twins in the secret room). And every day she tried to hold out a little bit longer. She never came down to talk to us.

Friday night Carlo and the kids came, and I was almost unprepared: I hadn't shopped for food, I hadn't thought of any games or excursions to keep them occupied over the two days; fortunately, on Sunday we had to go over to Grandma's. I took them to the mall to eat pizza, but Filippo whined the whole time because he wanted hamburgers and potato chips instead; Carlo was very agitated—the Americans had just bombed a hospital, and he said the Chinese embassy was one thing, but hospitals were something else altogether. Momo took advantage of our distraction to dart away, and I had to run and grab him at the exit a couple of times. Carlo barely touched his pizza. I finally got him to spit out what was wrong, but then he made me pay for asking. He asked when the hell I was going to start watching TV, saying it was inhuman to live the way I did, without knowing what was going on in the world, that I was lower than an animal. "Okay, okay, I'm lower than an animal," I admitted. It turned out that the Red Brigades had just surfaced again and killed someone; twenty years later there were still people running around shooting people, and that was what was troubling him. I leaned back in my chair with a sigh and said now I understood why he was so upset. He started shouting, "What do you understand? What do you think you understand? You don't understand shit! You're just blissing out with your flowers and your hedges—and you're nothing but a dick, a total dick!" The whole pizzeria turned to look at us, Filippo started crying, and the waiter came over to say we had to talk more quietly. I asked him for the check.

As soon as we got in the car, Carlo grabbed my arm and apologized. I told him that he could insult me as much as he wanted, he still wouldn't be able to make me mad. He even turned to the kids, who were watching us wide-eyed, and said, "Kids, Papa got mad at Uncle Claudio, but that was wrong because Claudio doesn't have anything to do with it. Papa's worried about other stuff, okay?" They nodded with great conviction; when kids nod like that, it means they deeply want to believe what the grown-ups are telling them. When we got home, Carlo put them to bed, and I didn't see them again. I poured myself a vodka, walked around the ground floor a bit, and then closed the shutters at the back of the house.

I light a fire in the fireplace from sheer habit, though I know I'll be too hot, and pull out a pile of magazines (back issues of *House & Garden*) to flip through, put them on the floor beside the armchair, pour myself another vodka, and turn off my cell phone. I don't know why I go then and lean against the windowpane—maybe I saw a flash of something; behind the reflection of my face, another face suddenly appears, just for a second, then there's only darkness, and the empty courtyard. Two seconds go by. I say "Fucking hell," and I run to the door, then run back to the hearth, hobbled by my mouse-shaped slippers, grab the poker, and run out, but see no one there: there's no one there *anymore*, if someone was there, but I don't know. Carlo, already in his pajamas, opens a window upstairs and looks at me like I'm crazy. "What's happening?"

"Nothing."

"So what are you doing with that thing?"

I look at the poker that's still in my hand, ready to strike. "I thought I saw a wild boar."

"And you want to kill it with that?" he asks, "or scare it away with your slippers?"

I shrug and go back inside. I close all the shutters. I go to sleep at 2:00 a.m.

My father often used to forget to close the front door of our apartment, on purpose. It was (and is) a double door, and when he was home during the day he liked to leave one half open so that daylight from our windows flowed out to the landing and the stairs. My mother and the tenants on the ground floor didn't appreciate his aesthetic approach; they rebuked him, and he would apologize, chalking it up to forgetfulness (but he wasn't at all forgetful). He was completely unable to distrust strangers: he had worked out a whole private system that didn't let him; it wasn't exactly that he *trusted* other people—he simply couldn't subscribe to the usual prejudices, even when they were well founded. He wasn't an expansive type, and he didn't make friends easily; he had gotten through the war unharmed because of his diffidence about choosing a precise position, about people who were too sure of themselves. But that was precisely why he never sat in judgment on anyone. Nothing had shaken him, not even the death of his beloved retriever, who'd been tied to a tree and butchered by somebody with a hatchet (after that, Grandpa decided to move his family down into the valley). I often think that there was something infantile about my father. (I dreamed that I suggested to Rossi and Elisabetta that we put a bronze statue of my father in the middle of their garden. They agreed.)

It's so strange to hug the little body of this miniature Filippo Fratta. At 8:00 a.m. they're already in my bed having a pillow fight, and soon afterward I'm fighting with them myself to get them dressed. Kids work on the principle of conservation of the status quo: they refuse to see the inevitability of shifting from pajamas to playing (even for their favorite game), or shifting from playing to lunch (even if their favorite food is on the table), or shifting from lunch to nap (even if they're exhausted), or shifting from nap to playing another game, and so on, until they tumble into sleep again at night, willy-nilly. So in the morning it's a battle for me to get them dressed and a battle to get them washed, but when they begin playing with the water in the sink, they don't want to stop, and then it's a battle for me to get them out of the bathroom, and when we're getting set to go to Malik's, they don't want to put on their shoes, even though they desperately want to go to Malik's—they wouldn't let me be if I didn't take them there. (Actually, saying that they want to go there isn't quite precise: they want to *be* there already, as soon as it's mentioned.) Carlo says that they live in an eternal present, that they don't have our sense of time as an arrow shooting from dawn to sunset, from Monday to Sunday, from autumn to summer, and, when they hear us talking about events in the past or the future, they really have no idea what we're talking about; yesterday and tomorrow are like people or things that aren't in the room: maybe they remember their shapes or their faces, but they don't pay them much attention because they're not around. At that point I ask him whether there are any adults who live in an eternal past, and he starts laughing and says, Yes, there are. But I wasn't trying to be funny, so I don't know what he thinks I meant; anyway, by this time we're at Malik's.

Our neighbor was wearing his dark blue, special-occasions turban, and his beard was combed and smooth; he was shining with pride over his new baby and even moving differently, more confidently. His wife, by contrast, scurried around the little apartment as if this were an official visit. It was Carlo who put her into a tizzy; he doesn't usually come. The baby girl was splendid; I had bought her a gift from me—a pink jumpsuit—and one from the kids—a plush tiger, of course. Filippo and Momo gave the baby a cursory glance, but Carlo turned out to be a perfectly sophisticated conversationalist: he told stories about when Filippo was born and how badly he and Cecilia fumbled the diaper changes. They offered us Indian sweets, but I was the only one who ate them, and then we went out.

In a celebratory mood, Malik put on Durga's muzzle and brought her out of her pen. The kids reached out dubiously to pet her back, keeping their bodies as far away as possible. She was tame, calm. "What's up with her?" I asked. Malik told me that she understood there was a pup around: that the new baby had softened her. That whenever his wife brought the carriage outside, Durga stopped moving around and just lay down and watched her. While telling me this, Malik scratched the dog beneath her jaw, and Durga shut her eyes blissfully. I said that I needed to get another dog; I felt like I was betraying Gustavo, but it was eight months now since he'd taken off. I needed a dog who'd bark if someone came into the courtyard at night. Malik shook his head and said that no one came around their place. "I'm not the one who scares them away," he added. Inside his house he has a remote control that he can use to open the Doberman's gate if he needs to. He put Durga back in her pen, and we went over to Filippo, Momo, and Carlo, who had gone to the other side of the yard to look for the dachshunds and the poor Shar-Pei, who had just had his eyelids operated on.

Now it's later; I'm playing with the kids in my courtyard and in the meadow. I have a straw hat to protect me from the sun. I'm sweating, and I keep having to stop and catch my breath. I don't need to think: Filippo is in charge, he tells me my lines as the game goes along—he's my prompter. But every now and then, the instructions are too wordy. "Okay, Uncle Claudio, now you say, 'Hey, we have to kill the bad guys,' and then you run to that bush over there, and Momo and I yell, 'Watch out!' and the bad guys *aren't* behind the bush, they come out of the woods instead, and you fall down, because they hurt you, and then you yell, 'Come help me, they hurt my leg,' and then Momo and I run over, and we shoot the bad guys and we get to you—okay?"

"Fine, but I don't remember what I'm supposed to say at the very beginning—"

"You're supposed to say, 'Hey, we have to kill the bad guys,' and I'm supposed to explain to you that they might *not* be over there, but you're *stubborn*, and you insist on attacking, and I don't—"

"Wait a sec, you're adding this new stuff now."

He stops and looks at me. "Yes," he admits.

"Okay. Should I start now?"

At the end of the morning, going back home through the tall grass, he says, "Uncle Claudio, you're really good at pretending to play with us."

I tell him I don't understand, that I'm not pretending, I'm playing for real. "Who gave you the idea I was just pretending?"

He shrugs his shoulders. He scampers up ahead. I think, I want him to stop and turn back, and I wave a cherry branch at him. And Filippo actually does stop, and turns around, and comes running back, and hugs my legs.

I promised I would do a barbecue lunch, and I started fiddling with a rusty old grill in the courtyard while the kids brushed flavored olive oil on the steaks, the sausages, and the vegetables, and Carlo got caught in the smoke and began coughing. It was a perfect day to eat outdoors, except that every five minutes a pallid face popped out from the front gate or the stone wall or the woods, and then immediately vanished into thin air. While I turned the pork cutlets and waved my big serving fork around to show everyone that I was ready to strike at any moment, Carlo came over to me with a half smile that looked both ironic and idiotic.

"They look tasty, don't they?" I said.

"Mmm," he replied, and then, "What a story, the thing about your client . . ."

I had been expecting it; I said nothing. I knew he would go on anyway.

"Tell me the truth: she really hasn't told you anything?"

"No."

"You could ask her."

"I don't want to."

"But"—with another smile—"maybe you're not intimate enough for that . . ."

I could respond in one of two ways: impassive or insinuating. When it comes to sex, insinuation is the way to go with Carlo. If you throw up a wall to block him, he'll never let you be. So I winked back at him.

"We're very intimate."

"Come on—tell me."

"Like hell. You know I'm as silent as a tomb."

"That's for sure. And what about her—is she a bit livelier than you?"

I laughed. But I knew I had to keep him on tenterhooks.

"'Lively' is putting it mildly."

"Wow." He shook his head. "Lucky dog." Then he said, "I have a funny idea to ask you about."

I turned the sausages over without offering him any encouragement.

"Listen: say you're Andreotti's wife—"

"Oh, for Christ's sake."

"No, wait—you're Andreotti's wife, and you find out that he's really guilty, that he actually did have that journalist, Pecorelli, assassinated. Do you still love him?"

And I picture Andreotti standing before me: the double-breasted suit of thick black wool, the hair still dark despite his age, the square skull, the pointy ears, the massive eyeglass frames, the hump on his back like Rigoletto's. "What the hell do I know?"

"Come on, it's a game . . ."

"Did I love him before?"

"You were crazy about him."

I laugh. "Okay, yeah, I think so: I'd still love him, even though it's pretty hard to put myself in her shoes."

"So here's another one."

"Last one, though."

"Last one—I promise. You find out your wife was a famous terrorist and once she even killed a man."

I look right into his eyes.

"Who?"

"Who did she kill? You mean, did she kill a shithead or a nice guy?"

"For example, yeah."

"It doesn't matter. Let's say she killed two people. A shithead *and* a nice guy."

"And I'm deeply in love with her?"

"Deeply."

"I'd go on loving her."

"And you wouldn't want her to be punished?"

"What do you mean?"

"I mean, would you want her to go to jail for murder, or would you want her to be acquitted?"

"But that has nothing to do with continuing to love her."

"It has nothing to do with it?"

"I don't think it does."

He shakes his head. "Would you be able to love her and let her go?"

"What the hell do I know? I'm cooking sausages—lay off me."

He smiles.

The kids were drumming their forks on their plates, and Momo was shouting "cookin' shaushage," and fortunately after lunch Carlo went back to stewing over things by himself. It's hard to get used to my brother's new silence. We used to roll our eyes, in my family, when he would get into his hour-long tirades, but deep down we were glad that someone had taken on the burden of talking. A completely mute household would have gone unnoticed. But we were proud of our parsimony with words, and Carlo made us see it more clearly when he came home from his university housing for the weekend. My mother maintained it was a question of genes and chromosomes, but I don't think she ever pinpointed which ancestor had given Carlo the gift of gab. Fabio tempted fate once, by making fun of him; it was the only time Carlo really gave him a thrashing. We were playing office, and Fabio was doing his own thing as usual, not participating; he wasn't actually boycotting the game, though, and Carlo tolerated him. All of a sudden

Fabio picked up the phone (an old black Bakelite phone that was nothing but an empty shell) and began talking. But he wasn't saying anything real. He was imitating Carlo's speeches but using nonexistent words, or words that existed in some language we didn't know. We stood there, not playing, just listening to him: I fascinated, Carlo growing more and more irritated. Even when Carlo grabbed the phone away, Fabio didn't stop. He looked at Carlo in surprise and said, "Biggle opty hatpat?" And Carlo began punching him, and kept hammering away until I pulled them apart.

The next day, when we got to my mother's house, we found her in a great mood; I hadn't seen her this way for months. She told us that she had been organizing the attic and had made a pile in the courtyard of all the stuff she thought could be thrown away; that we should go down immediately and pick out whatever we wanted to rescue and take back to our houses. Carlo tried to ask her why the attic needed to be emptied out, but she was no longer listening; she had begun talking to the kids.

We rooted about a bit in the pile of old stuff; I was afraid I would come across something bad, and Carlo kept exclaiming in surprise. There was a slide-projection screen (torn), a backpack, two sleeping bags, a tent (torn), a record player, an amplifier (broken), two speakers, whole collections of car-racing magazines and rock-music magazines, a fishing rod, and posters for rock groups and concerts and protest marches. After a moment I sat down on the steps, overcome by the weight of the junk, rendered mute by emotion, by sadness about the simple presence of years past, which wafted up with the dust as soon as you touched anything, and stuck to our fingers just like the dust. But Carlo was getting into it; ultimately he'd toss it all out, but in the meantime he was having fun rediscovering objects that he hadn't held in his hands for twenty years. I was looking at the tumbledown wall at the end of the courtyard, and the leaves of the paulownia tree peering over curiously from the neighbor's garden, when I heard him yell with excitement, calling me the way he used to do when he needed a hand with one of the games that we'd invented right here as kids.

He had found the cardboard box in which he had carefully packed away the bedsheets he'd stolen from my mother's linen closet and hung in his university's main lecture hall during a sit-in. He asked me to hold one end so he could unfold the whole thing, which turned out to be three sheets sewn together for twenty or twenty-five feet of slogans. But, being Carlo's slogans, they weren't immediately recognizable—nothing as simple as "Death to the Bosses" or "Fascist Swine." They said:

THE PRICE OF IDENTIFYING EVERYTHING WITH EVERYTHING
IS THAT NOTHING IS IDENTICAL TO ITSELF ANY LONGER.
ALL THAT IS SOLID MELTS INTO AIR,
ALL THAT IS HOLY IS PROFANED.
THE TIME IS OUT OF JOINT.

He explained to me that these were famous phrases, used for educational purposes.

"Before the sit-in ended, I pulled down the sheets and took them home; I was so proud, and I had spent so much time writing them. I didn't want them to end up in the garbage right away."

Even now they didn't end up in the garbage: he took them when he and the kids left for the city later.

As soon as Carlo was gone, my mother pretended to recall another nagging problem. My grandfather had found an American pistol in his vineyard; our father hadn't ever wanted to get rid of it, and she was afraid that some Albanian might break into her house and steal it. I took it unwillingly, thinking that I'd throw it in some canal. But instead I brought it home and hid it in my basement. Then I spent the afternoon going around my house and yard with the poker in hand.

At ten that night I got into position near the abandoned factory; maybe Elisabetta wouldn't come out, maybe she'd spent the whole day with Mosca and I would just see her coming in, without daring to stop her and tell her I couldn't stand it any longer. I had intended to do two things during the weekend: ask my brother if it had really been him driving the gray Clio around the countryside at 3:00 a.m. last week, and ask my mother if there was another name besides Conti that I should remember, and if the other name was Mosca. But the questions were too hard to ask; I had to ask them in some other way—I had to try something more diplomatic.

When her Ka comes out onto the road, I've already given up waiting for her; I have resigned myself to going home to sleep. She zooms off as if she'd just robbed a bank; something must have happened—this time she could really end up killing herself. She skids and runs red lights and stop signs, and in the heat of the moment I think that she's not running away—no one runs away that fast—she just really wants to die, she's trying to fly off the road. I tremble as we pass a row of poplars, I tremble as we turn onto a bridge; I keep waiting for her car to swerve violently and crash, or leap into the void. There's a curve up ahead that I know pretty well: you can't take it at this speed, and that's where she's going to crash.

But instead I'm suddenly the one spinning through a planetarium of stars and explosions, in a cloud of glass shards—I'm the one having an accident, my E270 is being destroyed, the air bag explodes against my stomach all red and sticky with blood, and I'm the one gasping in the silence and the dark, blanketed with windshield fragments like a mirrored disco ball. Everything is still—I've landed—I'm afraid to move, I'm afraid I've broken in half, I'm afraid my throat has been slit, that these are the final moments of my life. Then a car stops on the side of the road and shines its lights on me, making me sparkle all over, and someone comes closer, a silhouette against the brightness who manages to force my door open, the hinges coming apart, the door folding and flipping over and dropping to the grass.

Now she's leaning over me, whispering in my ear. "Everything's okay now, don't worry." She tries to unbuckle my belt, practically hugging me, and says, "I had to pay you back for rescuing me, right? Now it's my turn to take you to the hospital."

4

THE NEXT MORNING MY COLLEAGUES, RELATIVES, AND FRIENDS WERE WHIPPED UP into a maelstrom of worry: for two hours they flooded the nearby hospitals with phone calls; some calls were anguished (from Witold's wife, while he was out searching for me in the emergency rooms), some were furious (Carlo, threatening lawsuits and digressing into an attack on the regional governor for his irresponsible decentralization of health services), and some were warbling, shrill, nearly incomprehensible (Malik gets like this when he panics); and while all this was happening I was asleep in my own bed, Monday morning; I had a cut on my cheekbone and a bruise on my left thigh, but otherwise I was beatific. The problem was that the tow truck, which I had called the night before, didn't reach the body shop until midnight, after closing time, and so it towed my E270 back to my courtyard. It looked pitiful: it was completely destroyed. They say cars that look this bad are often dumped on the ocean floor to make playgrounds for the fish.

The first one to arrive, at 7:45, was Witold, who drove over in his Fiat Panda because he was alarmed that I didn't show up at our usual appointment and didn't answer my cell phone or my house phone (both of which were turned off). He grew even more alarmed when he saw the jagged, twisted, stripped, mutilated Mercedes, with its blood-spattered air bag dangling from the steering wheel like the tongue of a cow impaled on a butcher's hook; then he panicked completely when no one answered the doorbell (I didn't hear it; I'd taken a sleeping pill at six when I couldn't get back to sleep). My R4, parked under the canopy, proved that I hadn't driven off somewhere under my own steam, so therefore I must have been in a hospital, or staying with friends or relatives to recover from the accident. Malik was the nearest possibility. He got back in his car, drove around the hill, and rang at the famous photographer's gate. He poured all his panic through the video intercom onto Malik (who's always very susceptible to other people's anxiety), and then drove off to check the nearest emergency room.

At 8:15, Malik stepped out of the chestnut woods and appeared in my courtyard together with Indra, the striped dachshund who had fathered the new litter. Malik walked around the carcass of the E270 three times, weeping in pain as he pictured my torn and lifeless body in some morgue; he tried ringing the doorbell and knocking weakly on all the shutters, and noted with surprise that the ones in the back were all closed: that didn't augur well. Meanwhile Indra pissed on Gustavo's dog bed, an unpleasant detail that did nothing to unravel the mystery. Then they both went home. Malik tried to call a few hospitals, but—as he himself later reported—he was so upset he couldn't make himself understood.

After searching for me fruitlessly in one hospital, Witold thought it might be best to alert my family; but to avoid alarming my mother, who wouldn't have been able to help search anyway, he called Carlo at 8:40. My brother immediately concluded that I must have taken refuge in our childhood home, and he devised a scheme with Witold: he would call my mother on some pretext, without mentioning the wreck of the Mercedes, and if I were there with her, surely she would tell him about it. But my mother saw through his pretext—first of all because Carlo almost never calls her (especially not at 9:00 a.m. on Monday), and second because he mumbled that he wanted to thank her for Sunday lunch, on his behalf and the children's. That was too far-fetched.

"Is someone hurt?" she asked, without wasting words. Carlo denied it, but he wasn't very persuasive, and my mother was now sure that something was up.

After an hour, during which she considered and then discarded all the simple explanations, she concluded that Carlo was hiding something from her, and she gave in and called me; I'd woken up by then, so I answered the phone, telling her that I'd had a little accident, nothing serious . . . and Carlo? No, Carlo couldn't have known about it, I really didn't think so.

"So was he calling to tell me something about Cecilia?" my mother asked me.

"I don't think there's anything new," I said, and we were silent for thirty seconds, which was our way of commenting on their separation, Carlo's errors, Cecilia's revenge, the possibility of a reconciliation, the risks that Carlo would run if he stayed single. After having thought about these things together, and having tacitly agreed that Carlo should persist in trying to win her back, and Cecilia should give in honorably, that this would be best for the kids (but I don't agree, not completely: sometimes I think exactly the opposite, and my mother thinks I agree only because I don't have to speak out loud), we said goodbye and I made myself a big cup of coffee and got a chair and went out to settle down in the sun, battered but happy, next to the wreck of the Mercedes. I got a certain pleasure from seeing how the smooth lines of the car had gotten all smashed up; it was tangible proof of change, a satisfying sign that my old life was finally shattered.

After talking with our mother, Carlo checked back with Witold, who was driving over to the second local hospital (which his wife, moreover, had already phoned). They decided that Carlo would try calling the hospitals in the city, from the biggest to the smallest, and then he would contact the highway patrols (Witold preferred not to—he doesn't like authorities, because, he says, his surname makes them suspicious; I think he's just irritated because they always spell it wrong). All this searching turned up nothing. In the last of his calls, Carlo found time to accuse a male nurse of being a right-wing flunky, and the nurse retorted that he had been a card-carrying union man for the past twenty-five years, at which point Carlo's tone softened and he said, "I'm sorry, comrade, I'm just scared because I don't know what happened to my brother"; and when the left-wing nurse answered kindly, Carlo added, "I've already lost one brother, to drugs; please try to understand." It was ages since he had last called someone "comrade"; he must really have been distraught. I keep thinking about what Carlo said (what he himself reported to me) not because it's funny (though it is) but because it moves me. When he told me about that phone call, I had to pinch my inner thigh to keep from crying.

At 10:15, exhausted and disheartened, Witold drove his Panda into the farmhouse courtyard a second time. He was giving it one last try before Carlo called the police. But there I sat, coffee in hand, calm and sore, pondering my life and the events of the night before, and feeling the sun on my bare arms. Witold squeezed my arms with relief when he found me safe and sound, and kept asking me obsessively if I was okay; there was no way to reassure him: he wanted to take me right back to the hospital for tests. "I'm fine, really, don't worry," I said, "no bones are broken, I'm just a bit banged up," but I realized that he wasn't listening, or he didn't believe me, because if the car looked that bad, then I must have hit my head, and clearly I could not be the one to decide if I was okay or not.

Next came the clarifications and explanations and play-by-plays: I called Carlo, I called Malik, Witold called his wife. I would have been happy to spend a few more minutes outside, contemplating my car, but Witold threw himself into the role of nurse and insisted that I get back into bed, and, although I refused categorically, he did manage to settle me in my armchair indoors. Meanwhile he arranged for the Mercedes to be towed out of the courtyard: he convinced the body shop to come get it right away, by threatening more or less explicitly to call one of their competitors. I heard him talking on the phone in the kitchen as I sat in the living room, enjoying the air that spiraled in through the open windows and the squares of light hitting the terra-cotta tiles, lost in my thoughts, seduced by Witold's caretaking; I knew that if I didn't chase him out immediately he would never leave, but I didn't have the strength to stop daydreaming: I kept picturing sections of the Renal garden—the parts we had already begun to shape, and the parts still left to do, had all come clear to me now, as if I'd visited the perfect garden last night in a dream and all I had to do was remember the details of it and reproduce them in real life.

So I let the day go on without me; Witold took control, and after an hour his wife came too, and they confined me to the kitchen sofa and had me eat some broth and a hamburger with insipid mashed potatoes, when I would have happily devoured a couple of steaks instead; they took me to bed, closed the shutters, and managed to make me fall asleep, though I don't know how—I haven't slept in the afternoon for ages. After an hour I awoke with a start and staggered woozily downstairs, and at the foot of the steps, by the front door, I found a cardboard carton full of all kinds of liquor: bottles of vodka and gin, some still sealed and others half empty. I thought that Carlo had come with a gift for me, or that Malik had cleared all this stuff out of the famous photographer's pantry, but each scenario was less plausible than the last, and the only likely explanation—which was confirmed by the sounds coming from the kitchen—was that Witold and his wife had set about cleaning, and that those were *my* bottles, waiting to be eliminated the wrong way: in the garbage.

I bend over to pick up the carton, but dizziness topples me toward the wall; I buck backward to straighten up and then stand there, unmoving, while the walls of the corridor swell and contract; I feel like

I'm inside the lungs of an asthmatic animal. Slowly the things around me stop moving: first the coat rack and the mirror, then the shelves and the daguerreotypes in their matched frames depicting a couple of strangers (him with his mustache, her with her chignon) that I bought last year at a flea market (no one understands why: they're not my great-grandparents—no pictures of them exist—and these photographs aren't even particularly decorative). It's outrageous that two strangers should dare to clean out the special stash I use for nighttime distress; it's absurd that I should have hung portraits of unknown people in my entryway just because they seemed to belong to these walls, as if they lived in this farmhouse before me; it's unbearable that the happiness which ran through every cell of my being this morning, through every capillary, through every muscle fiber, has already been burnt away, evaporated, lost. I have to call Elisabetta Renal immediately.

Instead I walk unsteadily into the kitchen and assault the two Poles who are scrubbing my house clean; not only don't I thank them but I accuse them of sticking their noses into my business and of being moralistic zealots; I order Witold to put the liquor right back where he found it. Witold reddens and silently does so; his wife finishes drying two dishes and leaves the room without saying goodbye to me. Before leaving, Witold walks past me and says, "Don't drive after drinking." His tone is not at all punitive or sarcastic: he sounds so chagrined, so genuinely worried, that I cannot reply. After I hear them leave, I drop exhausted onto the sofa and successfully stare at nothing for at least half an hour.

And I don't know how the day would have ended if my cell phone hadn't started ringing, if she hadn't decided to come see me, and if we hadn't talked about what had really happened the night before.

The night before, she tried to pull me out of the Mercedes but she couldn't: I was too heavy, she couldn't even lift me out of the seat, so she asked me whether my legs hurt, if they felt trapped, and when through the foggy veil of shock I answered: "Too fat . . . ," she didn't get it, she didn't understand that I was talking about myself, she thought I was delirious. I surprised her, and myself, by managing to turn partway around and throw both my feet out of the car like a pair of grappling hooks thrown by a pirate boarding a ship, in the hope that they'd land on something solid. Elisabetta stood a few feet away and watched to see whether I could get up by myself, or whether I'd fall to the ground as she had done on that rainy night many months before. I pulled myself up and looked at her, wobbling, and held my hand out toward her with my palm down, as if I were showing her the height of some child—the child I was when my father lost his factory, or Filippo was when his parents split up, or the child that I had become now, because of the accident, who needed care. Elisabetta took my hand in her two hands, then moved next to me and held me up and largely directed my steps toward her Ka, which waited on the edge of the road with its brights on, illuminating the scene of the disaster. I moved jerkily, gathering all my strength to tug each leg up, because with every step I seemed to sink into mud, and each time I lifted my feet they felt soldered to the grass with ultra-superglue.

Getting into the Ka was even harder, maybe, than getting out of the E270, and when I found myself huddled just a few inches from the dashboard, before realizing I had to slide the seat back, there wasn't an ounce of my flesh that didn't hurt. She began to talk right away, and I listened with my eyes closed; the lights of the passing cars jabbed through my eyelids and into my head—suddenly I had no armor to protect me from the world. I had never been afraid of riding in cars, and now I felt I would always be afraid.

It's incredible that Elisabetta Renal had such an urge to talk, that she didn't ask herself whether I was in any condition to listen, that she didn't ask *me* if I was; and I didn't have the strength to protest. She told me about the night I had brought her to the emergency room: she hadn't seen my face clearly until we were in the hospital, but she didn't forget it later, and, when she stumbled across my picture in that magazine, she recognized me immediately, and it was a relief, because she had started dreaming about me at night—she was afraid I would turn up asking for a reward. She imagined that she would see me and that I'd threaten her, or simply stare at her silently; she felt she owed me something that I would have claimed with blackmail or by force. On the one hand, she tried to forget me, and on the other hand, she knew she wouldn't be able to, that to get me out of her dreams she would have to get me into her life somehow, and so she had started a long campaign to convince Alberto that the foundation needed a garden to celebrate Alfredo Renal.

"Reward?" I whispered. "Blackmail?"

In the emergency room they told her that the person who had brought her in hadn't waited around, which was fairly common. Apparently, anonymous rescuers fall into three categories: some are diligent and selfless, and they wait to hear that the accident victim is safe; some want gratitude from the victim; and some just get the victim to the doctor and wash their hands of it all. But she sensed that I didn't belong to the third category, that I was a different thing altogether, there was something in my attitude that didn't fit.

"What 'something'?"

"Your air of indifference. You pretended to be there by chance."

"But I *was* there by chance."

"Really? I don't know why, but I got the opposite impression. As if you were following me."

"But if I didn't even know you yet . . ."

"And why did you leave?"

"Because I really am in the third category of anonymous rescuers. I don't want to get involved."

"And why were you following me now?"

I don't answer. After a moment of silence, Elisabetta goes on with her story. That night, the night I abandoned her in the ER, she called Alberto, and when one of the twins had been sent to get her, she almost forgot about the danger that I might come back to pester her. She was distraught: all she wanted to do was sleep, to get home and take a pill and fall asleep until the next day. But the next day she started thinking about me, and she never stopped. "Thinking," though, was the wrong word. She was *afraid* of me.

"Afraid?"

"Yes, afraid that you knew something."

"Knew what?"

"Something you shouldn't know until I decide to tell you about it. Unless you already know it."

"I don't want to know anyway."

"Why?"

"Because then you'll be afraid I'll tell someone else."

"No, I'm not afraid of that. I'm afraid of you, not of other people."

I didn't understand why she should be afraid of me: I had never made anybody afraid, I felt completely inoffensive, and she was much too excited; I couldn't take her chattering anymore, and I asked her please to keep quiet until we got to the hospital.

Then I immediately began to think that it wasn't true, that someone had once been afraid of me—or rather, I had been afraid that someone was afraid of me, no matter how strange and unnatural it was. In his final years my father seemed to have become my assistant: I was the contact person for the clients, and I determined the job priorities, on the assumption that he was getting more distracted or losing his memory, so that having a son to help him was a big advantage—but I read in his eyes that that wasn't the truth. He was afraid of becoming useless, and that's why he was afraid of me: afraid that I could do without him, that I would find myself another helper and leave him at home, in that house, all day long, every day—so he refused to listen to me and always insisted on doing the most dangerous jobs. (As it happened, I actually had found a helper: Witold, freshly arrived from Poland with his literary, antique opera lover's Italian; Papa and I thought he was sort of delirious until Carlo explained things for us. According to Carlo, Witold's linguistic "normalization" was a tragedy as great as the disappearance of a dialect.)

When I finished up in the emergency room, I found her sitting on the edge of a bench, gnawing on her already-chewed-down fingernails and sighing like someone about to take an exam. She belonged to the second category of anonymous rescuers, even though obviously there was nothing anonymous about this.

"They scolded me."

"Who?"

"The nurses, because I moved you . . . took you out of the car . . ."

"And what should you have done?"

"Left you where you were and called an ambulance."

"You should have said I was the one who taught you to move victims away from the scene . . ."

I looked around: there was only one couple in the waiting room, a fiftyish husband doubled over with a kidney stone and his drowsy wife watching him. In a piercing voice the man said, "Fortunately I have a high pain threshold."

I asked Elisabetta to take me home.

We sat down in the kitchen, at opposite ends of the sofa, with a bottle of vodka on the table. She wanted to know why there was a sofa next to the dining table, how long I'd lived in that old farmhouse, why I lived there alone, why I hadn't rented out the other wing, which I had restored though I didn't live in it.

"Do you want to come live in it?"

She went on with her questions. Why did I have all those toys scattered around the house, why all the fairy tales, why the Disney videos, why the dog bowl, and did I cook for myself? And did I clean for myself?

"Does it look to you like anyone cleans here?"

She poured herself another drink. I did too. I stared into her eyes—by this point I had nothing left to lose. The worst she could do was leave. But maybe I would have stopped her before she got to the door.

"Was there anything else you wanted to know?"

"Yes, I wanted to know why you didn't recognize me immediately . . . why you pretended not to recognize me . . . when I came here to your courtyard to invite you to dinner, that Sunday evening."

I closed my eyes and leaned my head back; I'd claimed that the overhead light bothered me, so I'd turned off all the lights except the spotlight over the stove. I could have sat her in the living room, where I had another sofa that was probably more comfortable. But when we walked in, I suddenly felt it was very important that Elisabetta should sit in the guest's place. Even though I had never imagined the guest with any particular face—except maybe my own face as an old man—and certainly not a female one.

"Well, I almost never know why I do what I do. Do you?"

"No, not always."

I told her that I didn't know why, because I had recognized her immediately—I had even recognized her voice on the phone.

"My voice? But we had never talked on the phone . . ."

I told her how I had fantasized about her voice and her way of talking. I told her that I had expected her to recognize me too, when we saw each other, that I wondered about the very things she was asking me about now.

"I always had the impression you were avoiding me. Until I realized you were following me."

"When was that?"

She poured herself a drink, and I did the same.

"Mosca pointed out that it was strange for someone like you to be at that club at that time of night."

I nodded; I had expected it.

"And why were you following me?"

I don't understand why she keeps asking me that. I'm no good at replying without actually answering—I don't know the evasive answers that reveal nothing at all. I wasn't trained in that sort of conversation. I can't do it. Either I tell her the truth—that I need her—or I keep quiet. I keep quiet. And to cut the conversation short, I decide to get up and saunter around the kitchen looking nonchalant.

But I fell down as soon as I stood up. The floor rose to greet me, tipped right up to my chin, and I banged my head violently for the second time that night. I didn't faint—but I found myself on all fours, humiliated. Elisabetta was crouched down talking to me as if she were trying to console a huge, sad dog, and I stared at a tile and thought that one universe wasn't big enough to hold both the geometric perfection of the square and the turbulence vibrating within me.

She guided me to my big, useless bed. I lay down and knocked off my shoes, but I couldn't undress. The last memory I have is of her, at 1:30, sitting on the edge of my bed and holding my hand.

When I woke it was 4:00 a.m. and I felt much better. My head was no longer spinning. It was pitch-black, but I sensed that someone was lying next to me. It had been ages since someone else slept in my bed, and it's not a feeling you can re-create any other way, not even with a mannequin. It's a beautiful feeling.

So I didn't want to wake her. But I desperately needed to piss, so I got up cautiously and went out of the room and into the bathroom. I looked at myself in the mirror for ten minutes, thinking back on my arrival at the hospital and the point when I went into the exam room on a gurney: they X-rayed me and clipped the films up on a light box. The doctor was a woman so young that she seemed like a child, but her colleagues and the nurses obeyed her, and clearly they respected her; she came across like a little general, pointing to the X-ray of my cranium as if it were a battle map; and while talking to another doctor she named the tiny bones of my face, one by one, with childish glee, entertaining herself in the midst of the sad, boring night. I had no fractures, and my life wasn't in danger. A solicitous nurse dressed the wound on my cheekbone, and the girl-doctor discharged me with her sleepy eyes half shut: the entertainment was done.

I undressed and put on the T-shirt and boxer shorts that I sleep in.

The room was no longer so dark—there was a faint glow now, or maybe I'd just gotten used to the gloom, so I could see the outline of Elisabetta Renal's body stretched out on the right side of my bed, the deserted side.

Until the moment I touched the bed, I'd merely intended to lie down again in my spot and fall back asleep, and if she were to wake up, I'd ask her why she had stayed to sleep, whether she had drunk too much vodka to drive or whether she was afraid I might still need her, or a doctor, or a hospital.

But as soon as I touched the bed my intentions changed. I sat down on her side and stared at her. Maybe she wasn't sleeping, I thought. Her eyelids trembled with the effort of staying shut. I slowly moved closer and kissed her lids. She didn't move. So I began kissing her whole face. Her nose and her cheeks, her lips and her chin. She had a hand on her belly, and I went down to kiss the hand. I brushed against the fabric of her blouse, tracing the line of her bra. I saw a naked foot, and, gripped by some kind of euphoria, I began kissing that too. The euphoria had a caption to it, like the display photos in a plant catalog: "There's a woman in my bed, I can kiss her." I rested my lips on her toes, then touched them softly, one by one, with my lips, breathing against her skin.

When in the dimness I saw that her eyes were open and watching me with a serious and astonished and curious look, when I understood that she was waiting for something, I glided up her calves, lifted her skirt, roamed around between her thighs, and reached her white underpants, where I stopped to await her reaction. She began moving her hips up and down, pressing her sex against my mouth.

I slipped her undies off. I kissed her and licked her, and she grabbed my hair and pulled it. I squeezed her buttocks between my hands, crushed my whole face against her, and penetrated her with my tongue; my wound reopened, and I felt blood bathing my face and her thigh, but I didn't stop kissing her until she arched her back like a branch loaded with flowers and then fell back onto the bed and pushed me aside. A moment later she was bowing down over my belly, and I was staring incredulously at the ceiling. I came in thirty seconds.

I asked, "Where are you going?"

"That's enough."

"Why 'enough'?"

She got up and went into the bathroom. I lay down on my side, covering my belly with a corner of the sheet. Why "enough"? I wondered.

Coming out of the bathroom, she left the light on, and now we could see each other's faces. She came back with a damp towel, cotton, and alcohol, cleaned the blood off me, disinfected the wound, and put another Band-Aid on my cheekbone. She lay down again on the other side. It really was all over.

"Why 'enough'?"

"Enough. You've been in an accident."

She looked at me like a concerned nurse, and I was irritated but too weak to protest.

What accident was she talking about? She seemed to be distancing herself already: "You've been in an accident" was a way of saying "This was just an accident."

At some point I must have fallen asleep.

At 5:15 I heard the sound of the Ka's engine and its tires on the gravel, and I awoke with a start.

At 6:00 I took a sleeping pill.

This is what I told her about the night we spent together, what I told her the next evening, when she came to see me and we ate together in the kitchen for the first time. Elisabetta sat at my place, because she found the sofa too uncomfortable for eating. She listened in silence. She was embarrassed, but smiling. Then she told me that she had to think about it, that she wasn't sure it was a good idea for either of us. "Speak for yourself," I said. But I thought it was the end.

In those final days of May, the Renal construction site became a garden. There's always a point when a project you've designed and so often pictured in your imagination comes to life and takes the last few steps on its own; when your imaginative effort is suddenly interrupted, and a stranger—the garden—decides everything for you, decides everything for itself; it takes shape and suddenly has its own unique face, not exactly like the face in the frame hung on your mental wall, but it's still a friendly and familiar face; it turns out your only task was to recognize that face in the crowd and tease it out and set it in the foreground: the garden itself is like the real person, while the design project is just like a memory. But sometimes it remains nothing but an impression and never springs to life. Sometimes you get all the way to the end of a job, and you're still the one and only person responsible for what you've made, and the garden is just an inert heap of crude or sophisticated plants and dirt and materials that you've intentionally or unintentionally given some kind of shape to, which arouses some kind of emotion in the clients (or maybe no emotion at all). Then your attitude changes, and exhaustion makes you self-indulgent, and you no longer have the strength to solve problems, except when your errors leap out at you—like a flower bed built wrong—and force you to find a remedy. You finish the job on inertia alone. Or sometimes both things are true.

But it just so happened that the night of the accident (of the accidents) was the milestone marking off "before" from "after." Before I understood what the Renal garden meant to me, and after. (I had long worried about its precarious, impalpable, accidental nature, but now I saw it as a passageway, a subterranean tunnel that would take me elsewhere, and so I was more willing than usual to let myself be carried along on the inertia of the final stages.) Before sleeping in my bed with Elisabetta, and after.

Almost every night she came to my place. She was always the one who called me, from her cell phone, to say she was coming. She came at 7:30, stayed for dinner, and left at 10:00. Or I wouldn't hear from her till 11:00, when she would call from who-knows-where to ask whether she could come by for a drink—but she never stayed past 1:00 a.m. She'd leave the car half in and half out of the gate, which I always left open; I don't know if she did it on purpose, whether she was trying to tell me that she hadn't yet come all the way into my life, or whether she simply wanted to keep any other car from going in or out of the courtyard. I would wait for her in the doorway, and she always came in with her eyes on the ground, not looking at me until I had shut the door behind her. Roiling in her wake was a magnetic trail of anxiety like the train of an evening gown, and I always checked outside to see whether some of it had been left behind before I closed the door; I would glance around my deserted courtyard with a feeling of alienation. She would rub her hands together, tuck her hair behind her ears, cross and uncross her arms, pinch at her cheeks and her neck; it took her at least half an hour to calm down, and then she would slowly begin to smile. I didn't want to ask her where she'd just been, who she'd been with, or where she went after leaving my house; I didn't want to ask her to stay the night:

maybe I was simply afraid she'd say no. I asked her how she spent her day, what she did.

Four days a week she went to the foundation's office in the city. She was the one who dealt with the charitable operations, the funding requests, and the awarding of academic grants. No one had asked her to do it. But after Alberto's accident she thought it was the perfectly normal thing to do.

"It's bookkeeping; I like it, it keeps me busy . . ."

"And Alberto?"

Nowadays Alberto devoted himself to the management of Alfredo's intellectual legacy.

"And what does Mosca have to do with the foundation?"

Mosca had always been in charge of the Renals' money; he was an old family friend. He occasionally went in to the foundation's office, where he mistreated the secretaries and generally made a mess of things.

I asked her where the foundation's office was. She looked up from her plate and stared at me without answering. Then she smiled. "You followed me there too . . ."

"No, I don't know where it is—I swear."

"In the city, in the old Renal apartment."

It would have been stupid for me to deny it; at that moment it seemed that she could read my mind. "Oh, then, yes, I followed you there too, but I didn't know it was the foundation's office."

"How many times did you follow me?"

"Into the city, just once . . . I almost got found out. I was on the landing when the door opened and someone came out, a woman, who mistook me for one of those guys who put flyers in people's mail slots . . . For a moment I thought she was your mother."

She stares at me, unmoving, her fork halfway to her plate with the tines pointed at me, and I picture her stabbing me in the face.

"And what else?"

"What else what?"

"Did you investigate?" she murmurs.

"What do you mean?"

"Did you investigate me?"

"Well, I asked about the Renals . . . I always ask about clients . . . To protect myself."

"What do you ask?"

"I find out whether they'll pay my bill in the end," I say, without much conviction in my voice.

Again I get the look from her, and an ironic smile. "I don't believe that you're such a busybody. And you don't think about money. When you need information, who's your informant?"

"All right, it's true. I don't always investigate. This time I asked because"—I stop myself from lying again—"because I didn't even know that you were once Alfredo's wife—"

"You thought I was his sister?"

"Yes."

"Everybody thinks so . . . And maybe it's not far from the truth."

"What do you mean?"

"I mean, maybe it's not far from the truth. What else did you ask about?"

"I wanted to know about Alfredo, about his friendship with Alberto . . . He himself made me wonder about it . . ."

"But that's not why you asked around."

"No."

"You wanted to know about me—where I come from, why I married Alfredo—isn't that true?"

"Yes."

"You haven't told me who your informant is."

"I don't want to tell you."

"Okay. Don't tell me. What else did you find out?"

"Nothing."

"Well, then, your informant isn't very good."

"Why?"

"Because there are other interesting things to find out."

I asked her what they were, but she shook her head. Now she was distracted. Her anxiety would grip her all of a sudden, and I would see her staring at her glass, or at one of my copper pots hanging on the wall, and then the dinner was over: there was no way to bring her back. She was afraid that someone else was following her around those days, and she made me swear I had stopped following her; she felt there was always another car tailing her. "What kind of car?" I asked. She didn't know. If she had been able to identify one in particular, whether or not she knew whose it was, her fear would have been more direct, sharp, and controllable.

"You say that as if you've never had any real reason to be afraid."

She replied that a real reason produces a real but limited fear, no matter how terrible it may be, but that false, irrational fear is more flexible: it shapes itself to fit any situation, and it spreads across your whole landscape, blanketing everything.

I too had recently had the impression I was being followed; one night when I was parked with Cecilia outside the hypermarket, I had trouble concentrating on her words because it seemed that a gray Fiat Brava had trailed me all the way there and then disappeared, and that there was now a yellow Renault Scénic with some guy reading a newspaper—I watched him in the right-side mirror.

Cecilia had finally met with Carlo, so I had a thousand reasons for listening to what she said, but this thing was too strong: my eyes kept snapping back to the mirror. Carlo had met with his wife, whom he claimed he wanted to get back together with, not only for the children's sake but because he really still loved her, because she was the love of his life; he didn't care about other women, other women just vanish without leaving a trace. ("But what if *he* leaves a trace?" Cecilia once said to me. "What if he has a love child hidden somewhere—do you really think these girls are using protection? Because if you think *he's* using protection, you're wrong; he's the classic egotist who just wants to shoot his wad." "Shoot his *wad*?" "Shoot his load, ejaculate, come— Good god, Claudio, you're like a ten-year-old.") Carlo had met with this perfect woman after months of having doors slammed in his face and telephones slammed down, and it was his one chance to talk to her, this meeting that was arranged partly because I'd interceded for him. And what had he done? He'd told her how anguished he was by the war. The Americans had bombed a hospital.

The man I saw at the wheel of the Scénic seemed more and more familiar, especially in the position of his head: he seemed to be asserting the superiority of the rigid over the flexible, as if a tree is superior to a shrub, or brick is superior to gravel.

"Are you telling me that you didn't talk about the two of you?"

"I'm saying that he walked into that bar with a depressed look that was clearly fake, moaned for five minutes about how lonely he was and how much he missed me, and then launched into this half-hour diatribe about how the war changed his life, how he realizes now what's been happening in the Balkans in recent years, and that's the worst part of it, this is our punishment, and—"

"Okay, but then he must have asked you what you thought—"

"About the war?"

"No, about the idea—I mean, the possibility of—"

"Of him moving back in? No, no, no, he didn't ask—don't you get it? Don't you get what he's like—don't you see what your brother is really like? Don't you see what a massive shithead he is?"

I nodded. I looked in the mirror. It was one of the twins: Rossi was having me trailed by the twins. He had figured out what I really was— that I was a traitor.

"Plus, I don't really believe him . . ."

"About what?"

"I think he's got someone else. Or at least he's got someone else in mind. By now I can sense these things."

I should have said that she'd gone fifteen years without sensing these things, and that it seemed strange to me she'd suddenly become so perceptive. But I reassured her instead: "No, really, I think that's really unlikely, you can see how confused he is, he doesn't talk about anything but disasters and catastrophes and conspiracies . . ."

I had looked away for a moment, and now the Scénic was gone.

One evening when Elisabetta was eating with me in the kitchen, I asked her whether she could give me Mosca's number; he had spoken to me at the party about a hanging garden and I was interested, partly because I needed the income. Elisabetta wasn't happy about giving me the number, but she pulled out her address book and read it to me anyway, and as soon as I'd saved the number in my cell-phone memory with the name Mosca, the screen lit up and his name flashed on it: he was already phoning me.

Surprised by the coincidence, I answered jovially, saying that he really must have ESP; and like a cowardly prisoner who blurts out his accomplices' names in the very first interrogation, I said that he wasn't disturbing me at all, that I'd just finished dinner with Elisabetta Renal, who was sitting right here. I realized how stupid that was immediately, even before she rose in a fury and left the room.

Mosca spoke, and I held the cell phone against my ear with two fingers. It felt lighter, as if the swirl of his words swallowed the air inside my ear and made it into a suction cup or a tiny tabletop vacuum cleaner. I fiddled with the crumbs on the table and peeked toward the black rectangle of the door that Elisabetta had disappeared behind; I hadn't yet heard the sound of the front door, or the Ka starting up. Mosca was saying that he'd seen the hanging garden I'd done for the Gallo house two years ago, that he had visited it (nothing was impossible for him: he had called the owner and drowned him in a flood of words), that he'd been very impressed, and that he was interested, even enthusiastic, about the idea of having me design a garden for him. Hanging gardens are a godsend for me: they require very precise planning, but building them is effortless. Ultimately I would turn him down, but for the time being I said Okay, not to worry, I wouldn't forget about him.

I go looking for Elisabetta right away, and I find her in front of the fireplace, sitting in Carlo's favorite chair with a hand over her eyes. I don't know what to say, so I don't say anything, and I go back to the kitchen to clear the plates and put out fresh ones. I hope that the clinking sounds will bring her back in. But she doesn't come, she stays in the armchair. That's certainly the most popular piece of furniture I have. Even perfect strangers who come to my living room usually go straight to it and sit down, although it's not particularly comfortable; you can't say it has aged gracefully, despite the cracking leather on the back and the beaten-down seat cushion. It's just an old armchair in front of a hearth.

"He knew I was here, and he wanted to let me know that he knew," said Elisabetta when she came back into the kitchen ten minutes later. I had sat down to eat some fruit, and while she was gone I'd poured myself two glasses of wine and drunk them both. I told her that I was sorry I'd told him, but that he'd taken me by surprise.

"It doesn't matter what you said." She repeated, "He already knew I was here."

I said nothing.

"Why aren't you saying anything?"

I shrugged.

"Come on, tell me what you're thinking."

"I'm not thinking anything."

"Well, if you're thinking what I think you're thinking, you're wrong."

I rolled my head over onto the backrest of the sofa and stared at the ceiling. Why did my eyes always run toward the corners, like water running down a gutter? With my thoughts like little paper boats capsizing in the current. No, I hadn't really believed they were lovers, but I was relieved anyway. I mumbled that it was none of my business. Untrue.

She shook her head. "He's dangerous."

"I could tell."

"Do you know why he always goes around with Giletti?"

"No."

"Because he's afraid of being alone."

"What do you mean?"

"He's afraid, he never wants to be alone. He always needs to have someone with him."

"I don't believe that."

"Well, naturally he'll never admit he's afraid. He's not the type."

"So how does he account for it?"

"He has some long story to justify it, but I don't remember it. First he bought a dog—a thing like a big white rat—but that wasn't good enough."

"This is like your story about the two dentists."

"The story about the two dentists was completely true!"

She picks up a piece of apple peel and tosses it at me, and then she throws the bread crusts that were left on the tabletop. I grab her wrists before she can fling a glass of wine at me. She slips out of my grasp, smiling.

"So now you think I'm a silly person who makes things up . . ."

"No, I don't think that."

"A silly person who doesn't know what to say, who should just keep quiet . . ."

"I rarely think, and I think only nice things about you."

She smiles. "No, really, do you think I talk nonsense?"

"No, I don't think that."

"Yes, I do talk nonsense, but often I can't help it."

"You don't have to justify yourself to me."

"I'm not justifying myself," she says, and tosses another apple peel at me. "I'm explaining why sometimes it's worse if I don't say anything at all."

She stares me in the eye.

I say, "Okay, so tell me why you and Alberto pretend you're married."

"Oh, now your informant is getting better information."

"It's my brother, not an informant."

"And who told him the whole story?"

"An old professor of his."

"A gossip."

"I don't know; I've never met him."

"What else did this gossip tell him?"

"That you and Alberto had an accident that paralyzed him."

"Did he tell you who was driving?"

"No."

A pause.

"But why do you two say you're married?"

"He does it. And I can't always correct him. Did I ever tell you I was his wife? Actually, I introduced myself as Renal, didn't I?"

"Maybe he would like to have the name Renal too; marry you and take the name."

"Yes, he would like to *be* Alfredo. But I can't blame him for that."

I look at her.

"Why don't you come and live here with me?"

She starts laughing, and I laugh too; it suddenly sounds so ingenuous.

"Where would you put me?"

"The other wing of the house is empty."

"Oh, I see. It's interesting that you want to put me on the far side of the courtyard—"

"Oh no, there's room here too, if you prefer."

She told me to forget about it, but I kept thinking about it, and the next day I opened up the other wing of the farmhouse and aired out the rooms, picturing how she would use them, and then picturing her knocking on my door in the morning to have breakfast with me, and then picturing her waking up in my bed every now and then and having to cross the courtyard in her nightgown to go back to her house to dress.

Late on Saturday night I woke abruptly. I wasn't sure I had closed the ground-floor shutters firmly, or rather I had a perfectly clear memory of shutting them, but I didn't trust myself anymore. I glanced into the kids' room, where there's always an orange night-light glowing. They were sleeping, Momo crouched over like a praying Muslim, Filippo across the middle of the bed with his legs dangling in space. I went downstairs and toured the rooms. Then I opened the front door and shut it again, locking it all the way with four turns of the great key. Just as I was pulling the key out of the lock, I realized what kind of noise must have woken me. I opened the front door again. I breathed a lungful of air moist with rain. Beneath the canopy in the courtyard was the E270 that I'd bought secondhand to replace my unfixable one. The Clio wasn't there.

Carlo wasn't in his bedroom. But I had promised myself I would never follow anyone again.

The night Fabio died it wasn't my mother who told me to follow him. I was already asleep: I had fallen asleep in front of the little black-and-white TV at the foot of my bed; on its yellowish screen, I occasionally watched the strip shows and old R-rated movies that the local stations ran after midnight. I woke with a start to see my father bending over me, touching my shoulder and whispering my name. He told me that a neighbor on his way home had stopped to knock on our door and let us know that Fabio was in the parking lot behind the town hall, sitting on the ground between two cars. "Go get him, bring him home."

I got dressed again, in a pair of jeans and a T-shirt, and my Adidas without socks, and I went down to the street and I took the R4 and drove without haste through the narrow streets of the village (you couldn't do that now, the whole thing has become a pedestrian zone), obeying all the lights and stop signs even though there was no one around: it was 1:00 a.m. It was a warm, peaceful September night; some driveways and courtyards held camper vans or trailers carrying fiberglass boats (which were the big new thing, at the time, for people who got to the seaside only in summer), and dangling from the balconies were freshly washed sleeping bags hung out to dry—symbols that summer was over and that people were slowly, reluctantly winding up their vacations. How had we spent the summer? As usual, my parents hadn't left home. I had spent two weeks camping with four old classmates, under the pine trees near some beach. Was it the year I went to Tuscany? Or the year I went to Corsica? One or the other.

Fabio had roamed around the local countryside, sleeping with friends here and there ("Did you sleep in the fields?" I asked, and he nodded). He was very direct. He counted someone as his friend if he had met the guy just that morning and spent the day hanging out and chatting with him. What did I see him do, when I followed him secretly? Nothing. I spied on him. I didn't like the people he hung out with; it only made me angry to think about why he hung out with them. But actually I hardly looked at those people. I watched only him. He had the same serene, absent look he'd had when we were kids. He had nothing in common with those people. He didn't share their frenzy, their gluttonous energy. As I spied on him, I couldn't help thinking that he was happy. The idea was unbearable to me, but I kept turning it over in my mind; I held it close, like an ugly gift from someone I loved— something I couldn't shake.

When he got back home that summer, we saw that he'd had a "total relapse" (that was my mother's only comment on it, one evening after he came home; my father and I said nothing). Before the summer she had said, "He's having a relapse" (though it wasn't clear at the time that she was talking about Fabio: she was looking out the window when she said it). Summer wasn't good for him. Summertime usually brings relapses, I thought as I drove languidly through the village: there's something in the air. In February he had come home from his second stint in detox, and he had persuaded us that working in the factory wasn't a good fit for him, that he wanted to finish high school. We believed him. He had turned cagey.

The windows of the houses facing the piazza behind the town hall were all dark and shuttered. Four flickering streetlamps shone down on the parking lot, which didn't have even one empty parking spot left, and I thought how much I disliked empty or half-empty parking lots: a full lot is like a completed crossword puzzle, with every word in its place. It took me a while to find him, sitting with his back against some car's left front wheel; he had arranged all his tools on the right front wheel of the neighboring car, in the small gap between the tire and the fender, as if he didn't want to lay them on the ground: the lighter, the spoon, even the needle's tiny green protective tip. The needle was still in his vein, the belt still tight on his arm. After shooting up he would always fall into a blissful sleep. To wake him you just had to give him a shake, or grab his shoulder, or squeeze his hand. It had worked for me twice before, and I was sure it would work again. It didn't work.

There wasn't much room, and I didn't want to risk kicking him in the head if I stepped over him; I was on the side where he had the needle in his arm, the left side, and I wanted to talk to him on the healthy side, the clean, intact side; talk to him without raising my voice, maybe give him a little slap on the cheek. So I walked all the way around the car and kneeled down next to him. He was wearing a Shell Oil T-shirt with a big yellow shell on the back and a little shell on the front, above his heart. He had the same jeans I did, and Adidas with three red stripes (mine were blue). I said his name twice. I stroked his face with the back of my hand. I said his name again. I pushed his bangs back off his forehead. A strand of drool dripped from his mouth onto his T-shirt. I wiped it away with my own shirt.

I slapped him twice, without putting any muscle into it. He didn't wake up; he was breathing noisily, with a little groan, barely audible, on the exhale. I decided to lift him up, thinking that I would lean him against the car to see if he could stand. But first I had to get the needle out of his arm. I went back around to the other side. I pulled out the needle with a sharp tug and laid it down on Fabio's little night table (the tire) just as he would have done. I undid the belt from his arm and laid it on the hood of the other car. The metal buckle made a slight *click* against the hood. I looked up, but the lot was deserted, the night was still warm and calm. A tiny drop of blood blossomed from the hole in his arm.

Fabio was shorter and slimmer than Carlo and I. He had straight, almost black hair, dark brown eyes, fair skin. Carlo and I, at the time, had wavy but not quite curly light brown hair, hazel eyes, and darker skin. Every time I thought about that, I recalled my old idea that he wasn't really our brother. But that night, as I tried to get him up on his feet, by hugging him beneath his arms, pushing with my legs and my back, I felt his jawbone against my cheek, and I fit my cheekbone in under his cheekbone, pressing my face against his, and I understood that we were made from the same mold, that we fit together exactly. Lifting a body up from the ground is one of the most difficult tasks there is, and I had only a few feet of space between the two cars to work in.

I leaned him against the fender, but he didn't wake up, and I was afraid he would slide back down again to the pavement; I made another enormous effort and somehow dragged him to the R4. It took me about twenty minutes, but I finally loaded him in, sitting down with his head thrown back. I returned to his spot and tidied it up, throwing away the needle and its protective tip and the lighter and the spoon in a trash can. I took back the belt. (And during all this back-and-forth I didn't doubt for a single instant that we would spend more time together: other sunny days, other trips to the supermarket, other lunches, other TV movies—I didn't doubt for an instant that we would go on living and seeing each other and knowing each other.)

When I got to the house, my father was waiting for us outside. I told him that Fabio hadn't woken up, and only then did I think, We'd better take him to the emergency room. But I didn't say it. I waited for my father to say it. My father said, "Let's bring him inside." I don't recall thinking anything else. But that's impossible. I must have thought that he was only sleeping, that he was going to wake up.

We brought him up to his bed, undressed him, put on his pajamas, and tucked him in under the sheet. My mother didn't wake up, or at least she didn't come in.

My father went out of our bedroom, and I stayed and watched Fabio for a while. He inhaled, exhaled, held still for a second—uncertain about whether to draw another breath—but then he inhaled, exhaled, hesitated, and began again.

I found my father sitting in the kitchen, his hands clasped on the table. He was staring straight ahead. I took three steps into the dark hallway, toward our bedroom. And didn't go in. I couldn't have fallen asleep anyway, with Fabio breathing that way. I could have gone to sleep in Carlo's room, but instead I came back toward the light. I sat down in the kitchen, at the head of the table, tracing the blurry arabesques of the veined marble surface, spellbound by them just as I had been in childhood.

Considering that I must have brought Fabio home at two and we didn't call the doctor until six, we must have spent four hours sitting at the table without talking. When I looked up, I saw my father's profile. He was holding back the tears, sobbing silently. Who knows what he was thinking?

Who knows what I was thinking? Besides the fact that I wanted to tell my father we should take Fabio to the emergency room, I must have thought about something else. But I don't remember. I remember only that I couldn't speak. I should have said something, and I didn't.

At six my father stood up and went out of the kitchen. I heard him go to Fabio. He came right back out and called the doctor. He told me to put on my pajamas, and he did so too. When the doctor arrived, Fabio was dead. While I was standing there, my father told him that I had found my brother in the parking lot and brought him home, that he was sleeping but that we weren't worried because he woke up as soon as he got home and put on his pajamas by himself. I don't know if the doctor believed it—maybe he didn't even wonder whether we had any reason to lie, and he surely didn't notice that our pajamas weren't wrinkled from a night of sleep; he wasn't a police detective or anything.

When he left I went back into our room. I sat down on the bed next to Fabio. Without thinking about it, without thinking that he was dead—as if he were just sleeping and he might awake at any moment—I took him under the arms, lifted him up, and embraced him. I squeezed him tight. I could feel my father's gaze on my back.

I make a habit of presenting my gardens to the clients before I've put on the finishing touches. My initial reason was insecurity: in my earliest jobs I kept some wiggle room for myself so that I could change substantial elements if I saw that the client was unhappy. Now I'm famous enough that clients rarely dare to make suggestions, let alone criticize my work. With the Renals, though, I acted in a new and even more arrogant way: I presented a design and then built something completely different, without saying anything to the person who commissioned it. I didn't even really grasp who had commissioned this. Was it Rossi? Elisabetta? Alfredo's ghost? The foundation—and therefore Mosca? Who should I have talked to, to say that I wasn't executing any of the elements that, by the way, I had actually designed for the data center of a bank? Elements that appeared on the plans Rossi had displayed on an easel at the party celebrating Alfredo Renal's book; elements that will ultimately come to life in the space they were originally designed for.

And Thursday turned out to be the perfect day, because it had rained for the first two days of the week, and Wednesday had been one of those June days when the rain-cleansed air is scrubbed even cleaner by the wind, making it so crystalline that even myopic people feel they can see for miles, and distant objects look so sharply chiseled that it throws you off balance, tumbling you forward—as if the horizon were a nearby shelf and you could reach right out and grasp those things. I knew that the garden would look splendid, the still-damp stone would shine in the sunlight, the crushed glass would spray rainbow glimmers all around, the wet metal surfaces would reflect the plants, the shells would be perfectly clean, and the boxwood hedges would be decorated with minuscule globes of water scattered across the tiny leaves. And that a garden like this one always looks better with dark, moisture-soaked earth than with the dry earth of a breathless July or a snowless January.

At 10:00 a.m. Witold and I stood near the balustrade with our backs to the garden, smiling at Rossi, the twins, and even the assistant, who for the occasion had replaced her usual skirt suit with jeans and a T-shirt that had LISA written in rhinestones on the front. By now I'd figured out that Rossi always dressed the same, as if to say, "This is the paraplegic's uniform": a blue cardigan, a white shirt, sweatpants. He had come down in his electric wheelchair, and now the twins, both dressed as gardeners, muttered something behind his back, pointing to the motor and the heavy struts of the chair, worrying about how they were to lift it. "There's never more than a five-degree slope," I said. "It's designed so that an electric chair can easily get around the whole garden."

Rossi burst out laughing, and when I realized what I had said, I laughed too. The others smiled in embarrassment.

"You're right, it is sort of like a penal sentence," he said. "If you want to avoid faux pas, you can call it a motorized chair."

I was happy to see him in a good mood; I had run into him only a couple of times recently, and each time I felt guilty about wanting to steal his wife away; I was afraid he had already begun to hate me. He seemed quite calm and eager to proceed with the tour. He turned and said to his assistant: "Lisa, please go see whether my wife—" She was the only thing holding us up, and just at that moment she appeared, smiling and out of breath, her hair still wet from the shower, with shorts and a tank top and flip-flops. I tried not to look at her again for the rest of the tour.

"There are seven sections, and the transition from one to the next is very important." I paused. "If you agree, I'd suggest going all the way though the garden without talking, and then on the way back I'll tell you what I was trying to achieve."

They all nodded except the twins, but by now I was accustomed to their inexpressiveness.

As we moved along, the only sounds were our footsteps on the different paving surfaces, the hum of Rossi's chair, and the trills and whistles of sparrows, magpies, and blackbirds.

This is what we saw:

In the first part, seven aluminum canals, each twenty feet long, bordered by lamb's ears and brick paths just four feet wide, so that only one person can walk along the path at a time.

In the second part, three wavy Gaudi-style archways of concrete covered with shells and tiny mirrors of all colors, sizes, and shapes, the largest of which reflect the house and the paths that we were on; beyond the arches is a round area marked off by ten tall, narrow buckets of zinc-galvanized iron with tufts of thistle and belladonna plants.

In the third part, six great boulders of pink and gray granite, all about six feet high, with a walkway of teak strips snaking between them. The boulders were quarried in a seaside cave, and they're covered with pink and yellow moss; they have seats carved into them, where you can set cushions. At the feet of the boulders are patches of mallow flowers and tricolor violas.

In the fourth part, the old boxwood walls have been sculpted into uneven, curvy waves, and there's black and white gravel; at the center stand the roots of the walnut tree framed in a glass vitrine; the hedges of cotoneaster and holly are in bad shape and will need a long period of loving attention if they're going to heal.

In the fifth part are a funnel-like corridor of cages of galvanized steel, each filled with white, red, and green pebbles; beds of hart's tongue fern sprinkled with luminous little wells of water; and a small forest of tree trunks bleached by salty seawater spray.

In the sixth part is a square tube of opaque glass that runs toward the pond, supported by carved rocks; short slabs of dull copper growing upright in beds of fiddlehead fern, royal fern, and sweet fern; and a path made of stone split along its natural cleavage planes.

The seventh part has the cistern, now an ornamental pond studded with conical heaps of crushed white glass rising a foot and a half above the surface of the water; long, narrow beds fanning out from the water like sunrays; and stands of bamboo in purply black patches of mussel shells.

I talked to them about the Garden as Experience, about the kind of garden you can move through as if it represents a whole lifetime, like a set of memories; of the hardness of stone shattering against water and against the transparency of glass; about new elements versus old elements that deserve to be preserved and reshaped; about the three-way axis point in the fourth part, which is simply a reinterpretation of an old-fashioned garden, with the plant elements confronting the mineral elements and ultimately mixing and interpenetrating; about the marine elements as the memory of these plains where we live, a reference to their fossilized past; about the light and shadow that we simply have to accept; about the nuanced, indeterminate areas; about the unresolved elements; about the warped reflections and the ferns' symmetrical chaos; and I concluded by calling it a Garden as Dream.

Rossi turns his palms up to the sky and shakes his head slowly, smiling slightly. Now he's going to tell me it's all nonsense, I think, surprised to find myself anxious about a client's opinion, which I never have been before.

But "It's marvelous," says he, "it's evocative and . . ." He looks for some other adjective, shakes his head, "marvelous."

From the sound of it, Witold must have been worried too: I hear him sigh with relief. Everyone smiles and relaxes.

Then, still looking at the garden, Rossi says, "And what do you think, darling?"

Elisabetta is standing off to one side; out of the corner of my eye, I had seen her stroking the tiger flowers, shaking the ferns as if she wanted to wake them up, closely inspecting the shells embedded in the concrete, playing with the mirror shards that shifted one of her eyes away from her face.

"Yes, it's marvelous," she says.

I look down. I picture myself in my kitchen, Elisabetta across the table from me, and me asking her, "What did you really think of the garden, back then?" Ten or fifteen years have gone by, and we're living together. "It was marvelous," she says.

Rossi asked me back to his study for a cup of coffee. Before going up in the elevator, he calls over one of the twins and whispers something in his ear. Once we get to the study, he has me sit on the red sofa.

He says, "I understand, and . . . thank you."

I don't know what he's talking about. I smile, just barely. I hope he'll explain quickly.

"Alfredo is watching us from up there," he says, pointing heavenward.

I nod. The secretary comes in with the coffee.

"Congratulations, Mr. Fratta," she says, more cordial than ever before. "It's really splendid. We were all speechless."

I smile and thank her. She leaves.

"It's the story of Alfredo's life—I understood that right away. The three archways are the three choices he made: scholar, benefactor, and head of the family . . . and the labyrinth is the world, where a fragile human being gets tossed against the hard, sharp rocks . . . and the mysterious ways of the Lord . . . the pull of the basic essence of things . . . the bleached wood is splendid . . . and that final image of bliss, the clouds upside down in the pond . . . his spirit really hovers through the whole garden . . . I didn't dare to hope for something so good . . . and I can't wait to show it to some friends, the friends who will understand . . ."

I try to stay perfectly still; anyway, he doesn't need any confirmation from me. The twins come in, and one of them takes away the tray of coffee cups; the other is carrying a rectangular package wrapped in paper, which he sets on the floor, leaning up against the wheelchair.

"But the garden will also be good for my wife, so we're thankful to you for that too. She's so fragile and unstable. She needs peace and quiet."

A pause.

"She needs to spend some time alone, thinking about her life. But how can I help her with that, in the condition I'm in?"

He no longer has the plaid blanket across his legs; he smooths the rumples in his sweatpants.

"She has a very sad family history, you know. They wrung her dry, wiped her out, erased her. She has no ambitions, no dreams, as if the future didn't exist."

A pause.

"I don't know what she wants, and I'm afraid she doesn't want anything. Isn't that terrible? Isn't it terrible to want nothing? Or to want only small, simple things?"

Obviously I wasn't supposed to respond that there was nothing terrible about it—that you just had to get used to it. I stayed quiet.

Rossi picked up the package.

"This is a gift; I'm deeply indebted to you," he said, offering it to me.

"You shouldn't have—"

"Yes, I should."

He had tears in his eyes. "Please," he said, "take it."

I got up and took the package; I could feel a frame inside—it was a picture.

Afterward, I drove Witold home; he was excited and proud, humming the aria from some opera, and every so often he turned to me and said, "So everything's good, right?"

"Everything's good."

In the rearview mirror I kept my eye on the black Ka that was following me.

When I got home I brought the package right inside, shut my front door, and unwrapped the picture in the front hall. I heard the tires crackling across the courtyard gravel. It was the painting of the country house covered with climbing plants and immersed in dense, bright green foliage. Someone rang the bell. I set the painting on the floor against the wall and went toward the door. I asked who it was. No one answered. I didn't open it. They rang again.

"Who is it?"

No answer. I let her in.

She came in without looking at me. She was still wearing her shorts, top, and flip-flops. She looked at the painting. She turned around. She came close and embraced me. She squeezed me tight, hiding her face in the crook of my neck, pressing her breasts against me.

I took her hair in my fist and pulled it gently, forcing her head back. I kissed her. I felt her tongue slide around mine. I wished that I had a new life, with a kiss like that every evening. It seemed like a simple wish that could easily come true.

That Thursday night, Elisabetta went home again, but on Friday she was back, and for the first time she stayed the whole night, and Saturday, and until Sunday morning. She told Alberto she was going to visit her aunts up at the lake. She wanted to hide the Ka under a tarp in case someone came around here looking for her; I told her it was useless because anybody who might be following her regularly would already know she was here, but I pulled out an old camouflage tarp anyway, one that I covered the R4 with whenever I spent a few days away from home, in case any savvy vintage-car collector commissioned someone to steal it.

We didn't leave the house for thirty-six hours; we didn't even open the shutters, and when we weren't in bed we left the rooms dimly lit, and when moving from kitchen to living room, we crossed the few shafts of light that slanted through the shutters; in the whirling dust her hips and back were tiger-striped by the sun.

Sunday morning, in a corner of the living room, Elisabetta found the pile of fairy tales from the *Tales Told* series; I had recently seen a display of the same series I had as a kid (rereleased on tape, with the accompanying picture booklets), and I'd bought them for the boys. She and I reminisced about hearing the tales on the record player, on 45 rpm records, and then we listened to "Bluebeard" and "Snow White" and "Puss in Boots," which both of us remembered perfectly, especially the musical breaks, the jazzy rhythms, and the funny rhymes: "Little Red Riding Hood, head as hard as a block of wood"; "My love is growing day by day: let's get married right away"; "Jewels and gems! Gimme dese, dose, and dems."

She had inherited the tales from an older cousin, the original 1966 edition, published when I was six, Carlo was nine, and she, Elisabetta, wasn't yet born. At one point she asked me which one was my tale—which one told the story of my life. I told her that I didn't know, that I hadn't ever identified with any character.

"That's impossible," she said. "You must have done it, but you just don't remember."

"And how about you?"

Hers was "Sleeping Beauty."

Her father was a successful accounting professional who had started his own firm. This was a big deal, and his son was supposed to carry on after him, naturally; there has to be a succession, there has to be a king or, at worst, a queen.

She had grown up with four women. The good fairies were her mother and the two aunts who lived right next door. There was a connecting door between them that was always left open, as if it were all one big apartment; she never had a sense that there was any border between their lives. The bad fairy was the father's lover, who came to lunch every Sunday and spent a month with them at the seaside in the summer. She called her ma'am, and only when she was thirteen, when the lover disappeared from their lives, did she understand how the woman had been linked to her father, how much humiliation her mother had accepted, and what price the lover had paid.

The three good fairies made sure the daughter was raised to worship her father and his firm. Not because of any respect for abstract intellectual activity: the firm existed simply to produce money—money was the ultimate good as far as the father was concerned, and the three good fairies taught the girl to respect work and money. The bad fairy was very likable. The father didn't want to leave the mother and marry her, even though the kingdom had recently begun permitting divorces, perhaps because the good fairies had threatened to steal his daughter away, and that was unthinkable. The bad fairy loved the girl, and the girl sensed it. But she was a bad fairy, and her position meant that she had to wreak vengeance on the family.

Every Sunday afternoon the girl went out with the father and the father's lover. They would have hot cocoa, walk in the park, window-shop downtown. Wherever they were, at some point the father would suddenly need to stop by his office to fetch some forgotten papers or look over some urgent business. So then the bad fairy would take the girl into a church run by missionary priests whom she knew and teach her about loving her neighbor and about compassion for poor African children with big eyes and skinny legs. It was their secret, a secret between friends. The girl was happy to have a secret; deep inside a box of books she hid the pamphlets about life in the African missions, the minuscule carved wooden crucifixes, and the microscopic straw collages of Christmas crèches.

When the bad fairy began taking her along on Wednesday afternoons, too, the good fairies sighed in resignation. Then they got irritated. They observed that the girl was acting "strange." When they found out about the deception and interrogated the girl, they discovered that she wanted to grow up to be a missionary nun, and they spoke to the king. The king drove the bad fairy away and decreed that all compassion, mercy, generosity, and love for one's neighbor, as well as most of the crucifixes and crèches, be banned from the kingdom. People were to go to church only on Sunday morning, and only in a plain, bare church (it had walls of reinforced cement).

So in the era when other rich families were afraid of kidnappers and the Red Brigades, Mr. Valserra's family was afraid of priests. Africa was a taboo topic: it was never to be mentioned, and the girl was encouraged to learn nothing about geography. Eventually the girl was encouraged to learn nothing about any subject; she changed schools several times and spent the last years of high school in one of those private diploma mills where all you had to do was pay the tuition.

By now she was eighteen; her father had had heart surgery, and the good fairies insisted that she matriculate in economics and business at university, to avoid giving him "any more grief." Did that mean she had given him grief before?

She made new friends at the university, and one afternoon she happened to be at a charity event organized by Alfredo Renal. It turned out that not all compassion had been banned from the kingdom, and not all mercy had been destroyed. The king's soldiers had overlooked one small scrap, which was left behind in a tall tower where no one ever ventured. And the princess got pricked by it, and fell in love, and got married without her parents' permission. The king died of grief (or a heart attack), and the good fairies sold the firm to the king's courtiers and withdrew to live near the lake.

"And did the bride and groom live happily ever after?"

"No—not the bride, anyway."

"Why?"

"Because Alfredo could love humanity but not one woman, not one particular woman."

"And the bride . . . ?"

"The bride found a way to console herself."

Sometimes she thought that she had woken from her long sleep, and she would say: My real life starts here, everything else has been just a dream that will slowly fade away. But it was never true. Not until last fall.

I'm sitting on the floor with my back against the sofa she's curled up on; the *Tales Told* are scattered around us, and while listening to her story I've been leafing through the booklet that went with "The Three Musicians," without looking up, and even now I don't turn to face her—I don't look her in the eyes when I ask:

"What happened last fall?"

"What happened was . . . A bunch of things happened . . . Well, to start with, I killed a man . . . more or less . . ."

I try to assume an incredulous tone—not frightened, just affectionately ironic: "*You did what?*"

"I killed a man."

I have to be more convincing, and not give myself away. "I don't believe it. *More or less?*"

"I'm pretty sure."

"What do you mean? Did you kill him or didn't you?"

"Yes, I killed him."

"How?"

"I hit him . . . I hit him with my car . . . Well, actually he was already on the ground when I ran him over . . ."

I turn and look at her as if I want to see whether she's pulling my leg. "What was he doing on the ground?"

She waves it away. "It's too complicated to explain . . ."

She's leafing through "Little Red Riding Hood," so I can look at her without fear that she'll look back at me: she's gazing down at the booklet and its illustrations. I lower my eyes too, and look at her feet.

"Did you know who he was?"

"Of course I knew, I had an appointment with him, in the parking lot of a supermarket . . ."

She told me that one day she got a call from a man who said he wanted to talk to her about an important donation; an old widow had died without heirs, and he claimed to be her butler; he said there was a handwritten will, but before turning it over for probate he had to meet with her because he was afraid something shady might happen and the money might not get to the Renal Foundation as the lady had wished. Elisabetta suggested that he talk to Mosca, but the butler had insisted on seeing her. "That's why I called you, because I cannot meet with that man," he said, giving her to understand that it was Mosca he was concerned about. The story didn't ring true, and Elisabetta thought that if she met the butler once she could persuade him—she pictured him as old, frightened, and anxious—to proceed in the normal way and trust the probate system and Mosca.

They agreed to meet in a café downtown, and as soon as the man bent down to greet her—he was fiftyish, tall, and stout, in a gray summerweight wool suit and camel-hair coat—Elisabetta saw that he certainly was no butler and there must have been something else going on. The man introduced himself as Mariano Conti, the owner—"for how much longer I don't know"—of an investment company. He apologized for having lied to her, but the things he had to tell her were too delicate and important to say over the phone. He told her about a betrayal: he had worked a lot with Mosca, done a lot of favors for him, sent a lot of money his way, and now his former partner had tired of him and was dumping him. Elisabetta said that Mosca's business had nothing to do with her; she didn't see the point of this meeting, and she wanted to leave.

"Wait," he told her. "If in five minutes you still think the thing has nothing to do with you, then you can go." And he explained how Mosca had used the foundation from the very start for his own money laundering. He asked her to tell Rossi, to call a meeting of the foundation's board and expose Mosca. Again Elisabetta got up to go, but then something made her pause. She thought that exploiting the foundation to cover up illegal activity was like abusing a child, the child Alfredo had never had. And that wasn't all: the bookkeeper in her demanded that she straighten things out simply for the satisfaction of a job well done, and that was the funniest aspect of the indignation she felt: this reconciliation with her father's spirit. She told Conti that she needed documents to show to Alberto, that they needed proof. And Conti promised to furnish documents. They decided to meet not far from the villa a few nights later, in a supermarket parking lot.

She got to the supermarket, saw Conti waiting for her near a car, and parked, but she had no intention of getting out; she was waiting for him to come over, get into her Ka, and show her the documents. Maybe he had left them in his car: he turned as if to get them.

Then Elisabetta heard the sound of a car revving up and saw the white van shooting down the driveway; she heard the sound of the impact, a thud that she'll never forget, and saw Conti's body fly through the air.

She looked at the body; maybe he was dead, or maybe not. Panicking, she turned on her engine and ran over him by mistake as she fled. Then he was certainly dead.

"And what about the driver of the van?"

"I didn't see him. It was rainy and dark."

"Did they catch him?"

"No. In the paper the next day they said that Conti had a lot of enemies but that the police thought it was an accident."

"Did you think that they might have wanted to kill you too?"

"Yes, I thought of that, but I'm not so sure anymore."

"So what do you mean? . . . Why do you say this made you think that you'd woken from your slumber?"

"Because for the first time I thought that I had to leave: I began to dream of another house, anywhere else, and a job—another life. But then there's Alberto. He needs me."

"Are you sure he does?"

"What do you mean?"

"You can't leave him?"

"No, I don't *want to* leave him," she replies.

And maybe it's because I'm so crushed by this—maybe to hide my disappointment—that I say the words that spell my ruin: "Weren't you afraid that the police would track you down when they looked at the log of car accidents that happened that night?"

She looks up from "Little Red Riding Hood." She smiles bitterly: she built a trap for me without even meaning to, and I fell right into it.

She says slowly, "Who says it was the *same* night?"

She's wearing one of my old striped pajamas; I have no top on, and I feel ugly and fat.

"Well . . . I just assumed it . . . you were driving like you were drunk . . ."

"You'd been following me for a while when you saw me go off the road—"

"I wasn't following you, I just happened to be driving behind you . . ."

Her tone changes: she doesn't raise her voice, but she's clearly furious; she freezes me with an icy rage that she'd kept hidden until it was the right moment to strike. Now the moment has come, and it erases everything that came before; it's as if all her loving actions were only building up to this attack.

"All you do is ask questions, and tell lies, and clam up, but the result is always the same: the upshot is that I tell you my whole life story and you've never told me anything about yourself."

"I don't know what I'm supposed to tell you . . . Nothing has ever happened in my life."

"Explain why Mosca knew your father."

"My father?" I stutter. "Mosca? I haven't the foggiest idea why."

She doesn't believe me.

"Mosca told me he remembers your father very clearly. He recalls that he had a furniture factory."

Now I don't need any further confirmation; I should be satisfied, but I haven't got time for this.

"It's true, but it didn't do very well; he sold it and then started working as a gardener. I was just a kid. I don't know anything else."

"About your father? You don't know anything else about your father?"

"That's right. He didn't talk, and I didn't ask. None of us asked, and he rarely talked. None of us ever talked much."

"That must have been quite a cheerful household."

I hurl the *Tales Told* booklet across the room. "Don't say another word about my family."

She gets up from the sofa. She goes upstairs. After a bit she comes down, fully dressed, and goes out the front door without saying goodbye. I follow her without speaking. I help her drag the tarp off the Ka. I fold it up with my back to her; I hear her get in the car, back out, and leave.

I stand there in the courtyard, half naked, in the shadow of the canopy. There's no sound, and unless I talk to myself, I haven't any hope of hearing another person's voice for the rest of the day.

My paternal grandparents' famous silence was quite different from my maternal grandparents' famous silence. My paternal grandparents came from peasant and artisan stock, mountain people accustomed to working hard without wasting time chatting; they lived by the principle that you're better off not talking unless you have something really important to say, something vital, something crucial for survival, for the task at hand, or for the running of the household; that it's best to communicate without words, to do instead of say. As Carlo joked, "It's a cross between peasant traditions and lofty philosophy." My maternal grandparents lived in a small provincial city where my grandfather taught music in a school and my grandmother was a dressmaker. She wasn't naturally taciturn: at work she was considered a great gossip, but her husband obliged her to be quiet at home, in front of their daughters, so they wouldn't pick up the vice of talking about other people's business. My mother's two sisters were housewives who cooked and mended and embroidered, but as far as I can tell—we didn't see them much—their father's policy had no effect on them. My mother was her father's favorite, the only one who had the patience to learn to play the piano. For Grandfather, silence wasn't a question of age-old peasant distrust for words: his reticence was self-taught. He hated teaching at school— hated his clamorous students and his petty colleagues—but he loved giving private lessons to musically gifted children. For him, teaching was about showing rather than telling. He hated opera, which he didn't consider real music; he complained that Italy was musically backward, and he admired the Germans and, to a lesser degree, the French. A great piece of music shouldn't have to use stories to evoke emotion (and then the stories used in opera were full of hysterical women and laughably fat lovers and stabbing deaths); he considered music, like math, to be an abstract art that fostered pure feelings. Even today, when my mother hears a TV reporter telling a story in a way that she finds too fervid or sentimental, she'll shake her head and mutter, "Italy, home of melodrama." That was her father's expression.

On Monday I worked on the Renal garden with Witold, but I didn't see Elisabetta; I didn't go looking for her, and she didn't come looking for me. We held off until Tuesday afternoon; at three o'clock I was talking to a client on my cell phone, and I'd rambled away from Witold and was crossing the open meadow toward the woods. After the conversation was over, I pictured myself spending another evening alone, and

I thought that my dinners with the guest were over for good, so I might as well send her a text message. "Come over tonight," I typed. After a few seconds my voice-message indicator flashed: she had called while the line was busy and left a voice message saying that she had hardly eaten the night before and she was hungry. I called her right back and told her our messages had crossed. I was afraid she didn't believe me, so I said, "Really, we thought of each other at the exact same moment."

"I believe it—I saw you."

"What do you mean?"

"I'm in the house, I saw you on the monitor; I called you on purpose because I saw that you were on the phone and I wouldn't have to talk to you directly—"

I started laughing. "So that's how you spend your time . . ."

"Not always . . ."

"Can you see me now?"

"Of course, I'm keeping an eye on you."

"What am I doing?" I said, swinging my arm around.

"You're waving at me."

I was concentrating on her voice, looking toward the garden but thinking only about the warmth of her voice and how it stoked my desire. And then, through my vision of Elisabetta standing somewhere in the house, I made out a real figure: Witold. He was at the edge of the garden with his arm up, and even from far away I could see that he was confused: he didn't understand why I was waving at him, but he felt he had to respond. I had caught him staring at me in recent days; maybe he understood what was going on, and the idea of me with a woman must have worried him, because he was a creature of habit and my isolation had been a reassuring element for years.

So on Tuesday, and all the rest of the evenings that week, Elisabetta came over, and she didn't accuse me of lying or keeping silent anymore, even though I continued to do both, and everything seemed to be going fine. I knew that I wouldn't see her on the weekend—she and Alberto were going to the seaside, to their beach house—but I had the kids coming to stay, so I didn't expect to miss her too much.

Carlo was agitated. I asked him why he wasn't happy that the war was over, and he said he was very happy that the bombing had stopped, but the people of Serbia, Kosovo, and Albania still weren't okay, their lives were miserable, and even without the bombs there were traffickers throwing refugees off their boats, and even without ethnic cleansing they faced nothing but violence and hardship.

Of course he was right. It's not like I ever thought he was wrong, but usually I just listened and nodded, because he always exaggerated. And he was exaggerating now, too, but not about the facts—that was the point: the injustice that made him react so melodramatically was real and awful, it wasn't a figment of his imagination. I felt kind of dizzy and nauseated: how could I have thought that Carlo invented everything? That on top of his posture of anger and shock and misery, he had also invented all the ills of the world that made him so angry and shocked and miserable?

I left Carlo in my study, slumped in one of his favorite armchairs, chewing on his fingernails. The TV was on in the living room; the kids were watching *The Lion King* for the hundredth time. Rafiki, the shamanic baboon, was making Simba look into the water at the reflection of his father's face. I knew this part by heart. When Simba decided to go back to Pride Rock, Filippo turned to me and said: "Papa's worried about the war."

"Well, the war is over. You'll see, everything will be better now."

"Papa is very *sensitive*. You're more *stable*."

"Thank you."

We finished watching the cartoon, and I put them to bed. When I came back downstairs, Carlo was still in my study, and he was holding the book of Alfredo Renal's writings. It seemed like a good opportunity to talk about something else, so I asked him what he thought of the idea of the landscape of the plains being a big hodgepodge. He shrugged. "That's old news."

"Old news that's wrong, or right?"

"The picture is right, but the conclusions are all wrong. Who says it was better before? Why should we go back to the past?"

"Right, of course; but I don't even think the picture is right."

"Oh, finally you have an opinion," he said. "When did you decide to start having opinions?"

I ignore him and press on. "It's not true that this landscape is a hodgepodge, it's not true that it's all the same; maybe it looks that way from the outside, but each of us has places that we love, places where we feel at home. It's not all interchangeable. Right?"

"Maybe so. But this isn't about your personal memories; this is about looking at the world objectively. At least I think so."

"And what's it like, objectively?"

"Objectively, it's pretty much of a hodgepodge."

"So what if it is? Can't we get along okay in a hodgepodge?"

"I guess some people can: you wallow in it. For someone else it might be hell."

"Hell? Really?"

"And even if there were only a single person who couldn't stand it, it would be your human duty to try to change the hodgepodge. Rather than justifying the way things are just because you're okay with it."

I don't speak, so then he regrets having been so harsh, and he tries to make amends. "But you're right, people are better off now than they were a hundred years ago, in Alfredo Renal's arcadia. The only thing that's been lost is sociability: conversations in the piazza, stories around the fire. It's quite a loss, no?"

"Peasants led isolated lives too; they didn't talk."

"You're wrong, they talked a lot."

"But our grandparents—"

"Forget about our ancestors: they were from tainted stock."

I try to find some issue with which to continue the conversation. Nothing comes to mind. Then I think of the artificial piazza at the mall near here.

"People end up talking at malls."

He bursts out laughing. "Of course, of course, and in supermarkets too . . . A quick chat with the cashier . . . You've always liked supermarkets, haven't you?"

I smile as if he's being affectionately sarcastic, but he's getting on my nerves.

"People meet on the Web too," he says. "They become friends, they spend their whole lives online . . . So what are we complaining about?"

It's like he said the magic words and unlocked all my rage. "I'm not complaining about anything. I just live here quietly and handle my own problems by myself; I work, and I mostly just keep my mouth shut."

"What do you mean by that?"

I raise my voice. "I mean that if I go to the supermarket sometimes, it doesn't mean I'm an idiot. A lot of the time I have to buy food for three extra guests."

"Hey, calm down—"

"I'm calm, I'm very calm. I keep my mouth shut and I don't complain and I go to the supermarket. I trust I'm not offending anyone."

"You misunderstood me—"

"I don't think so," I yell. I've gotten to my feet and I'm yelling. Carlo is floored by my reaction; his mouth is hanging open. "I don't think I can misunderstand you, I know you too well to misunderstand you!"

"Come on, cut it out," he murmurs.

"I'm not doing anything; I mostly keep my mouth shut, and I stay quiet, and occasionally I go to the supermarket."

"Okay, I'm sorry, forgive me." He shakes his head. "I'm sorry. You can go to the supermarket all you want. But don't yell, you'll wake the kids."

"I'm not yelling, I rarely talk, and for once I'm talking and not keeping my mouth shut."

And I sweep out theatrically; finally I'm being melodramatic too; I go up to my room to sleep. Actually, I lie on my bed for two hours with my eyes open in the dark, bewildered, asking myself what got into me.

The next day I took the kids over to Malik's. We finally met the new Doberman, Kalki. He was supposed to be a companion for Durga, but they were being kept apart for the time being. I told Malik that this Kalki had a strange expression, that he didn't seem very likable. Malik chuckled and said that I didn't like him because I was in love with Durga and I was jealous. The dog was so stripy that it looked like his stripes had been painted on. "It's a little bit fake," said Malik, whispering in my ear as if the famous photographer might hear. Momo kept saying, "Sake, sake," and Filippo was very worried. "Will he be a good husband?" he asked us. Ever since Kalki had arrived, Durga had been restless again. She hadn't seen him, but she smelled his scent, and they barked canine messages to each other day and night. "What do they say?" Filippo asked. Malik always takes Filippo's questions seriously; he said they talked about their kids, the children that they would have someday. "How many do they want?" Filippo asked. "Oh, a lot. But they're afraid the babies won't be stripy and their owner will get mad."

Before dinner I surprised Carlo as he was fiddling with his cell phone, writing a text message. Later, but not as late as last time, just slightly after midnight, I heard someone open and shut a car door with excessive, useless caution, and then an engine start up and tires crackle on gravel. I got up and went to check that Carlo wasn't in his room, but we were the only adults in the house—who else could it have been? Unless someone had just stolen a car from us.

I went down; Carlo wasn't in any of his armchairs. At first I thought I'd wait up for him and ask where he'd been, and for half an hour I tried to prepare a speech; it's not like I'd never meddled in his business—I certainly had—but I'd never done my meddling directly at him, so it was hard for me to find the right words. But why wait for him to come back? I could talk to him on the phone, I could call right away. So I called him; I was sure that if he were with a woman he wouldn't answer. But he answered immediately.

"Where are you?"

"Claudio," he said, and he paused. "Claudio, I need you."

"Where are you? Why did you go out?"

"Claudio"—now I could hear that he was scared. "Claudio, I need your help."

"Okay, but come home, I'll wait for you here."

I hung up and laid the phone on the arm of the chair. I looked at the cold, sooty fireplace.

Breaking the silence is always a bad idea, I thought; never do that again. Words set things in motion: any equilibrium of whatever kind is always shattered by words. So many more words are needed to bring back the peace.

This was basically why I didn't tell Elisabetta Renal all about myself, and I understood her resentment, because she couldn't accept that I didn't want her involvement.

Carlo got home at 1:30. With him was a girl about twenty years old, or maybe eighteen. He was very agitated, and he kept trying to reassure her by saying, "Don't worry, you're safe here, calm down." She had a bruise under her left eye. She was blond, thin, and tall. She wore a leather jacket, a miniskirt, and clunky Doc Martens boots.

They ignored me for the first five minutes. Carlo seated her in the armchair. The girl took off her boots and curled up to hug her knees, trembling, with her face turned to the wall. Carlo asked her whether she wanted a glass of water or a real drink. She said a glass of water.

I followed my brother into the kitchen. "Now I'll explain," he said. But he didn't explain anything. I had never seen him like this.

He asked whether he could keep her here for an hour or two.

I closed myself in my study and waited until they left. I leafed through rose catalogs the whole time. I was still awake when Carlo came back from driving her to I don't know where. But he didn't feel like talking anymore.

The next day they left right after lunch; it was election day, and Carlo wanted to go vote. He hadn't said another word about what had happened. He seemed much calmer. I had prepared myself in the shower and figured out what I would say. As time went on and the morning became lunchtime and lunch gave way to coffee, I felt a growing unease. I was afraid he no longer needed me, as he had said he did over the phone last night. "I need you." That's what I had liked, what had thrown me into turmoil. We were the first people in our family to say such things to each other. Before us, no one had ever confessed that he needed another family member (not even my father had used such a strong expression when he asked me to help him with his work), and I was afraid that Carlo had already forgotten it.

I was still nervous on Monday morning; further agitated because I hadn't heard from Elisabetta—her cell phone was always off. We got to the Villa Renal, and the cars, even the Ka, were all parked in the garage, and I unloaded the stuff with Witold and we set off for the garden. We began working in two different spots: he was by the cistern, setting up the circulating pump, and I was near the cotoneaster hedges, calibrating the drip irrigator.

I don't know how the man could have crossed through the garden without my realizing it, but he must have passed just a few feet away from me. At about 8:30 I heard a splash in the water and a frightened shout, or maybe a call for help, and I began running downhill, cursing the maze of paths I had designed. When I got to the cistern, I found Witold standing in waist-deep water, the motorized chair overturned against one of the cones of crushed glass, and Rossi floundering in water up to his neck, flapping his arms on the surface like a duck about to take flight.

5

IF SHE AND I WERE MERELY TELLING FAIRY TALES—WITHOUT TOUCHING ON THE REAL truth, or including only bits of the truth—then I could play the game too. My favorite one of the *Tales Told* was "The Three Musicians." Two nights after Rossi's accident we were in bed: she was leaning back against a couple of pillows, and I was lying on my side, supporting my head with my left hand. As I told my story, I ran my right index finger along her skin.

So: there were three musicians—the first played the violin, the second played the trumpet, and the third played the flute. They traveled from town to town and performed in the piazza wherever they went (my finger danced across her thighs).

"You're tickling me."

"I can't help it."

They got to a city known for its enchanted castle, which stood on the far side of a dark, dense forest—my finger slid up through her patch of hair—and they found a place to sleep: in this cozy . . . little . . . inn.

"Cozy like my belly button?"

"More or less."

At the inn they asked about the castle, for through the window they could see its two towers in the distance (my finger traced the slope of her breasts). The innkeeper told them that a beautiful princess was imprisoned there. She was guarded by a friendly, harmless old man. But everyone who tried to visit the castle was thrashed so soundly that he fled forever. The three musicians decided to go and see it. The first one, the violinist, set off (my finger took a roundabout way), only to return that evening battered and in pain. He told the others that the old man had fed him like a king but that when the musician asked to see the princess, a magical stick had appeared out of nowhere and begun beating him, so he fled. The castle had some kind of magic spell over it. And what about the old man? asked the other two. Oh, the old man can't do anything about it. He's short and skinny with a beard three feet long—and he's mute.

The next morning the second musician set off. (My finger dipped down again before rising toward her breasts.)

"I don't understand why they have to go through the woods to get to the castle from the inn: the woods are in the other direction."

"Because it's a fairy tale."

The trumpet player was cleverer than the violinist: he thought the old man was responsible for the beating. "It must be the beard: his beard probably gives him superhuman strength." He got to the castle, and the old man opened the door and ushered him into the tower. He gestured to the lavishly laid table and sat down with him as he ate. The musician told the old man about where he'd come from and all the lands he'd traveled through, and bragged about the marvels he had seen. Every so often he asked the old man about the castle, and who lived there, and what great lord it had belonged to. The old man didn't answer, but he kept smiling and stroking his beard wordlessly. He ate nothing: he just stared at the musician in silence, with a completely innocent and disturbing expression. How can someone be both innocent and disturbing? wondered the trumpeter. "Kind old man," he said, "maybe since you've been living alone here you've fallen out of the habit of shaving, but I'm an expert barber, and if you like I can give you a shave to repay your hospitality." The old man agreed and allowed himself to be shaved. "Now take me to the princess," the musician ordered him. The beardless old man pointed to a door, and the musician—delighted by his success—prepared to step through it. But as soon as he turned his back, he was hit by a hail of blows, and he fled, stunned.

"I don't remember the story that way—you're making it up."

"Could be."

The flute player was the cleverest of all: listening to his friend's story, he understood that the old man had some secret. "If it's not the beard, then what is it?" he asked himself as he went toward the forest.

"There's that forest again."

"It's got to be there."

He got to the castle, and the old man opened the door and led him to the table. The flutist was struck by the old man's ambiguous attitude, which the trumpeter had perceived only vaguely. He noticed that the old man kept quiet but obliged the other person to talk: he forced you to talk by the simple strength of his silence. As the two sat at the table, the musician decided that it would be wisest for him to ask no questions and volunteer nothing about himself. He went on eating heartily, ignoring the old man staring at him. The old man's gaze gradually became weaker and weaker. The musician finished eating and stood up. Without asking permission, he went toward the door that his friends had described, the door that must lead to the castle's other tower and the princess's gilded prison. (My finger slid up her other breast.) And the old man couldn't stop him.

"How did you choose which of the two towers the princess was in?"

I move my fingertip around her nipple. She closes her eyes.

"You see? It opens out here along the edge, like the corolla of a flower."

"Is that the end of the story?"

The musician got to the princess, but the princess was mute like the old man. The musician didn't like mute women, and he got annoyed and took off.

"What kind of women did he like?"

"Women who occasionally told absurd stories."

Later she whispers to me that I'll have to be patient, that I'll have to be good and wait for her here, that we can talk on the phone, but that she won't be able to see me for a while. The doctor has prescribed at least two weeks of complete rest for Alberto, and they've decided to leave for the beach earlier than usual this year. I don't think Rossi will heal in two weeks.

"I promise that in any case I'll come back to see you in two weeks."

"And you'll call me every day?"

"Every day."

"And you'll call if you need me? I can get there in two hours."

"Without crashing your car?"

"Without crashing my car."

"I told Mosca to look you up, for the hanging garden."

"Pardon me?"

"I spoke with Mosca, and I told him to get in touch with you. You should go to his place, to see if the job interests you."

"Why did you think of that?"

"You told me that you really wanted to do it . . . remember? When you asked me for his phone number."

"Yes, but why did you think of it now?"

"Now when?"

I was irritated, but I didn't know why. I made her swear to be careful, not to go out at night, not to go to isolated spots, to let me know if anyone was following her.

"But when will you tell me the true story of the mute old man?"

"I don't know."

"Tell me now."

"It's too late."

"It's not late."

"It's not late, but it's too early to tell you."

"But I told you my story."

"You already knew yours. I never thought I had one; I wasn't ready."

By now she was in the Ka, and she asked me about Rossi again.

"You don't think he wanted to throw himself in, do you?"

"Witold told me it was the edge of the cistern that tripped him up. It was a terrible mistake, to design such a detail at an invalid's house. I'll never forgive myself."

So I was lying to her again. But I thought: I was used to silence; now I talk, and I lie because I'm not used to talking.

Witold told me right away what happened. Rossi suddenly appeared, heading for the pond, ignoring Witold's shout of alarm; he lurched across the raised border of white pebbles, his wheelchair overturned, and he shot forward into the water. Witold dove in and tried to grab him under the arms, Rossi struggled, I got there, and the two of us managed to lift him and pull him out. We didn't have any time to consider what to do with him, where to lay him down, before one of the twins came running, followed by the other twin carrying a robe and towels. They wrapped Rossi in the robe and took him in their arms and carried him off with their usual efficiency, without saying a word.

Some towels are left on the ground, and Witold and I look at them, still panting. We certainly can't dry our clothes with towels. I ask him what happened, but he doesn't answer right away; he shakes his head and simply gestures, pointing at the garden and then at the pond. We look at each other, standing there, breathing hard, water dripping down into two matching puddles. I ask him how Rossi fell into the pond. He shakes his head. "He didn't fall—he threw himself." While I try with some difficulty to link words to the action he saw, and the action to its consequences, and consequences to a noun as thin and solid as a rope, Elisabetta appears, barefoot in jeans and a sweatshirt.

She leads us into the house, into one of the guest bedrooms, and insists that we shower right away; she brings us shampoo and two robes. She's scared: she never looks me in the eye, and I stare down at the ground. After washing, we sit on the two beds with our naked, hairy legs sticking out beneath the light blue robes. Elisabetta took away our clothes before we could stop her—how does she plan to dry them? Witold giggles and says that maybe they'll forget about us and we'll be stuck in here for a week, but then he gets serious again and I know he's thinking about what he saw. One of the twins brings in two cups of coffee and sets them down on a little table; he asks us if we want a cognac and says that our clothes will be ready in half an hour. I glance at Witold and say No, thanks, the coffee is all we need.

The second twin appears in the doorway, mirroring the figure standing next to our beds, and says that Rossi wants to speak to us. We follow him, walking barefoot across the cold floors. In the dim room Elisabetta is sitting on the edge of the bed and holding Rossi's hand; he's stretched out under the covers. Elisabetta says that Alberto wants to thank us. His eyes are closed; it looks like he's sleeping. There's half a minute of silence. Does she really have to hold his hand?

"Remind me of your name, please," Rossi says.

Witold doesn't react; I touch his arm and whisper that Rossi's talking to him.

"Witold Witkiewicz," he says feebly.

"Witold," Rossi repeats.

Silence falls again. It's the first time I've been in this room; it looks identical to Alfredo Renal's room, which Rossi showed me more than a month ago: the same furniture, in the same arrangement, but not the same room—the other one is at the end of the hall. I think, He should have simply gone and slept in that room. There is a photograph of Alfredo Renal on the bedside table, another one standing on a dresser, and one hanging on the wall behind me, next to the armoire with the mirrored door; that's the picture I want to inspect more closely, because from the corner of my eye I see that there's someone standing next to Renal.

"Witold," says Rossi, "what country are you from?"

"Poland."

"It must be a beautiful country."

I take one step to the side and peek at the photo; no one sees me do it. They are eighteen or twenty. Both wearing jackets and ties, clothes that look more adult than they are themselves. They're smiling. Renal has his arms down at his sides and his head lowered a little bit, as if the light bothers him. Rossi, standing next to him, looks like the older brother, with a hand in his pocket swelling one flank of his jacket, the other arm held out, with a cigarette between his index and middle fingers.

"I've never been there," Rossi speaks up again, "but it must be beautiful."

Soon we'll be out of here. I'm not cold, but I'm shivering. I want to get dressed. Elisabetta strokes Rossi's still damp hair, readjusts the pillows behind his back, and then takes his hand in hers again and squeezes it. She doesn't turn even slightly to look at me.

"Not as beautiful as yours," says Witold, surprising everybody. "Italy is an extraordinary country."

"Witold is an expert in Italian literature." I feel I have to clarify this, to justify his enthusiasm.

"Italy has given the world a wealth of literature," Witold goes on, smiling. "And most of all it has given us opera. Rossini, Verdi, Puccini. I think there's nothing greater; sometimes . . . sometimes I think I would like to have been an Italian in the nineteenth century, to have been a patriot during the Risorgimento, going to the theater at night to hear the *Trovatore* or *Rigoletto*."

Standing in the midst of us gray Italians, the Pole suddenly seemed taller: he stood there wrapped in his robe as if it were a hero's mantle. We looked at his smile with something like deference, and then Rossi began to cry.

"Calm down, quiet down," Elisabetta said to comfort him, and she waved us out of the room.

We went out, nearly pushed along by one of the twins. In the guest room were our clothes, magically washed and ironed and laid out tidily on the beds. Witold wasn't smiling anymore. "What did I say that was wrong?"

"First you save him, then you make him cry," I remarked, shaking my head.

We worked on the Renal garden for two more days, and Jan came back to help us re-create the cone of crushed glass that the wheelchair had crashed into; we left many little details unfinished, which didn't actually bother me since I didn't want to think about the ending: the end of the job and the end of coming to the villa and the end of the affair with Elisabetta, despite her assurances. We could have gone on working even with the villa closed up for the summer, but Rossi's assistant told us it would be better to finish in September, right before they organized a nice party to inaugurate it; and she smiled—she always smiled at me now. During the summer the property was patrolled by security guards, and it just created trouble for them if there were people coming and going. "If we're not here, they can shoot on sight?" I asked her seriously. She was taken aback and stared at me for a second, then burst out laughing; she must have decided that I was a joker (but I wasn't laughing).

We finished restoring the pond on Thursday evening, and on Friday morning we drove to the villa in the R4. I wanted to say goodbye to Rossi again, check on him, and see Elisabetta one more time, just to squeeze her hand for a brief moment. It had been very hot for the last few days, and the idea of leaving these hills to go work down on the plain, near a highway intersection, was dreadful. Driving along the tunnel of plane trees, I felt absolutely sure that this was the last time I would go to the villa, but I didn't believe my premonition—I've never believed in premonitions, whether mute and vague and imprecise or detailed descriptions of disasters and calamities.

One of the twins was coming toward us with a wheelbarrow that held a suspicious shape inside a black bag. Apparently they had found a drowned dog in the pond; before dying he had jumped from one cone of crushed glass to another, cutting his feet and going mad with pain. The man lifted the edge of the bag to show us the mutilated paws. For the first time his tone was not neutral; it sounded like he was blaming me, and since I don't think he cared particularly about the dog, he might have been accusing me of being responsible for Rossi's accident. I wanted to say, "Finally you have an opinion; when did you decide to start having opinions?" but instead I just stuttered, "Are the cones badly damaged?" His eyes flew open wide—for once they showed an expression—but the rest of his face stayed inert; his stunned eyes were like early snowdrops blooming long before any other flower. He didn't answer me but just started walking again with his wheelbarrow hearse, the dog paws jouncing along outside the bag.

I didn't want to go see the damage; Elisabetta came down to say goodbye to us, and we helped her load the last bags into the old Lancia Thema. Rossi came down at the last minute and simply waved to us; he looked very depressed. We left right after they did and spent the rest of the day at the data center garden site, talking as little as possible, taking measurements and making lists of the materials and tools we would need. I felt like I'd been sent to a penal colony: I sweated and drank and drank and sweated, and my head boiled under my straw hat. As we were going home, I decided it was my duty to say something: Witold was gloomy—the Renal job had been special for him too, and it had ended on the wrong note; also, the roads were bubbling with vacation traffic, as if we were the only people on the plains who'd been left out. I began telling him about the plans I had in mind, the clients who had called in the last few weeks, the magazine that wanted to do a story about us. I purposely said "us" because I knew it was the quickest, most direct way to put Witold in a good mood. It did me good too.

At a stoplight I drew up next to a woman driving a yellow Fiat Punto convertible; she wasn't pretty, but she was smiling as she looked at the road and didn't notice me spying on her; maybe she was thinking about the evening ahead. For the first time since I'd blown up at him and his wife about the liquor bottles, Witold asked me how I'd be spending the weekend, and whether I'd like to eat with them on Saturday night or at lunch on Sunday. Then all my sadness about Elisabetta's departure suddenly hit me, and I dropped him off and said goodbye in a hurry, saying I'd get back to him by phone, and I went home to the arid desert of two empty days stretching before me. I could have spent the days drinking cold white wine, but instead I worked late in the empty wing of the farmhouse, fixing up the electrical wiring. I talked to Elisabetta; I sent her text messages that attempted to be funny; I thought about her. The sun was merciless, and there wasn't a breath of wind; on Sunday night I went to see my mother, and I wished I had the courage to ask her about Mosca at some point, but down on the plain it was even worse than at my place—you just couldn't breathe—and she was paler and looked older than I'd ever seen her look (she had always suffered from the heat), and maybe just the fact that she wasn't crying was good enough for me: it was already something.

I was so eager to spend the following weekend with the kids that on my way home from work on Tuesday night I stopped by the hypermarket and bought a huge supply of meat: beef, pork, sausages, ribs. I bought six 1.5 liter bottles of Coca-Cola, all kinds of flavored chips, popcorn, mayonnaise, ketchup, snack foods, pudding, and ice cream. I filled my cart to the brim, and then when I got home I described everything I'd bought to Elisabetta, item by item. She didn't have much to report: she spent her mornings tanning and then went down to swim in the afternoons, while Alberto was resting. She didn't want to go far from him, and I wanted to ask her exactly why not, why she felt she had to hold his hand; I didn't understand it, but I couldn't have her explain over the phone.

The blow came halfway through the week, when Carlo called to let me know that he and Cecilia had decided on the spur of the moment to spend four days at the beach with the kids.

"Together?" I asked skeptically.

"We got here this evening. I don't know how it'll go, but we had to try."

He was speaking softly; I don't know where he was, and I hadn't ever been to Cecilia's house at the beach, but it can't have been very big; I could hear the kids yelling in the background.

"Are the kids happy?"

"As you can imagine: they're wild with joy."

My stomach clenches—pure jealousy feels like taking a gulp of vinegar by mistake.

"So you're not coming . . ."

"I'm sorry I didn't tell you earlier, I wasn't sure that—" He breaks off, I hear Cecilia's voice in the background, and Carlo says, "It's Claudio . . . Cecilia says hello . . ."

"Whatever happened to that girl?"

"Hold on." I hear him walking through the house. "Kids, do you want to say hello to Uncle Claudio?" The voices and noises get closer to the phone and then fade off. Then he's speaking softly again. "What in the world were you thinking?"

"Well, it's not like she could hear—"

"Nothing ever happened to that girl—"

"Are you still seeing her?"

"Listen"—he's still walking around the house, like a terrorist darting to a new safe house every night—"are you pissed off that I didn't tell you earlier? I'm sorry, you're right, I behave like shit, I act like you're always available whenever we want you, and I know perfectly well that's not true, that you have a life of your own."

A life of my own. I'd never considered it.

"No, I'm not mad, it's just that I bought a ton of meat . . . and I really did want to know what happened, about that bruise . . ."

"She's got a sort of violent father, but— Listen, I'm sorry"—he's never begged my pardon so many times—"I shouldn't have dragged you into it—" He breaks off. I hear footsteps and Cecilia's voice saying to him, "Are you still on the phone?" and him saying again, "It's Claudio," as if I were a justification for the length of the call—incredible.

"And have you heard the latest news?" He's started whispering again like a conspirator.

I tell him that I've had a lot of work to do.

"Didn't you see that the right wing won the elections for the European Parliament? And then just three days later the court absolved Craxi . . . The wind is changing direction."

"There's no wind at all around here: it's impossible to breathe—"

"It's going to get even harder to breathe, you wait and see . . . No one in this country ever pays for what they've done, never; they usually just find some scapegoat, every time: Mussolini, or Moro—all the other Christian Democrats got away with it—they have gotten away or they will get away with it . . . Tambroni, Donat-Cattin, Fanfani, Leone, Cossiga, Piccoli, De Mita, Forlani, Gava . . ."

I'm stretched out on the sofa in my kitchen, and my brother is on the phone whispering an endless list of names; I close my eyes, I see Elisabetta's naked breast, I see the girl with the black eye, I see myself standing in the middle of the meadow, with Carlo holding the pistol and me saying to him, "I need you." And I embrace him, even though brothers don't do that anymore.

"I have to go now," I say, interrupting him.

"Yeah, yeah, me too. I'll say hi to the kids for you . . . No, wait, Filippo needs to talk to you. His voice is a bit hoarse: he spent too much time in the water."

"Uncle Claudio?"

"Hi, little mouse. What's up?"

"My voice is an old Magic Marker: sometimes it gets worn out and you can't hear it anymore."

"Wow. We'll have to buy some new markers—"

"No, no, Uncle Claudio, it was a *metaphor*."

"Oh. A metaphor . . . Listen, pass the phone back to your father—"
Carlo gets back on the line.

I say: "I'm going to call you in a few days; I need to talk to you about something important."

"The Renals again?"

"No, a different issue."

Cecilia's voice is in the background again. But this time Carlo ignores her; he wants to know. "What's going on—is something wrong?"

"I told you, I want to talk to you."

"Papa wants to talk to you," my mother would say, and she would push the wheelchair over near me. Usually I was working in the courtyard of our house, or outside the farmhouse I had just bought; it was the year after he'd had his accident, falling off a ladder that was leaning unsteadily between the branches of a tree. He'd hit his head and had surgery, and the doctors had removed a blood clot; he could walk, he could step from one chair to another and go very slowly up and down the stairs in the house, but he used the wheelchair whenever possible. My mother would push him outdoors for some fresh air, and they would circle me, and then, even without my noticing my father speak to her, without my hearing them approach, there they'd be in front of me, and she would report what he wanted. But she didn't stay to hear what he had to say to me; she would add that she was going to take the opportunity to get something done, or go and fetch something she'd forgotten indoors. She would leave my father with me, and leave me with my father—and did she really think that we would talk? That he would say all the things he so needed to tell me? Or did she know we would just stay silent while I went on with my work and my father observed my hands, the tools I was using, the pots I was filling with earth, and the trellises I was building for the climbing plants? Maybe she didn't even wonder. And I never asked her about it, later.

One time, for example, I was in the farmhouse courtyard on a spring day when I had brought them over to see it; I'd bought the place as soon as I had some savings. I was very proud of having bought it, and though it needed to be completely restored, I was in no hurry: I had no intention of leaving my mother to look after my father alone, so I really wasn't planning to move out; I thought maybe I'd rent it when it was ready. My father had already been using the wheelchair for several months, and my mother was pushing it around the sunny courtyard while I scraped old paint off a shutter laid across two sawhorses. "Papa wants to talk to you," my mother said. "I'm going to tidy up indoors." So we were left alone. His hands lay inert in his lap; they were traced with bluish veins like rivers on a relief map. His legs were nothing but skin and bones: he just didn't want to use them anymore. I was concentrating on my work: the scraper I was gripping and the flakes of dry paint that lifted off to reveal the naked wood beneath. My father didn't talk, and I didn't ask him what he wanted to tell me.

I could have asked him if he liked the farmhouse.

I could have talked about the weather.

Asked him if he wanted to talk to me about Carlo.

If he wanted a glass of water or wine.

If he was pleased with me, with my work, with my gardens.

If he wanted to go home.

I kept quiet with my father facing me in a wheelchair.

I could have asked him any old thing, but the one thing I *should* have asked him kept me from talking at all.

I should have asked my father if he wanted to talk about the night Fabio died. I should have asked him to explain to me what we had done, he and I, and how it was possible to go on living. I should have asked him, and he would have had to explain it to me. If your father doesn't explain it, who will? If your father doesn't explain why he let his son die, how can a son wish to live?

In the last few weeks, especially since Elisabetta left, I was tormented by imagining that conversation that never happened. When I pictured my father, I no longer saw him sitting next to me in the car, as usual, with our four eyes playing the world like the four hands of a pair of pianists in a duet. Now we were facing each other, I standing and he trapped in his wheelchair, I as both judge and defendant, he as both judge and defendant, I weak and strong because I was standing, he weak and strong because he was seated. As long as we were in the car we kept moving forward, our eyes never met, and there was never any threat to the silence. Now we were planted in each other's paths, though, and the silence became unbearable. But which of us should have broken the silence?

So I imagined someone else in my place, and someone else in his, to distract myself and give me some relief. I pictured Renal and my father. What would they have told each other? About the indifference of a man who becomes a gardener so he'll never again run the risk of thanking the loan shark who ruined him. About the saintliness of a man who can love all humanity but can't love the woman who chose to marry him. I pictured Elisabetta and my mother. The Sleeping Beauty who can never leave her enchanted castle because she wants to look after a paralyzed Prince Charming. The pianist who studies Bach and detests melodrama because feelings should be kept in the heart, under lock and key. I pictured Witold and Rossi. The Pole who proclaims his love for Italy in order to forget his longing for his homeland. The man who had the misfortune of seeing his ideal of perfection personified in another man.

But all of them would have had something to say to one another, if only because they'd never met. They would have started talking about the weather, then they would have told one another the stories of their lives, maybe using *Tales Told* as a springboard. I pictured them all together in one room, and the sound of their voices suffocated me. Only my father and I were condemned to spend eternity in the places where my mother had left us, wordless, in the most perfect and lacerating silence.

But no, now I'm getting carried away. I'm too fond of silence to betray it this way.

There are lots of ways of communicating. True. You can say things without speaking. True. For example, Fabio's favorite places to shoot up. Some of them I knew about because they were where all the junkies went, protected places where they wouldn't be bothered. Others were places I'd followed him to, where I'd waited for him and spied on him. But I think the places he liked best were an untilled field behind my father's old factory and a bench in the public park in town (my father had worked for the town for a while). And it's true that these messages are no more vague and imprecise than a statement full of words.

"Biggle opty hatpat?" can mean a thousand things.

But did my father's silence mean something?

There are two different versions of the fairy tale. One is that our father is offended by the world and won't recognize that he has any responsibility for his bankruptcy and the death of his son: he's silent because he has nothing to say, because there's no point getting upset about fate, you simply have to bow your head and carry on. The second is that our father knows perfectly well it was partly his fault he lost the factory, and feels guilty for not being able to get his son off drugs and for having let him die: he's silent because he lacks the courage to speak, because he thinks that admitting his guilt would lose him the affection of his wife and sons.

The first version is reassuring; it's Carlo's version. The second is not reassuring; it's mine. The first version does nothing to redeem our father, or rather it redeems him by transforming him into a victim of his own upbringing, of his own history, of his background: a marionette. The second does too much to redeem him, because it seems intolerable to think that the old man died without ever understanding what he had lived through. So then, maybe—thinking about it now—I see that this one is reassuring too.

But we'll never know which of the two is closer to the truth, if indeed there was only one truth in our father's head, because he doesn't talk, not even with himself, he doesn't articulate his feelings in words, he never runs the risk of lying to himself or anyone else; all he does is keep everyone from laying bare his lies, perhaps, and thus perceiving what he feels. He is the owner of his own silence, and he gave birth to my silence: he's the father of my silence.

(But no, now I'm getting carried away.)

Mosca eventually called me, and without showing too much eagerness, I agreed to go to his house to see the site. The elevator opened directly into the apartment, and as soon as the doors parted, a nervous little white terrier slipped between my legs so that Mosca had to kick at it to get it back in the house. The apartment took up the whole top floor of a building in the center of the city. Mosca explained that he'd had all the interior walls ripped out, and then he himself, with an architect friend, had designed the layout of the rooms. It was a checkerboard based on the principle that every space should be the same size—3.1416 yards square—and that all the spaces should flow into one another without any corridors or foyers; and he wanted the hanging garden to follow the same philosophy. Well, I'll design any kind of garden if the money is right. If I needed cash and someone asked me to, I'd design a garden with succulent plants topped by Corinthian capitals with red velvet drapes. But I didn't need money at the moment. I could turn down a job and shop around carefully for my next victim.

On the great terrace surrounded by a palisade of silver firs, where some haggard azaleas and yellowing gardenias were suffocating slowly, we stopped to watch the yellow disk of the sun diving into the city's haze. The air was terribly close. I asked why he didn't have air-conditioning, and he said that there was nothing worse for the health, and that his checkerboard idea fostered excellent air circulation: he had been inspired by houses in India and the Minoan palace of Knossos. He took me on a guided tour, presenting each room by name, as if this were Versailles: "the little reading room," "the writing room," "the music room," "the screening room," "the bedroom," "the bathroom," "the steam room," and so on. "The rooms are also balanced by the number of furniture pieces in each one." I nodded. We turned left and ran into Giletti, stretched out on a chaise longue reading a newspaper, holding the pages up and away from the terrier, who was trying to rip them. Mosca gave the dog another kick, and Giletti rose to greet me while I was telling him not to bother getting up. We went on with the tour.

"The dining room," "the kitchen," "Mr. Giletti's rooms"; we turned left again and found ourselves in "the laundry room," then "the ironing room," where I saw a Peruvian woman in a white apron who didn't seem to be benefiting from the excellent air circulation system: she was grunting and sweating over her steam iron. We went back to the little reading room and sat at a round table with a smoked glass top that held a carafe filled with ice cubes and lemonade. I asked whether I could add some gin, and Mosca turned to his right and murmured at the wall, "Do you know if we have any gin in the house?" and the wall answered with a muffled voice, "Not as far as I know." I didn't give him the satisfaction of asking how it worked. But he went on for a bit singing the house's praises, and I sipped my lemonade in silence.

Suddenly he broke off, his brow furrowed. He pretended to cast about for the right words, but there was no way he hadn't already chosen them.

"You must be wondering about Mr. Giletti's role in my life . . ."

I put on a sincerely amazed expression. "No, really, I'm not."

"At first I thought I could solve the problem by buying a dog, so I got that terrier, Hello, but he wasn't enough."

Another pause.

I say, "Dogs are good company; I had one myself, but—"

"No, no, you misunderstand me. It wasn't for company. I'm not lonely, I'm perfectly self-sufficient." He smiled. I smiled too, reflexively, but without knowing why. "What I needed was a witness."

"A witness?"

"An eyewitness. Someone to see me living my life. When I turned fifty I began to feel strange. And I thought, I'm not the type of person who gets clinically depressed."

A pause.

Was that a question? I shake my head: no, he's not the type.

"And then I understood: I've always lived alone, I've been working and earning—earning a lot of money, if I do say so myself—but I don't like spending money just to show how rich I am, that's just not the way I was raised. I don't show off my money; it's hidden. So where does that leave me? I was like a buried land mine: no one knows where it is, anybody might step on it. I was about to explode. But then I had this idea: a witness, a biographer, a documentary filmmaker. Giletti is all that. He tells the story of my life."

A pause; a sip of lemonade.

"Don't get me wrong, it's not for posterity. I don't give a damn about posterity. It's for me. For me alone. You have no idea how my life has been enriched since Giletti started following me. In the evening he tells me what I did that day. The objective account of my life. And then I go to bed with this new awareness: I exist."

I was now sweating diligently and consistently, very focused on the task of sweating; I was like a piece of cheese left on the counter outside the fridge.

"A lush green garden would help make the house fresher," I said. "I'm also thinking about some stands of reeds, and some small palm trees that you could bring inside during the winter."

He stared at me to see whether I was making fun of him or whether I really hadn't understood any of what he had said.

"Come, let me take you into the multimedia room; I want to show you a tape that I received anonymously in the mail."

Giletti appeared with a laptop computer under his arm.

"It was a VHS video, but Mr. Giletti copied it digitally so we could examine it more closely. He's really a technical wizard."

It was nighttime, with fog and fluorescent lights, but I immediately recognized the lot at the supermarket, and Conti standing and smoking, and the parked cars.

"Last fall an acquaintance of mine, Mariano Conti, was hit by a car in the parking lot of a mini-mall. It was very sad. This Conti wasn't the most honest of men, but he certainly didn't deserve to end up like that. He got his start lending money, with interest rates that were a bit high, but not unreasonable. Then he set up an actual investment company, and I helped him out. That was a mistake. I couldn't ever shake him. He was a hard man to shake."

The film rolls for a few more minutes, and nothing happens until the Ka appears.

"The quality is really dreadful. Look, you see, only at this point did I realize that this had anything to do with me. That's Elisabetta Renal's car."

Giletti froze the image, fiddled with the computer mouse, and enlarged the Ka's license plate.

"I recognized that the standing man was Conti, and I thought she was going to hit him, but now wait . . . in just a moment there'll be another surprise . . ."

The white van shoots down the driveway, hits Conti full on, and hurls him thirty feet away. After a moment the Ka starts up again and runs him over.

I sit there without moving, just sweating, and say nothing.

"It's a nasty business," Mosca says, "but I still didn't understand why I'd been sent the tape, until . . . There, watch the car that starts moving now . . ."

My Mercedes leaves the parking lot with its lights off. Giletti enlarges the license plate. It's fuzzy but legible.

"So you were there too, and you saw everything even better than this camera did. But don't worry; I'm not going to ask you to tell me about it. I'm not even going to ask you whether you knew the driver of the van, or whether you were there to make sure he did a good job—" He puts out his hand as if to stop me, but I haven't moved; I don't feel offended or accused, and I have nothing to say.

Giletti shuts the laptop.

"Thank you," Mosca says to him. Giletti leaves the room. "And don't worry, I've already found out who sent me the tape, and I've met his terms. But, you see, I cannot keep on tidying up that woman's messes. She'd gotten it into her head that she was going to find out something or other."

I look at him without speaking.

"Yes, I understand. You're in love with her. But Elisabetta doesn't deserve it. She's a very superficial woman. When he married her, Alfredo made the biggest mistake of his life, a colossal, incomparable mistake, and even though he really loved her—in his own way, of course—I can't help thinking that she made him die. At first she was just a young girl, but she has never grown up. She's a woman of no character, and she's not even very clever." He stopped and looked at me, struck by a sudden thought. "You do know you're not the first, don't you?"

I couldn't flush with anger. I was already purple.

"Of course, you're thinking that Elisabetta has the right to do whatever she wants. But you're wrong. A woman doesn't outlive a husband like Alfredo Renal."

I run my eyes along the edge of the table, and I count circles around the carafe where the ice cubes have all melted by now.

"Forget about her. Let me explain: I care about the foundation. And the foundation is held by Elisabetta and Rossi: two people who for very different reasons are both extremely fragile. Alberto, in particular, is on the edge of a nervous breakdown."

I drop my gaze to my crossed legs.

"Well, I don't want to keep you here any longer. The work on the garden is finished, isn't it? More or less."

I nod.

"I was sure you'd understand right away; you're an intelligent man."

Then I'm in the elevator with Hello the dog nipping at my ankles. I kick him out of the elevator. Mosca laughs. "Good, good, that's the way: kick the past away, send it packing. Please do think about my hanging garden; I'll keep bothering you until you design it for me. And keep in mind that I have lots of contacts."

He stares at me. I stare at him.

"Compliments on your house," I say. "It's really phenomenal."

• • •

As soon as I got into my car, I called Elisabetta; I was very agitated, and to avoid talking about the video while I was still working through my agitation, I told her that someday I'd tell her about my brother who died of an overdose.

"You're upset—what happened?"

"Nothing, I'm just a little dejected. I miss you."

"Are you in the city?"

"How can you tell?"

"I heard a tram going by."

I hadn't even noticed it passing. I wasn't somebody who really noticed things happening around me.

"Is it hot?"

"Terribly."

"Are you feeling better now?"

"Yes, talking makes it better."

Talking never hurts. Talking hurts a lot.

I corrected myself. "Talking *to you* makes it better."

"Why did you go to the city? Did you go to Mosca's?"

"No, I had to meet the people from the bank."

"But he called you; do you have an appointment to meet?"

"Yes, he called me . . ."

"And?"

"We're getting together tomorrow or the next day—he still has to confirm it."

"I can't tell whether you're still interested."

"In Mosca?"

"In the hanging garden . . ."

"Yes, of course; it's just a question of how much time I have . . . and how much I want it . . . I'm a bit tired."

"What do you mean, you're 'a little dejected'? Why were you thinking about your brother?"

"I think about him. He comes to mind. I don't know."

And while I'm talking I imagine her sitting in the same perfectly square room where Giletti showed me what his laptop could do, and I imagine the words that Mosca must have used, months ago, to blackmail her. And her surprise and her fear when she saw my Mercedes appear in the video. And her searching for my address and phone number. And then our meeting, and her waiting for me to tell her what Conti meant to me. Her disappointment and her rage.

She promises to come back on Sunday: she'll leave in the afternoon, as soon as Alberto goes to lie down, and she'll stay till Monday morning.

Her promise keeps me going all the way home, and through the evening and the next day, and it makes me accept Witold's invitation to lunch on Saturday, and makes me spend some time with Malik and his wife that evening. Malik tells me all the details about the little girl's development, and he puts her in my arms, even though the baby objects. "How about Durga?" I ask; I didn't see her because I came by the road. "I haven't heard her barking recently." Durga's very angry, apparently. She met her husband, and she doesn't like him. "Not a bit," says Malik. And how about Kalki? "He's a fake dog—he has no love in him," says Malik. What happened, exactly? "What happened is that Durga got angry," he repeats; Malik seems to want to leave things vague. But ultimately, he tells me: "He's not the right one, and she knows it, and she goes for his throat." She tried to kill him?! "Yes, if I don't save him the husband is eaten," he says, laughing. But isn't Durga dangerous? Malik nods. "Durga is always dangerous." I look at the portrait of Shiva gazing down on us from a wall calendar that hangs next to a portrait of the guru Nanak Dev Ji. I smile. Malik chuckles and says, "You're happy because you're envious of the fake dog." Me, envious of Kalki? "You don't want

Durga to marry," he says, and he laughs, proud of having something to make fun of me about. I laugh too.

At eleven the next morning I went out in my underwear to drink my coffee in the courtyard; I sat on the stone bench, closed my eyes, turned my face to the sun, and tried to calculate how many hours were left before Elisabetta might arrive. I pictured my nose as the point of a sundial, and my teeth as the notches measuring the hours; the math was easy, but I couldn't do it because I was agitated. I started subtracting, but I couldn't finish because I suddenly thought that I'd like to stage a little welcome ceremony: I could be waiting for the Ka in the courtyard, I could drag a couple of wicker chairs out from the house, I could prepare an aperitif and wear something elegant (would you like people to notice you?). When I opened my eyes, I saw a line of people coming around the bend in the road and toward my gate, and the absolute light of July, plus the reddish, incandescent halos in my vision—my eyes were still flooded with the yellows and oranges that the sun had splashed on my lids—made them seem like human torches marching up silently and desperately; I was gripped by panic and dashed into the house, where I locked the door tight and peered out through the shutters.

As they came closer, they fizzled out like embers, turning into simple black silhouettes. It was a strange group: three guys and two girls and three dogs, with small military rucksacks and clothes that were not quite clean but weren't very dirty either—dark jeans and black T-shirts—and shaved heads; the dogs were short-haired mutts, black with a few white patches. It was as if they had purposely eliminated color from everything they had. They didn't seem dangerous, but still I was irritated that they had seen me escape into the house. I slipped on a pair of shorts and went out.

They were standing in the middle of the courtyard. "Hello," said the guy at the front of the line. "Can you give us some water?"

"Certainly." I brought them three bottles of mineral water. First they drank straight from the bottles, and then they pulled two bowls out from their backpacks and gave the dogs a drink.

"Water from your hose would have been okay," said one of the girls.

"At least for the dogs," I said, making a little joke.

"We share everything with them, we don't make any distinction. If you gave us champagne we would do the same thing."

"Champagne I don't have." I was trying playfully to coax out a smile. But it didn't work: they were restrained and serious.

I asked them where they came from. They had been protesting the war at an American military base, and now they were on their way back to the city. On foot? They traveled only on foot. How many miles did they cover each day? They didn't keep count. And how many days had it taken them? They had stopped a few times along the road, wherever someone would put them up, and they had been traveling for three weeks, ever since the bombing ended.

I smiled and said that my brother was very happy the bombing had ended.

They gave me puzzled looks, and then they smiled; one of them chuckled and said, "But not you?"

"Oh, yes, of course, me too, I am too—" I said, and I laughed.

I get the hose and refill the dog bowls, and the kids drink from the hose before I can offer to go inside and get them some more bottled water. Looking at them more closely, I see that one of the guys must not be part of the group, even though he's dressed in black like the others. He has Nikes instead of work boots, and he's wearing not a T-shirt but a short-sleeved blue shirt, and though his head too looks shaved, he is actually bald. He's less dirty and threadbare than the others.

"Why don't you all sit down and rest a while?" I say before I can stop myself, and I regret it immediately; this alien element has upset me again.

Thanks, they say, we'd be glad to, and they sit down with their backs against the wall of the farmhouse. I look at them, unsure whether I should offer them chairs, and then I go back inside. I don't shut the door.

I peer out at them through the shutters. I think, They're here to kill me. I watch them for ten minutes and I think, They're just kids, they've walked for days and days, they're worried about the war, and I have a fridge full of meat that's going to spoil.

So I went out and I suggested that they stay for lunch. I explained that I had been expecting my brother and his kids, but they didn't come, and I have a lot of meat for grilling if they want it. They looked at one another, conferring together in silence. I noticed that the outsider wasn't part of their exchange of glances.

"We're generally vegetarians, but we haven't eaten for two days, and maybe it would do us good," said the guy who had been leading the line at the beginning.

"Good, then that's decided. Would one o'clock be okay?"

They exchanged glances again.

"If you like, we can start the grill right away."

"Maybe that's better," a girl said. "Otherwise we'll fall asleep."

They helped me carry out a table, the girls started preparing the meat and vegetables, the guys started a fire in the barbecue, and the outsider fell asleep sitting against the wall with his head straight up—I don't know how he held it there. I wanted to ask if they ever ended up sleeping in the meadows, if they came across old shortcuts between the fields and the industrial sheds, if they were often invited to lunch or if the people who live here on the plains turned their backs instead and shooed the group away from their courtyards. But they said nothing and asked nothing; they weren't curious about my life—why all that gardening stuff? Why did I live alone? Why was the dog bed empty?

Even their dogs were calm and polite: they stayed near the table hoping for some scrap of meat. I remembered that I still had half a bag of Gustavo's biscuits; I went to fetch it and called the dogs to come to me under the canopy, but they didn't trust me and only when one of their owners joined me did they come over, wagging their tails and sniffing around suspiciously. These three black dogs were so tired that they didn't even bark when Indra appeared at the edge of the woods, drawn by the smell of the meat on the grill. The dachshund and I had become friends: he often came by to sniff around, and he never pissed where he shouldn't. But he was noisy and touchy and pretty unbearable. The group's dogs looked at him unperturbed for ten minutes while he went running up and down like mad, trying fruitlessly to provoke them, and then he went off. I explained that he was the neighbor's dog, and I would have liked to tell them about the famous photographer's obsession with tigers, but clearly my guests wouldn't have been interested. They were starving and couldn't wait to eat.

So we ate. We ate everything. At least this way we could communicate. Even the outsider ate, sitting apart from everyone else. I asked the others if he was unwell, and the spokesman said he was his cousin, who had some problems; he came along with them to get out of the house, but he didn't share their views and they didn't share his—still, they would help anyone who was standing against the system, one way or another. He was evasive and mysterious; or maybe not.

After we ate, I told them that the other wing of the house was empty, and if they wanted to rest for a few hours they could lay down their mattresses and sleeping bags on the floor in one of the rooms. They accepted. The outsider went back to sleeping outside, on the pavement.

I worked on the computer for a while, but I was distracted. I'd found several voice messages on my cell phone, and I'd played them back voraciously, thinking they were Elisabetta's. But instead it was just a whiny voice saying, "Sonia, we're stuck in traffic, you go on ahead, don't wait for us," and then, "Sonia, I left you a message, you go on ahead because we're stuck, there's been some kind of accident, okay, call back when you can," and then, "Sonia, why aren't you answering, are you at a truck stop? We're still in this traffic jam, maybe it's an accident or something." I tried to work, but I kept thinking about all the people moving around this weekend, about the radio waves bouncing over the landscape of the plains, waves pushing out ahead of the cars and following them like shadows, and about Elisabetta on the highway surrounded by those millions of strangers.

Every twenty minutes I got up to peek at the outsider through the shutters. At one point I saw that he'd woken up and was sitting with his legs crossed, having a smoke. He was tossing pebbles at the middle of the courtyard, snapping his wrist as if he were skipping stones on water. I went out and over to him. There was a fine smell of hashish in the air.

"Everything okay?"

"Great. We needed that."

I smile and look out toward the road.

"You wouldn't have some of that to sell me, would you?"

"Sure I do; and even better stuff if you want."

I don't tell him that I haven't smoked for more than twenty years, ever since my brother died. I pay him, and I go back inside.

With the bag of hashish next to the computer, I was calmer, and I worked uninterruptedly for two hours. Then I went into the kitchen and opened the fridge; there was a partially eaten chocolate pudding that looked like an ancient ruin, there was half of a Crescenza cheese, and a package of prosciutto: provisions that would be hard to keep fresh without a fridge. So I gathered some packages of cookies and crackers, as well as canned meat, peas, corn, and beans. I filled up a plastic bag; maybe my guests were opposed to using plastic, but I couldn't think of any other container.

Useless. They were gone. They had left the door half open and the room as clean as if no one had been there. I glanced around the court-yard, out of habit, but nothing was missing; they weren't the kind of people who would steal: they'd be more likely to die of hunger. I got mad. Why the hell did they leave like that, without saying goodbye? And then I thought, Who knows if Fabio said goodbye when he went around like a vagabond? That was good for a few tears. I wanted Elisabetta to come; it was four in the afternoon, and I couldn't take it anymore.

I tried to kill some time dragging out the wicker chairs and table; I mixed up two vodka martinis, but after half an hour they were warm and I drank them myself. Then I drank another, a cold one, because I was thirsty. I was too sad to stay outside, and too sad to go back in.

Then I thought I would go find my old self-inflating mattress in the basement and bring it outside. While looking for it, I went to check that the pistol I'd hidden was still where I'd put it, behind one of my father's metal cabinets. I unwrapped the newspaper and weighed the pistol in one hand. The newspaper was from the beginning of May, and it had headlines about the bombing of Belgrade. That meant my mother had wrapped it up and put it aside for a month before entrusting me with it. Who knew if it still worked? I could never use it anyway, because I didn't know where to get bullets.

I took the pistol and the newspaper and the mattress upstairs, left the pistol by the front door, under the portraits of the unknown couple, laid the mattress on the cement pavement outside, and read the eight pages of the two-month-old paper.

I turned on the stereo in the E270 and put on Witold's *Rigoletto* at top volume, with the car doors wide open. I waved my arms around and pretended to sing along.

Later on I heated up the hashish, crumbled it, and prepared a joint. I didn't smoke it. I looked at the blue sky instead, those endless days of early summer.

• • •

I'm sitting on the wicker chair waiting for Elisabetta; she can't be late. But the chair slowly sinks into the ground and disappears. I can't get back on my feet. The farmhouse also falls into a chasm. I struggle and drag myself up, but actually I'm just swimming in the dirt, which is crumbly, like corn kernels. I do the breaststroke. Then I see the shore, not far off, with two men on the beach.

One is dressed bizarrely in a lace bodice and puffy shorts, and shoes with big square buckles. The other is dressed as a Buddhist monk. They're arguing. I try to get their attention, but they don't see me. The first one tosses a pebble in the water, nearly hitting me. He says, "Who decides how it is?"

I recognize the other one immediately. It's the pope. He says, "No one. It's always been that way."

The concentric circles spread across the water and run out of energy, and the surface of the water goes flat again.

"That's not an answer," says the first one. "Tell me whether it smooths out again because the turbulence is suppressed by force, or whether there's a reconciliation between the pebble and the lake."

The pope looks irritated.

I finally manage to get out of the water. I shake hands with the pope and introduce myself: "Witold Witkiewicz."

"I've heard a lot about you," he replies. "Good, you're a fine young man."

Then he turns to go. The other one stops him by grabbing his arm. "And explain this to me, please. Does equilibrium come from revenge or from forgiveness?"

The pope rolls his eyes upward, takes a deep breath, and sings in a baritone voice:

Yes, revenge, terrible revenge
Is all my heart desires.
The moment of your punishment is near,
The hour that will be your last.

I fall down again. I want to get to Malik; he'll know how to save me. I drag myself through the chestnut woods by my hands, grabbing whatever I can reach—roots, low branches—painfully, ripping my nails off and bloodying my fingertips. I start cursing and punching the ground.

I look up. The man from before is standing in front of me, wearing a thick double-breasted suit of black wool. He's old, but his hair is still black, combed back close against his square skull with its pointy ears; on his small nose are a pair of glasses with heavy frames. He kneels down, washes my hands in a basin, and then disinfects them.

"Why are you so angry? You have to learn how to forgive," he says paternally.

I smile. "Hey, I know you—"

"Of course you do," he says, lowering his shoulder and jerking his thumb back toward his evident humpback. "Do come along"—as if we were already late for some appointment.

He leads me along the driveway going to the famous photographer's villa; the dogs aren't there—Malik must have taken them away for a holiday, and it doesn't surprise me. But the photographer's house isn't behind its gate. There's just a sort of dump with a dirt road rising and falling and twisting through it; they're building a garden here, I think.

On the edge of the road is a man sunk up to his waist in a mud puddle. He is encrusted with mud, all over his small head and massive body; there are only two narrow slits for his eyes. He's breathing with difficulty;

his mouth is wide open, and I can see the pink—red—inside, the broken teeth, the whitish tongue. He's gigantic and says nothing.

"There's nothing to be done," whispers the old man. "He wasn't forgiven." He shrugs.

After a while we come upon another man, sitting on the ground; he's naked and emaciated, and next to him is a pup tent; he's holding a notebook and writing in it, and the pup tent is full of crumpled-up pages; he doesn't look up to see who we are, he just goes on writing.

"Not him, either," the old man tells me.

The third man we encounter is hanging upside down from a cherry tree, struggling to right himself. My guide is about to speak, but I gesture for him to stop. He nods, as if to say, Of course, who wouldn't recognize him?

We walk through the desolate landscape. No one is visible any longer. The old man seems hot in his double-breasted suit, and more tired than I am. He falls behind, and every now and then I wait for him to catch up.

"Most of them are forgiven. Some are not so fortunate. What's wrong with forgiveness . . ."

I can't tell whether it's a question. We've been walking for hours. I'm exhausted, and I turn back to ask him what he meant to say, what he plans to do, where we are. He has disappeared.

I say loudly that I want to get to the crest of the next hill, and if I don't find Malik I'll turn back. Just so he'll know.

When I turn again and look up the road, I see a ghost a few feet away. I stop, and he doesn't come closer.

For the first time in my life I think how tall and strong my father was.

I see me crying from outside, as if I'm someone else watching me from behind. Then I'm not crying anymore.

The ghost nods. He disappears. I look at him until I realize that I've turned around and started down again along the dirt road that brought me here.

I'm calm. Tired. I drop to the ground. I sink down and start swimming again. I'm in the courtyard of my farmhouse.

My right cheek is resting on the gravel when I feel a vibration and see the Ka driving into the courtyard. Then Elisabetta is next to me, asking what happened—why am I asleep on the ground?

Because . . . I don't know; I don't know the reason for all the things that happen to me.

But didn't you see? I ask her: I didn't throw myself to the ground, I fell; and she caresses me and helps me up. She takes me into the house, and she's crying and I ask her why—don't cry, my angel, you don't have to cry, we're together again.

6

SHE KEPT STUDYING HER FAVORITE PIECES OF MUSIC, SITTING AT THE KITCHEN table and reading the scores, following their development and the turning points in the music, the quickening and the slackening pace; she rarely played now because arthritis had deformed her hands, but maybe she didn't need the piano anymore: it was satisfying enough for her to trace the thread of the notes pulsating along the staff like a faulty and unsteady heart, hypnotized by the counterpoint. Monday morning I showed up at my mother's door with an excuse even more far-fetched than the thing about the button: I told her that I had to look for an old manual, and she asked me what manual—there were no more books in either my room or Carlo's—and I mentioned an old gardening manual that I couldn't find but that I needed desperately, which might have ended up in the attic or the basement, in one of the storerooms she had begun emptying. "There are no books," she murmured.

But I was already moving around the apartment—it's one way to assert my presence in her house: walking up and down the hall and from room to room, looking for the cellar keys, making as if I were about to go out, shaking my head and reminding myself out loud that we had already moved the boxes of old schoolbooks over to my place—"how stupid of me." I passed by the kitchen again and asked her if she was sure that there were no books left in the attic; she didn't look up from her score when she answered yes, she was sure. I took the attic keys anyway, but I had no intention of going up there; I just held them and walked through the rooms again—through the world's last remaining display of

Fratta Furniture's products: the living room, my parents' room, Carlo's room, my room (where the bed had been turned into a sofa, as if to deny that anyone had ever slept there). And across from that one remaining bed was the desk that filled the space where Fabio's bed had been; after his bed was taken apart and stacked in the basement, it had disappeared; I lost track of it—maybe my father burnt it. So that no one could ever die in it again. On the desk was an electric sewing machine that had never or rarely been used.

I went back into the kitchen; now I had been in the house for a while, and my mother couldn't throw me out. As I sat facing her, looking at her, I felt on my neck the draft of the cross-ventilation, which she arranged so deftly that it didn't make the doors slam shut, and I got goose bumps—she knew the house the way a musician knows his instrument: she knew how to play it. I asked her if she recalled what year they had moved here, and she replied tartly, "I remember perfectly well, and you know when it was too"; but she didn't sound irritated.

"What was in our room before we were born?"

She looked up from her music, already alarmed. "We" meant Fabio and I, and that meant trouble. Furthermore, I knew that my father had bought the house when Carlo was two, and she knew that I knew. I also remembered the music she was reading, Bach's harpsichord partitas: I remembered her playing them, and her students mangling them.

"Carlo's crib was in there. It was his room."

"And what was in his room?"

"Nothing."

"Nothing?"

"We used it as a storeroom; we put old furniture in there."

"And when Fabio was born, why didn't I move into Carlo's room?"

"Carlo was already in school; he did his homework there in the afternoon."

"But we also went to school, later."

I'm just making a statement, but it sounds like a reproach. Have I ever reproached my mother for something like this?

"There were no other rooms."

"So Carlo's academic success comes from the fact that he had a room to himself."

And then, to shut me up, she says something terrible, and I see that I must have really angered her. "You had a room to yourself too, ultimately."

She goes back to reading the music. She desperately wants me to leave. But this time I really can't.

Yes, I remember Carlo doing his homework in the afternoon while I played. Naturally, he often slipped away from his desk and darted over to give me orders—quietly but as authoritatively as ever—after which he'd disappear and I would carry out the orders.

"You mean after Fabio died."

This is my terrible answer to her terrible answer. No one in this house has ever mentioned his death.

She begins to cry: her eyes tear up, the handkerchief appears in her fist, there's a quick gesture to swab the leak, the spurting emotions, the discomfort and embarrassment.

And I press on.

"I wasn't in school anymore, but you're right, I did get the room."

At this point I know I can't expect her to comment. There won't be any answers to my questions. But silence won't stop me from going on. I know where I'm heading, but I'm not sure about how to get there. I could, for example, tiptoe up to the topic slowly, carefully, circumspectly:

"Someday I'd like you to tell me something about your past—where you and Papa met, in what exact circumstances. What was the first thing he said to you?

"And what did you like about him?

"Men are often different when they're young.

"I mean, their character is different. Cheerier.

"First they make women laugh, so they can marry them, and then they become glum and depressed.

"But maybe Papa's character never changed—what do you think?

"No, I don't think he changed.

"He must have been taciturn even when he was young.

"But on the other hand, chatterboxes aren't reliable.

"Papa must have been sure he himself was reliable.

"That's why losing the factory was so hard for him.

"Not that he ever showed it.

"Because there are lots of ways of communicating.

"Words are not always necessary.

"A small-scale industrialist becomes a gardener after a bankruptcy. That's one way of saying something.

"Like the people who work at the university. They're out of the running too.

"Then again, the world is full of hidden dangers.

"And then there comes a point when you feel you've done your duty and you can't go on anymore.

"You even end up thanking the person who ruined you."

But then, at the last minute, I choose the most direct way of asking her. Not to be nasty. But because I think that she'd stop respecting me if she heard me talk so much. So I say:

"Do you remember that guy who ruined Papa? He was called Conti." She doesn't answer.

"Sure you remember. Conti is one name. And you know what? There was another one."

She doesn't react.

"Mosca. Does that mean anything to you? Was he the other guy?"

She gets up and goes out of the room. She takes her purse and an empty plastic shopping bag. She leaves the house.

I sat there for a while with my arms resting on the cold marble. I thought about the skills I'd developed in the last twenty-four hours: wounding people and driving them away.

The night before, Elisabetta had tears of fury in her eyes; she kept saying that I shouldn't let myself get so low, but she didn't explain why. It's not easy to find a reason not to, and it's even harder to help other people find reasons. I was dazed and didn't have the strength to answer her, but I kept murmuring that she shouldn't cry, that we were together again and nothing else mattered. But actually a lot of other things did matter; she had expected to find me wearing mouse slippers and a tiger apron, cheerful and satisfied, preparing a tasty dinner, with no weighty issues on the table—just some ice-cold white wine. There wasn't even that.

"What do you mean, you fell? You didn't throw yourself down on the ground?" she asked me. I didn't recall telling her that; she stroked my face, which was pocked by the gravel as if I'd survived smallpox; I must have rolled off the mattress in my sleep. I didn't know what to say: I was thinking about my dream, my quasi vision, and I was laughing at the idea of my father dressed as a ghost, but Elisabetta—looking at my dusty, filthy body and the pale streaks of dirt in my hair—just grew more irritated. "It's not funny, you know. How much did you drink?"

"Two or three."

"Two or three what?"

But meanwhile I was thinking of Andreotti and my father, and smiling.

I told her that I was going to shower and that if she really did belong to the second category of rescuers, she shouldn't leave; she didn't smile, and if she had actually taken off I would have simply gone to bed—maybe that would have been even better. The stairs up from the ground floor seemed to go on forever; I got undressed and got into the shower and let out a hoot (the water was scalding hot), and struggled with the old faucet without managing to turn it, and then the plastic handle broke off (the ultrasuperglue gave way—I knew it was going to happen sooner or later).

I went down in my bathrobe to find her sitting on the stone bench; without looking her in the face, I tried to describe something to her. I couldn't do it. The idea, more or less, was that sometimes it's important to fall down and lie in the dust; that the earth is always sucking you down, that the force of gravity pulls you all day and it's useless to resist; that it's horrible to stand up all the time, as if trying to demonstrate that you keep your thoughts above the rest of your body. "Take the trees," I said. "It seems like they're standing up, but it's not the same thing. You have to see the whole tree; the roots are just as important as the branches. So in a garden . . . you have to think of a garden as an organism with roots, and the roots are planted somewhere else, in the body of the person who made it, and you can only ever see half of it: you can't see the roots, you can't describe them."

"So every now and then the best thing to do is get drunk and throw yourself on the ground to sleep," she said with no trace of a smile. She shook her head and said that maybe if we ate something the alcohol would wear off. And at that very moment it did wear off, and I was sober. I told her that I was sober, that maybe I'd made a confusing speech but I was grateful to her for having listened. And then she gave in and hugged me.

The broiling heat of the day had produced a perfectly still evening, where each brief and pathetic breeze petered right out, and as we sat in the wicker chairs in the courtyard, eating prosciutto and cantaloupe, the plants and things seemed to stare at us stupidly. Indra did a little performance for us: he stood up on his hind legs and hopped forward like a tiny tiger-striped kangaroo, then got bored and ran off, barking and ululating, to the woods. It was getting dark. I said that maybe now the kitchen wasn't so hot.

We went into the house and glimpsed the pistol in the dimness, and both of us headed simultaneously toward the table where it lay, as if we each meant to grab it and use it; I was actually lunging in a desperate reflex to hide it, while she, I think, was just afraid. But neither of us touched it.

She asked me what it was.

"A pistol."

"Yes, but why do you have one in the house—where does it come from?"

I told her the story of my grandfather and the weapons the Allies had parachuted in to the partisans, and I pointed out the American army markings; I was anxious to prove that I hadn't gotten it in order to kill someone.

"I've never seen it here before; why did you pull it out?"

"I didn't have it before; my mother gave it to me this morning, and I'm thinking I'll wrap it up and throw it in a canal, or maybe in the river."

Without waiting for me to finish, she turned and walked outside; I thought that she'd forgotten something on the wicker table, but when I looked out the door I saw her gather up the pages of the two-month-old paper that were still lying next to the mattress.

"Look," she said sarcastically, "you can use this to wrap it. It's already the right shape." And she held the newspaper up toward the lamp over the doorway to show me that it was still molded into a triangle. Then she looked down again and stared at something on the ground. She bent over and picked up the joint, still intact and tidily rolled. She held it for a few seconds, as if she'd never seen one; then she let it fall.

I went back into the house, and after a moment she came in too.

I ask her what time she has to leave for the seaside tomorrow morning, and she says she doesn't have to go back there because they've all come home; Alberto was very agitated, he couldn't stand the beach, and he wanted to get home at all costs. She'd tried to convince him to stay, but it was impossible. So she would spend another half hour with me and then go back to the house.

"I thought you were going to sleep here. Why didn't you tell me sooner?"

"When? While you were lying on the ground?"

But beneath the thin surface of my disappointment I sense a thick layer of relief: I don't want to make love with her, I don't want her to sleep here.

And I want her to leave immediately; I'm about to ask her to go, saying that we can get together tomorrow, or the day after, or whenever we want. But before I can, she starts asking questions.

"Did you see Mosca?"

"Yes."

"What did he tell you?"

I talk about the house, about Giletti and Hello and the hanging garden that I actually don't want to make, and—lying—I tell her that Mosca offered me a lot of money.

"Did he tell you that he remembered your father?"

"No. Maybe he's not so sure anymore . . ."

She blushes. And stares at me. I don't blink.

"Tell me the story of your father."

"Not tonight—I don't have the strength."

"Just tell me one thing: is it possible that he ever got money from Conti?"

It's not only possible but certain: that's what happened, and so I answer:

"I don't think so. He was an old-fashioned sort: he'd rather have gone bankrupt than be in debt. And in fact, before he went bankrupt he sold everything. But anyway, I don't know. I told you, I was young."

"Do you think . . . Is it possible that Mosca had Conti killed, that night?"

It's not only possible but certain: that's what happened, while Giletti documented it all with his little video camera, and so I shrug and answer:

"I have no idea. From what you've told me, he might have had reason to do it. But he doesn't seem like the type." I pretend to consider it. "No, he's not the type to dirty his hands like that. It's more likely that a man like Conti had other enemies."

"You weren't the one who killed him?" she asks suddenly.

I don't have to pretend to be amazed: this time she really has surprised me. The answer seems so obvious that I don't think twice—I just blurt out:

"Me? I couldn't hurt any living thing, not even Hello, that yappy little dog."

Which is true, in a way.

"That's too bad," she says seriously. "You should consider doing it . . . to his master too."

"I don't know what you're talking about; I'm just exhausted, and I don't want this visit to end like the other one ended."

"What other one?"

"The one where you told me about Sleeping Beauty."

"Okay. But I don't understand why you won't let me into your life."

"But I want to let you in."

"It doesn't seem that way. You just need someone to fill your empty sofas and your chairs."

So I finally get her up and out, and only as she's leaving do I see her body and feel desire welling up, and I curse myself for not having wanted to keep her here.

I was in bed on Monday night, but not yet asleep, when I heard a car come into the courtyard and through the window I saw my mother getting out of a taxi and coming to ring my front doorbell. She has a set of my keys, in case of emergencies, but maybe she'd left them at home, or maybe she wanted to ring the bell to warn me that she was here—how can I tell what goes on in my mother's head?—maybe she imagines that I fill my lonely hours in some unseemly way; she never asks about my private life, and she must not want to find me in bed with a woman she doesn't know, a woman I haven't yet introduced her to. But if she wanted to avoid surprises she would have called, I thought as I slipped on my pants and left the room. She came in person, instead, which means that she has news too horrible to tell me by phone. Immediately I thought of Carlo and the children. What time was it? As the doorbell rang for the second time, I went back to get my watch from the night table and I saw it was past 1:00 a.m. I wondered where she found the taxi, and what she told the driver, and how much she paid him.

Barefoot, I nearly slipped on the stone staircase; when I opened the front door I saw her lit up by the lamp over the doorway: in a nice dress with green checks, she held her purse tightly against her stomach with two hands, as if she were afraid I'd steal it from her. "What's happened?" I asked.

"Nothing has happened," she said with an expression I'd never seen before. "Let me in."

Once inside, she shook off the fragile and insecure air that she'd had while getting out of the taxi; maybe it had only been the discomfort of spending all that money. And indeed the first thing she said was:

"I told him that you were sick and I had to come help you" (I assumed she was talking about the driver).

"Okay, but why did you come? What's going on?"

"I have to talk to you, but first I need a chamomile tea."

I took her into the kitchen, murmuring that it scared me when she showed up in the middle of the night—why hadn't she called?

She sat at the table and looked at the sofa across from her—she had always thought it was foolish: how can you eat comfortably on a sofa?

"This can't be said on the phone."

"What is 'this'?"

She sighed, but not because she was tired: she was awake and vigilant, and annoyed; she was angry with me now—after all those months of tears, she was angry.

I started some water boiling and looked in the cupboard for a chamomile tea bag.

"Kill him," she says.

At first I think that I misheard her, that I imagined her saying it because I've been thinking of nothing else; my mother can't have said such a thing.

"What did you say?"

"You were right to get rid of the other one. Kill this one too."

"Mamma," I stutter, "what are you talking about?"

But she has already said enough, and she even said it twice, and she doesn't intend to say anything more. She shakes her head as if it's already inevitable.

"Mamma, how can you possibly think that I killed someone?"

She glances up with a look that slices right through me, like a knife.

I imagine her one night, many years ago, when a neighbor rang to let her and Papa know that one of their sons was asleep or passed out or maybe dead in a parking lot. And she said to Papa, "Send Claudio to get him; bring him home," and then closed herself in her room.

"Listen, I don't know what you're talking about. If you mean that man, Conti—I didn't kill him. And this other character, Mosca, is just someone I met by chance; he wants me to fix up his terrace. I asked you if he was Conti's partner because I don't want to work for him and then discover later that he ruined Papa."

She shakes her head again.

"Well, then don't fix up his terrace, because he was the one. He ruined Papa."

I pour water into her cup and push the sugar bowl closer.

"So why did you tell me to remember only Conti's name when I was little?"

"I told you to remember . . . ? What are you talking about?" I tell her what I did with the old pistol: how I threw it into a hole where Witold and I were planting a sweet gum tree this afternoon. I don't know if she believes me.

I refused to take her back home and made her stay the night in Carlo's room, but I don't think she closed her eyes all night, and I didn't sleep either.

The next day I called Mosca and told him that I had a lot of ideas for his garden, that, in fact, I'd even built a little model and I'd be happy to show it to him if he could stop by my house some evening, before the beginning of August, so the work could begin in September. I thought he would say that we should meet in the city, and I had two other excuses ready (the project existed only on my computer; or I had some unusual plants in my courtyard that I was planning to use, if he liked them)—it was really better for him to stop by here whenever it was convenient. But he caught me off guard by accepting enthusiastically; the very next day he'd be in this neighborhood, in the early afternoon, and he could drop by. "Good, I'll expect you," I stuttered. But it wasn't okay at all for him to come by so soon—I wasn't ready.

After lunch I abandoned the site at the bank's data center; the sky was white with dense haze, and the air was stagnant; Witold's figure trembled like a candle flame in the distance. I drove twenty miles off and parked in the shade of some plane trees in a little public park, to stand surveillance over a shop marked MARTINO STATIONERY• CARDS•BOOKS•TOYS. As soon as I saw Martino come out—walking stiffly at first, then loosening up into a long stride; his torso was hunched slightly forward, and he was clearly unwell but as determined as a bull—I got out of the R4 and headed toward the store. Inside was the salesgirl, a tall, unattractive brunette who helped Martino in the afternoon; I had seen her only once: there was no way she would remember me. I asked her for a green cardboard expanding file because I knew they kept them in the back, on the topmost shelves, and she would have to get out the ladder. And indeed she sighed and said, "It'll take a minute." A minute was just what I needed.

When she disappeared I went around behind the counter and opened the drawer beneath the cash register. The pistol I was looking for was right there waiting for me, and I took it and slipped it into my pocket. Now I had to hope the girl wouldn't take too long, so that Martino wouldn't have time to come back. I began watching for him through the window full of toys; if I hadn't been in a hurry I would have bought something for the kids. She finally came back with the file, and I paid for it and left. I got home at four; it must have been 120 degrees inside my car, and I was longing for a cool shower, but the shower faucet was still stuck on the boiling hot setting.

I called Carlo and asked him to come, because I had an important appointment tomorrow and I wanted him to be there. He replied that he was busy. So I said that he wasn't allowed to say no to me, that if he had appointments, he had to cancel them, and if he had to give exams, or attend a thesis defense, he'd have to call in sick, and that I wouldn't accept any excuses—that I would erase him and the kids from my life. He was silent for a moment, trying to figure out if I was joking. "I'm not joking," I said. "Get in the car and come here."

"But why tonight? Isn't your appointment tomorrow?"

"I have to explain—it'll take a while."

"Can't you even tell me who you have the appointment with?"

"No. Come. I need you."

Things your parents say—or merely hint at—can lie dormant inside you for years and then suddenly come to life and ring out clearly above the clatter of words that regularly shout through your mind. They're like sleepers, the spies that the Soviets cultivated in the West, or the secret guardians of Italy who were poised to launch the Gladio coup against the Communists: only Andreotti knew who they were—the guardians themselves had almost forgotten. The problem with those dormant words is that when they come alive they're dangerous. Having survived oblivion simply strengthens them: they emerge from hibernation without having spent any energy—in fact, they've acquired more. When you first hear the words, your mind temporarily represses them; I can picture them going into a kid's head but knowing that they can't hope to be heard for years, so they find a little nook and patiently hunker down and doze, despite the din of all the other happy and angry and rude words in there with them. But they're always on the alert, and they pop out at the right moment, robust and strong, and rise up to the highest peak of your memory and can't be knocked off it: they shine their blinding light on every one of your thoughts and lead you toward your destiny.

Almost all the synonyms for my word have something to do with accounting: to settle accounts, to make him pay, to even things out. And the only reason I even have my word is an account being out of balance: too much interest due on a debt that was contracted in order to cover other debts. Martino the accountant must have understood such things; I wonder if he advised my father not to accept that loan . . . Wasn't it his job to warn against certain people and certain interest rates? No, maybe it wasn't his job. But anyway, he didn't save him. And in our childhood games, I was Martino the accountant. Carlo was the hero, the successful entrepreneur, and I was the sorcerer, the magician, the accountant who smoked like a chimney amid the bizarre tools of his job, and Fabio was the peasant in the background, the nameless worker on the assembly line; we could have put a cardboard dummy in his place, because he wasn't really there anyway—he was off playing by himself.

The last time we had seen Martino was at my father's funeral, and even then we'd noticed the signs of Parkinson's disease. We talked to him, Carlo and I first, asking him about his stationery store, and then my mother and I, reminiscing about the times at the factory and, before that, the carpentry shop; he was only a kid when my grandfather took him on as an errand boy, and he went to accountants' school at night— there was so much energy in those days, said Martino, postwar reconstruction and growth, nobody thinks about it anymore, it's better just to forget about it. And even though I'd always known, it was only at my father's funeral that I understood exactly where his store was, and I promised I'd stop by. I didn't make good on the promise until I read about Conti in the paper and thought I should find out whether he really was the same person who had ruined my father.

When I first went into the store, Martino was helping a young customer, a boy of about eight or nine who was transfixed by the movement of the stationer's hands. The old accountant seemed to be expecting me, because all he did was raise his bushy white brows and murmur, "Be with you in a moment." And the moment was lying there on the counter between us, beneath the trembling fingers trying to count out ten sheets from a ream of drawing paper and sell them to the boy. The task was to make time implode, to divide it into infinity, to make it collapse in on itself, because halting time would also halt the progress of his illness. "Ciao, Martino," I said, the way I had as a kid—I'd never shifted into formality with him, never stopped using the familiar *tu*—and he smiled.

He took me on a tour of the shop, shelf by shelf: the stationery—pens and notebooks and manila folders and drawing paper—and the toys—stuffed animals and toy cars and board games and children's books. It was the logical next step from his old office: here the tools of his trade finally revealed their playful side, showing that I had guessed right when I was a child: they did actually belong to the same category of merchandise.

Then he went behind the counter again, with his small, dragging steps, and gestured for me to follow him. He opened a drawer beneath the cash register. There was an automatic pistol inside. He didn't pick it up, but he pointed to it and explained, "I'm ready for anything that might happen; and it's all legal, see?" He showed me his gun permit. I wondered how they could give a permit to someone whose hands trembled so badly.

At that point I began to talk to him about Conti; I had read that he was in trouble, that there was an investigation, and talk of usury. I just assumed that he knew and remembered; and indeed he did know and he did remember. He looked at me fearfully, and shook his head without speaking.

"Do you remember this man Conti? Did you ever meet him?"

He had never seen him; he knew that my father had asked around for money and then filed away some documents about the money he got, but Martino had never had the courage to speak his mind.

"What do you mean, 'the courage'?"

"I was afraid of your father, you know?"

My picture of Martino the accountant—serious and self-sufficient, master of his office and independent of the factory owner—crumbled to bits. And I got a clearer picture of my father, so strong and proud in his silence, so much so that he struck fear into his workmen and other employees. (But not his wife? But not his children?)

Martino hadn't had the courage to tell my father that there was nothing to be done, that it would be better to sell right away, without getting into debt with those people. He was just an accountant, but he had heard plenty of stories of entrepreneurs ruined by loan sharks, stories that in those days were merely whispered in the café and the piazza, as if they were sex scandals.

Then Martino's face lit up with a sweet, disarming, childish smile. "But why dwell on these ugly memories? Come, I'll show you something."

He took me into the back and rolled a tall library ladder along the shelves, then told me to climb up and pull down an expanding file: "The one at the end isn't for sale; I keep newspaper clippings in there." The ladder creaked under my weight.

We laid the file on a table, and out popped a complete press kit on Claudio Fratta, garden designer—interviews, articles, portrait photos. "My niece brings them to me—you know, the one who works at the magazine." I nodded, even though I remembered nothing about her.

I said, "Do you remember when I used to come around and bother you in your office?"

He went on leafing through the clippings and looking at the photos of my gardens, his teary eyes hidden beneath the little canopy of his eyebrows.

Maybe it was that visit to Martino that got me started following Conti. I didn't even know why I was doing it. I didn't achieve anything by it—I just followed him and spied on him from a distance, as he went about what were probably the most innocent of activities. In the morning he left his house and went to the bar for a cappuccino. He went to the office. He drove around in his car. He made short trips to the towns within a twenty-mile radius. In the evening he sometimes went out with a woman. They didn't live together. He did one funny thing that made me smile: he never turned away the gypsies or Romanian panhandlers who approached him at stoplights, and he always bought something from the Moroccan vendors.

I don't think I learned anything about him by following him, and I wasn't even able to figure out for certain whether he was indeed the same Conti. I wanted to follow him. I didn't get any particular pleasure from it; I didn't feel I was holding his life in my hands. I didn't have any plan or idea—not even vague prospects—and I wasn't daydreaming about what might happen. But when it happened, when I saw him die, I realized that I had wished for it and that wishing could still work: all you had to do was be ready for it.

Carlo came at nine, and I offered him the couscous I'd prepared, but he didn't want any; he merely said, "Let's not waste time."

I said there wasn't any hurry, I had to talk to him about Fabio first.

He sighed. "Claudio, if you've decided to go crazy too, then it's all over. Don't you realize that you're the only solid element in my life? You can't get delirious on me."

I didn't know what he was talking about. "Don't worry, this isn't delirium. There are just some things you need to know about before I tell you some other things."

He gave in and dropped into his armchair. He opened his hands and gestured for me to begin.

I asked him if he remembered exactly how Fabio had died.

He closed his eyes for five seconds and then opened them up again. "Yes, I remember."

I told him we could have saved him.

He stared at me for so long that I had to look down. "It's nobody's fault," he said. "There are some kids who live through it and others who don't. It's not your fault."

I told him he didn't understand. Fabio had OD'd that night, but we could have saved him; all we had to do was take him to the hospital.

"Listen," he responded. "I'm sorry we never talked about it. I thought a million times about asking you how you felt, asking you whether you still thought about him. But there's no point going over it again now. It wasn't your fault. If you'd known he was in danger, you would have done everything possible. Just as you always did."

Again I said that he didn't understand. Papa and I had waited up all night for Fabio to die.

Carlo leaps from the armchair. "Jesus, Jesus, Jesus!" he rages. "Don't give me that bullshit—would you please not give me that bullshit? It wasn't your fault! He was a junkie, get it?" He's shouting at me.

"Okay, okay," I mutter. I reach out to get him to sit back down. "Okay. I wanted you to know."

"There's nothing to know," he says, sitting back down.

We're silent for a while.

"Do you want to eat something?"

He buries his face in his hands. "God, Claudio, I beg you—tell me why you made me come. Don't drive me crazy."

I tell him that I found the two loan sharks who bankrupted our father.

He springs up again. "I knew it, I knew it," he repeats, pacing up and down. "I knew that had something to do with it." He shakes his head. He waves his arms around. I've made him angry.

He stops short. "Give me something strong."

I pull two mini bottles of Schweppes from the fridge and get the blue gin bottle. Carlo isn't used to drinking. He asks how much gin he should put in. I pour in more than he will be able to handle. He takes a big gulp, as if it's just mineral water. After a few more trips up and down the living room, he sits in his chair again.

"You found them. And?"

I tell him that I found one, named Conti, who Martino remembered; it was the same guy. But before I could talk to him, somebody killed him; they ran him over with a truck.

I show him a newspaper clipping that I kept. He reads it.

"Okay, this guy is dead. And the other one?"

"Aren't you going to ask me whether I killed him?"

"No, I'm not going to ask you, because you didn't kill him. Get real. Who's the other one?"

I tell him about Mosca. And how I met him. And that Elisabetta Renal confirmed he was Conti's partner. And that he told her he remembered our father.

He shakes his head. "Yes, but . . . there's no proof, there aren't any documents anymore. It's twenty-five years ago. You can't catch him now. What are you trying to do?"

I tell him that the guy has a video showing my car in the parking lot where Conti was killed, *while* he was being killed.

"And why did he have that video?"

"Because he killed Conti himself, I think; he had to get rid of him."

He's grimacing in disgust. "What have you got to do with this story?" He waves his hands around. "What were you doing in the parking lot?"

I tell him that I was following Conti and I don't even know why.

He starts rubbing his forehead and mutters, "I knew it—I knew you shouldn't stay out here all alone. Spending all your time brooding about this crazy business. Instead of doing something more enjoyable. I shouldn't have left you here alone." He looks at me. "Okay, you were right to call me. Let's phone a lawyer right away. We'll go to the police with him. We'll tell them everything. We'll turn this Mosca in. What's he demanding?"

"Huh?"

"What does he want from you?"

"Huh?"

"Money?"

I don't understand.

"Why did he blackmail you? What does he want?" He's shouting again.

I wasn't expecting this. I'm unprepared. What does Mosca want?

"No, not money; no way. He's very rich."

"What then?"

"I'm not sure."

"What?"

"Maybe he asked me not to see Elisabetta anymore."

He stares at me, astounded. "What kind of blackmail is that? He's threatening to turn you in for murder, and all he's asking is that you stop seeing some woman?"

I finally wake up. "But who knows what he'll ask me for next—you see?"

"What does Elisabetta Renal say to do?"

"Elisabetta? I haven't told her anything."

"You haven't told her that Mosca is blackmailing you?"

"No, it's none of her business. And if I told her, I'd have to admit that I was in the parking lot too, not just her."

"She was there too?"

I tell him about the documents that Conti was supposed to turn over to Elisabetta.

"And anyway, that's not the problem. She has nothing to do with this. She has nothing to do with our thing."

"*Our* thing?"

"The thing about Papa. She's not part of it."

He shakes his head. "I get it. Unlike her, I *am* part of it. Naturally."

He covers his eyes with one hand. "Okay. We have to talk to Mario Banco—you remember him? We were friends when we both lived in university housing; he's a very good lawyer, and that's what we need here—we'll call him tomorrow, okay?"

"No, it's not okay."

"Why isn't it okay?"

I tell him that Mosca can't get away with it. That he has to end up like the other one.

He gets up and starts yelling at me again. "What are you saying? Jesus Christ, what are you saying? Do you want to kill him yourself? Are you gonna put fertilizer in his gin and tonic? Eh?"

I murmur, "Somehow. There's some way to do it."

"Listen: I don't want to hear any more bullshit for tonight. Right now I'm hungry. Give me that couscous and tomorrow we'll talk to Banco."

We moved into the kitchen. I served him some food while he told me about how much experience his lawyer friend had. I thought that after dinner I'd talk to him about the pistol.

But then, when he was on his second mouthful, his cell phone rang. I saw him blanch.

"Yes," he said; then, "And you let her in? Why? I told you not to answer the doorbell. What do you mean, me? I'm here; I'm fifty miles away. No, no, no," he shouted.

He got up and said he had to go back to the city right away, there was a hell of a mess there. Cecilia had turned up at his bachelor pad and found Anna—that student of his—there.

"Well, what was she doing there?"

"I can't explain it to you right now."

"But you were supposed to stay till tomorrow—"

"I can't— Tomorrow . . . we'll talk tomorrow—"

He ran out. I stood at the front door and watched him. He was already inside the Clio, he'd turned on the ignition, and then he rolled down the window and yelled out to me, "And don't you do a fucking thing, you hear? Don't pull any crazy shit!" He drove off, burning rubber.

After a whole night when I don't think I slept more than three hours, and never for more than half an hour at a time, I go down into the courtyard at 7:30 to lie to Witold, who's waiting for me near his Fiat Panda; I don't feel well, I tell him, maybe I'll join him in the afternoon. "I didn't get drunk, I promise," I say, making him blush. "It must have been the canned corn: I really shouldn't eat it, nine times out of ten it makes me sick." And it's true that I'm not drunk, and it's true that I look worn out (more worn out than usual), so Witold—honest, loyal, sincere Witold—believes me and doesn't think I'm lying and reassures me: he suggests I stay home all day and rest; I repeat that I'll try to come after lunch, and we go over the plans for the day again, and we agree about everything—or rather I agree with all his suggestions and I suggest things I already know he'll like, to get rid of him quicker. And I do get rid of him; he takes off. I wonder dispassionately whether I'll ever see him again.

Carlo won't get back before Mosca and Giletti arrive; he may not intend to come back at all; in fact, my problems are almost certainly the last thing on his mind right now, so I can't put this off any longer; I have to deal with it myself. And the first thing I have to deal with is my weapon. It's 8:00 a.m., the air is still fresh, and I go out to the courtyard a second time; who knows whether Martino has ever pulled the trigger on this pistol? There's a chance it might not work anymore. Guns have to be oiled, and he never did that, for sure. I cock the hammer.

I point the pistol at the sky. I try to pull the trigger, but I can't. I'm afraid of the sound it'll make, of the chance that the muzzle might flare, or that the gun might even explode and maybe kill me too. I run back inside and down to the basement to grab Carlo's old full-face motorcycle helmet. Outside again, I lower the visor, reach my arm as high as I can, and shoot. The recoil knocks the pistol to the ground, where it almost hits my foot; but it works.

At the edge of the woods I aim into the shade beneath the trees and shoot again, to learn how to keep from dropping the pistol. It's too big for shooting point-blank in an enclosed space; inside a car it would rupture my eardrums, and inside the house it would make huge holes in my walls. I was right to take it away from Martino before he got himself killed by some nutcase. I shoot into the woods without aiming at any particular tree; I shoot the woods straight in the heart.

I take off the helmet, and suddenly all the noises around me go back to normal volume: I can hear Malik's dogs barking furiously, the hysterical magpies, and the distant hum of the main road—it's the sound of people driving toward me, shocked and outraged by this sudden noise of mine, because I'm usually so silent . . . I must have been overcome by the heat. But the sound of moving cars doesn't subside into the aural background again, even as the animals calm down and the echoes die out; after a few minutes the car noise intensifies, modulates down, and breaks out of its monotone—second, third, second gear—someone is shifting gears on the road that leads up here. I go over to my gate and see the car appear around the curve: it's the black Ka.

I tuck the pistol into the helmet, and the helmet into a stand of hydrangeas, and go back to the middle of the courtyard and turn my head as if I've just noticed her; she parks next to the other cars, and I think back to the early days when she used to stop half in and half out of the gate. I go to meet her without smiling; I'm unshaven and my hair is tousled and I fear my hands and T-shirt stink of gunpowder. But even if she smelled it, she wouldn't say anything today; by now I recognize that anxious gaze fixed somewhere beyond my shoulder—she avoids my eyes and spins around me like a satellite.

An hour later we get to the villa, which makes no impression on me even though I haven't been there for three weeks; we go in through the greenhouse and up to the second floor, where one of the twins sits in a chair in front of the door to Rossi's room, waiting like an old-time valet. He immediately rises and gestures for me to take his seat, and I hesitate for a moment, flattering myself with the idea that the door will open as soon as the master of the house hears my voice; but Elisabetta pushes me toward the seat, too, so I give in unwillingly and look at my watch and think that I haven't got much time.

"Mr. Rossi," I said. "Mr. Rossi, can you hear me?"

Elisabetta gestured for me to lean toward the door.

"So you came," he said faintly through the door.

He said that he needed to talk to me but he didn't want to let the twins or his wife into the room because he knew this time they would take away his key. He made them go down to the garden, and when he saw them by the concrete balustrade on the terrace, he opened the door for me. He was in the old wheelchair, the one I'd seen the very first day, with the foam and the towel-wrapped cushion. Otherwise he was dressed as usual, in his habitual cardigan, where he pocketed the key after double-locking the bedroom door.

He asked me to let the others know that I was in the room, so I went to the window; Elisabetta was looking at the ground with her arms crossed, but one of the twins was on lookout, and when he saw me he touched her shoulder lightly and she looked up and I waved to her. Rossi told me to take a chair. We sat in silence for several minutes.

He starts talking about the garden: he was wrong, it wasn't the story of Alfredo Renal, right?—it's his own story, the story of Alberto Rossi. All his life he tried to be as good as his friend, but he believed it was hopeless. Then he realized that he wanted to be something more than his friend: he wanted to be him and also be something else, something more complete. But now he isn't sure whether the something more isn't in fact something missing, and in the condition he's in now, he can't do without that missing thing.

Without giving me time to react, he goes on.

Because the three arches are the road that bring three different people to the same house.

And the rocks represent the difficulty of moving through the world.

Then there are the roots, which are preserved in a glass vitrine instead of being forgotten.

And the squalid, bleached-out tree trunks show the danger of moral poverty.

Then there is a revelation, a new sense of life, in the water running through the glass tube, all the way to the cistern and its pile of treasures: treasures of the spirit, ready to shine.

"Is that what it is?"

How can I answer?

"I believe that everyone is free to see whatever he likes in it, so why not your life? But I didn't know anything about you, I couldn't have done it on purpose . . ."

He smiles. "No, you didn't do it on purpose," he says thoughtfully. "So maybe it's a portrait of *your* life. You've never told me anything about you. I know that you had two brothers; maybe the three arches have some meaning there? And the roots at the center of the garden are an homage to your father? I hear he was a gardener."

I shake my head; I don't think I was trying to say something about myself, at least not consciously.

We hear a knock at the door, and Elisabetta asks if everything's okay and if we want some coffee. Rossi makes a silent no, as if he's asking me to turn down the offer too.

Instead of spending the whole morning in this room, I might end up grabbing the key away from him and opening the door.

He starts talking to me about his wife again, whispering so she won't hear him. Then he asks, "Why don't you come and live here with us? Elisabetta has great respect for you."

I smile. "I'm glad to hear that," I say.

"I've already told you that my wife is a very fragile woman?"

"Yes, you told me."

"It's her family's fault."

"Is it?"

We go on like this for an hour; every now and then, one of the twins knocks and asks whether we need anything.

"Did you know that Alfredo Renal discovered them in prison?"

"The twins?"

"They were swindlers: they exploited the fact that they're identical. They're quite devoted to me, have you noticed? They were quite devoted to Alfredo as well."

I listen to Rossi's stories without any particular pity; I just sit and listen. I picture Elisabetta outside, and I try to imagine her at my house again or traveling with me, sometime in the future, or at the movies, or at a restaurant. They all seem like old images to me, as if we've already had that affair, and in the end she's decided to leave me and go back to her husband—non-husband . . . whatever he is to her. Or she's decided in a huff to leave me because I wanted to keep her on the margins of my life, because I didn't want her to be involved in it, because I didn't want to tell her the true fairy tale of the mute old man.

At a certain point Rossi confesses that he'd had to threaten suicide in order to get me brought over here. He chuckles. "I'll die childless. Aren't you sorry not to have had children?"

"I have two nephews, whom I see often."

"I don't have the strength to go on any longer," he says. "Alfredo left many things undone, and Elisabetta's not interested in them."

He closes his eyes. Lassitude hits me; I rest my elbows on my knees and drop my head into my hands. I, too, close my eyes. Then I open them.

Rossi's head is bowed down. It looks like he's asleep.

I reach out to take the key from his pocket.

Suddenly my cell phone began to ring, Rossi awoke with a start, and I pulled my hand back and answered the phone; it was Mosca.

He said they were outside my house and they'd rung the bell—maybe I hadn't heard it.

"I'm not home. I was expecting you in the early afternoon."

I had misunderstood: the appointment was at noon.

"Is it noon already?" I asked incredulously, looking at my watch.

"Where are you?"

"I'm working, I'm with a client . . ."

I wanted to ask him where exactly he was, whether he was near the stand of hydrangeas, whether he felt free just to walk around my courtyard as if the place were his.

"Do you think that you can get here in a reasonable amount of time?"

"No, I really don't think so; I'm too far away. I'm truly sorry, I was sure you'd be coming after lunch."

I heard a dog barking and Giletti shouting something in the background.

"No problem," Mosca said. "Let's talk later. We can get together another day." Then I heard him yell "Hello!" and I knew he was calling the terrier, but it was funny to hear it in the middle of a phone call. I thought of the prostitute who said "Hello?" to tell me that supper was ready.

"Pardon me," he said, "we've lost sight of the dog." I heard him walking across the gravel. "He went into the forest."

"It's not really a forest—it's not very big," I reassured him.

"This looks like . . . a path. Where does it go?"

"To a house nearby. It's about five minutes away."

"Is it an easy walk?"

"Completely. Go right ahead."

I hung up the phone and saw Rossi watching me; I wasn't disappointed that Mosca was leaving, but I wasn't relieved either; I simply thought, Today I'm not going to shoot him.

"Give me the key now, please," I said to Rossi.

I went out and gave the key to one of the twins. Elisabetta was watching me, but I kept my eyes on the ground.

I hold my hand out to her, and after a brief hesitation she shakes it.

"I'll call you," she says. And then, almost under her breath, "soon."

I start calculating the length of that "soon" as I leave.

Someday Witold will get fed up. After we finish the job at the data center, he'll announce that he's willing to take a risk, that there's enough demand, and that he's decided to launch out on his own; he doesn't claim to be a garden designer, but he could have a small garden-maintenance business with Jan; the work would be duller but continuous, and the market is bigger, because there are more *fake* gardens than *real* ones—far more, no? And I'll nod and say maybe the work isn't even that dull, and I understand: he's got a family to support, and I'm not so reliable.

Occasionally I explain to him exactly what he thinks of me, to make him feel guilty, and then he tries his hardest to convince me that working with me has been the best experience of his life, that I'm a fantastic person, that he'll never forget what I've done for him, and that if he ever leaves me he'll help me find someone to take his place. Sure, garden maintenance is much duller and more banal, but for some reason he's destined to do it. "Because I know very well that I'm a dull person," he will say. I picture myself bursting into laughter and hugging him; for the first time since we met, I feel like hugging him like a brother.

Then fall will come, and winter. I'll find another assistant, and anyway I'll be able to work less, and I can rent out the other wing of the farmhouse, maybe to someone who uses it only on weekends. I no longer want to be alone all the time: maybe it would be enough for me to see people from far away, to witness other people's lives. The courtyard will fill with icy puddles and patches of snow, I'll make a bonfire of the dead leaves in the meadow, I'll start using the wood-burning stove regularly, I'll put on my heavy clothes again, and count the moth holes in my sweaters. I'll roast chestnuts for the kids for All Saints' Day, and light firecrackers for them on New Year's Eve, but first I'll hide the firecrackers in the pile of old tires and deny until the last minute that I've bought any. In October or November, like every year, some English journalist will come and write an article about me, and I'll be very loquacious and hospitable.

I'll have the whole family here for Christmas. We'll do two trees: one outside, with strings of lights, and a little pine tree in the living room that's not too tall, so the kids can decorate it by themselves. My mother won't cry anymore. Cecilia will have taken Carlo back, and she'll look the happiest of all. Carlo will or won't smile; he will or won't talk; he will or won't be outraged about something. Neither my mother nor my sister-in-law has any idea how to cook a stuffed guinea hen—but for that matter they can't even make mashed potatoes. I'll have to cook; the kids count on me.

I think I'll start walking in the woods again, maybe because I'll get a new dog, maybe because I'll stop wanting to eat and drink for two. The kitchen guest won't come by anymore, but I won't miss him. I'll miss Durga when the famous photographer moves away; I'll remember her frustrated wish to be loved, and the fake dog that was supposed to be her husband, and her fascination with Malik's baby. I'll declare Gustavo officially lost, and I'll ask the famous photographer to sell me the dachshunds. I see dachshund eyes—Indra's eyes flashing a challenge from the edge of the woods, and Mosca's dog chasing him. Sure, Gustavo was a more satisfying dog: he was lovelier, more charming, more loyal, and he had no family. Dachshunds have secret, hidden ambitions, or ambitions tailored to fit the situation; they seem more suited to the times that lie ahead. Certainly to the life that lies ahead for me.

And when I'm out walking, I'll almost always choose the path that heads east, but every now and then, when I see that Indra is nostalgic and pining for home, I'll go down toward the famous photographer's house. It won't be an easy house to sell, but it'll be empty before fall. He'll get rid of all the animals, and the pens will be empty. Malik will leave too. There's an idea: I'll try to get Malik to replace Witold. In August I'll offer him the job; I'll even offer him a place to live. But he won't accept—I shouldn't kid myself: ever since the baby was born, Malik's wife has been wanting to move back closer to the Sikh community. And the famous photographer will be very generous to him.

But for now, as I drive into the courtyard of the farmhouse and park my E270 next to Mosca's A8, fall and winter are still far off. I get out of the car and head unhastening toward the woods, through the warm and acrid shade of the chestnut trees, along the path. Malik and I have been the ones keeping the path clear in the past few years; just a few seasons of neglect would allow the woods to devour it again, and bring back the natural disorder of things. The impassive tension of the plants, the continual pressure—the imperative is "Grow!" Some time ago, a local farmer asked me to sell him firewood from the forest: he said he'd bring over his power saw and clean the place up, cutting away all the young shoots and leaving only one big tree every twenty feet or so. I never called him back.

I reach the meadow above the famous photographer's house. The police van and the ambulance are parked on the driveway in front, just where I imagined they'd be; the wheels of the Land Rover Defender are turned sharply, showing off the deep treads carved into the tires, and the doors of the ambulance are flung open. Two carabinieri turn toward me without curiosity.

They brought me into the house where Malik and his wife were sitting off to one side, with fear in their eyes, and Giletti, the only eyewitness, was telling what happened.

They had been in my courtyard for five minutes; they'd tried ringing, but no one answered. Then Mosca had called me, and the misunderstanding was cleared up. At that point Giletti went into the woods after Hello, who had run off toward the chestnut trees for no apparent reason. Wandering in the woods, he didn't recall passing by the limestone bluff that hangs over the old ocelot enclosure, Durga's pen. After twenty minutes of looking in vain, though, he continued down the hill and emerged behind the famous photographer's villa; hearing a dog's bark, he entered the property by way of the meadow that I've so often walked across with the kids.

Then the long glass barrier caught his eye, and behind the glass the shape of a dog much bigger than Hello, standing motionless. For a moment he thought it was a ceramic dog, but as he got closer he noticed it was breathing hard—its torso was swelling rhythmically. He thought, I've never seen a striped Doberman before, but since he didn't know much about dogs, he wasn't particularly surprised. After looking at the Doberman, he rose up on tiptoes and saw Hello's corpse, the white fur striped with blood: Durga had ripped a fist-sized hole between the dog's throat and his belly. Giletti clearly recalled the Doberman turning her head toward him and then looking back at the rear of her pen, with the same petrified stance he'd first seen.

So Giletti, too, looked toward the bluff that closed off the rear of the horseshoe-shaped pen, and he came closer to the glass and cupped his hands around his face to block out the reflections. He saw a dark mass of rags stirring, and he recognized that it was Mosca trying to stand up. His nose was bleeding, his clothes were torn in more than one spot, and he'd lost a shoe. He had broken his ankle falling from the bluff, but despite the pain he managed to take four wobbly, fainting steps. Durga took off, trotting toward him, and when Mosca saw her he dropped to the ground. While Giletti ran toward the house to call for help, Durga crouched next to the corpse, standing guard, as if she would never let it go.

The policemen's reconstruction of events was detailed and almost totally complete. They would never find the missing piece. The missing piece was me. Sure, I couldn't have known what would happen; I didn't know that Indra would show up at the edge of the woods that morning, making Hello shoot off after him and dragging both the dog and Mosca toward death. But I wanted it to happen, just as I had wanted it to happen to Conti.

I didn't have to pretend to be pained, or shocked, or even simply surprised about what had happened. I was cold and indifferent through my whole deposition, and nobody asked me why.

But Mosca's demise has had an odd effect on my imagination. Whenever I thought about Fabio's death before, I was always distracted by something inside me. Now the image of Durga standing guard over Mosca's corpse is superimposed on the last hug I gave Fabio, and it makes it possible for me to look directly at that older memory. I picture the tiger-striped dog against the robust form of the man with the receding hairline, and I see my brother and me again, with my father watching us from the door; and then my mother coming in and sitting on the edge of the bed, behind Fabio's back, and taking him in her arms from behind, squeezing me into her embrace; and me pulling back and leaving Fabio in her lap; and her looking at me and then at my father. My mother is dressed; she hasn't slept, she spent the whole night shut up in her bedroom, on a chair, rigid, alone. Fabio's head drops back, and his arm is dangling loosely, and my mother is still supporting his weight, and I lower my eyes because I can't bear the look that passes between my parents; I lower my eyes and stroke my brother's hand for the last time.